PRAISE FOR TOM PICCIRILLI AND *HEXES*

"What I like about Piccirilli's work is the way it slips between your vertebrae while you read, starts you floating before you know it, and in the end leaves you haunted. Tom Piccirilli just keeps getting better."

—*Cemetery Dance*

"Piccirilli splices genres, combining elements of supernatural horror with hard-boiled fiction to produce a narrative that sizzles. This is whiplash fiction that takes dangerous curves at 150 m.p.h."

—*Deathrealm*

"Tom Piccirilli delivers the goods. I'm a big fan."

—Richard Laymon, Author of *The Midnight Tour*

"Tom Piccirilli is a master of the occult novel. *Hexes* is a wild detour through a hell that occupies the shadowy corners of our homes and our minds."

—Douglas Clegg, Author of *The Halloween Man*

"Armed with the cold brilliance of Jim Thompson, the stripped-down language of James M. Cain, and the wry observations of John D. MacDonald comes Tom Piccirilli, a writer who has staked out the darkest territory of the soul and made it his own."

—*Mystery News*

THE GIRL SCREAMED AGAIN

Matthew groaned and slowly turned his head in her direction, attempting to stand.

Joanne Sadler sat shuddering beside the closet door, her arms locked around her calves, moaning, staring at him, the rats dragging themselves across her feet, her eyes murky without pupils. Passages from the books recited themselves, chanting, *Aieth Gadol Leolam Adonai* . . .

Sobbing, Joanne hid her face against her knees, realizations of life and death fully upon her. Matthew took a step forward but stumbled.

He moved to her.

Telling her, *Forgive me.*

"It hurts," she said, her mouth moving, the voice exactly as it should be, except not a voice at all any longer, though he could hear it. He could imagine her reading poetry aloud to audiences who could appreciate what she had to offer, soft and humble in the dim lighting. She lifted her chin to face him, those colorless eyes full of pain and contempt. It had been a long time since he'd spoken with the deceased.

HEXES

TOM PICCIRILLI

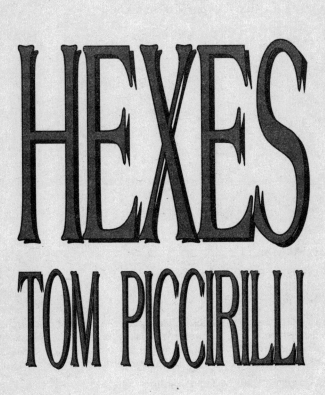

LEISURE BOOKS NEW YORK CITY

For my personal demons
payback's a bitch

A LEISURE BOOK®

February 1999

Published by

Dorchester Publishing Co., Inc.
276 Fifth Avenue
New York, NY 10001

ISBN 0-8439-4483-8

I would like to thank the following people for their friendship and encouragement during the writing of this novel: Diana Jackson, Matt Schwartz, Joe Arden, Gerard & Linda & Barbarian Barbie, Ken Abner, Ed Gorman, and Don D'Auria.

Chapter One

At least he thought he stood at his mother's grave.

But in Potter's Field one nameless marker abided as well as any other. Because of the weeds he couldn't clearly make out the chiseled numerals on the few shards of tombstones that remained standing in the area. It didn't make much of a difference. Their social security numbers, and perhaps a birth date, were the only way in which these dead were known.

Everyone in town realized that only a mile beyond Panecraft Hospital, somewhere on the hillside, hidden in the thickets beside the abandoned train station, there endured a graveyard of the anonymous, empty of remorse and family. Less gossiped about remained the section opposite the crumbling platform where another sunken meadow lay even more separate and untended. Along the trail were wildflower-covered graves of the stillborn, aborted, and murdered infants who'd never been given the chance to be held in their mad mothers' arms. Whispered rumors allowed that there were one or two elderly women who still wandered the wards cooing to their own broken fingers and rag-stuffed dolls.

It made for good theater.

Matthew Galen crossed himself out of habit. Rose petals flapped free in the breeze and swept against the empty October branches of the diseased sugar maples that leaned scattered across the field. He looked down from the hill and saw the lights of Summerfell coming on.

From here he could make out whatever sights there were to be seen on the edge of town, where you could catch a glimpse of your life unfolded.

He took the binoculars from his satchel and scanned his estranged home, feeling the nervous tension throb in him like his heart. He focused on the park and watched the lamplights lining the paths reflecting off the lake; benches and playgrounds slowly emptied with the arrival of evening. Glancing north, he noticed the windows of the high school gym glowing. He watched as orange flashes changed to a red that cooled to blue, cut to black, then lit up to white again. A school dance, possibly a costume ball if they still had the annual reception. Only the first week of the month, they were already set for the season of masquerades. They'd better be prepared, this year.

The Krunch Burger fast-food joint prevailed, spelled out in twenty-foot-high letters of blinding neon you could see as far away as Gallows, six miles across the river. A greasy short-order restaurant managed by Frankie "Screw with me and I'll yank yer tonsils outtayashitter" Farlessi, with a region-wide reputation for hitting on teenage girls and killing dogs that wandered into his trash bins. Some of the Summerfell studs hung around the Krunch in hopes that Frankie's wife, who occasionally flashed the boys extra thigh from her slit skirt, would cast her heated, luscious gaze their way.

Jazz Metzner used to make it with her, Matthew thought.

From the promontory he observed a full scope of events unseen anywhere else in town. Did they realize just how close Panecraft stood to the high school and park? It almost seemed that the asylum had drifted farther into the community. He couldn't remember any parents ever having taken up signs and picketing the way they would have anywhere else. There'd been no real controversy, petitions, or outright hostility. His father had been a masterful spin doctor, placating the county.

Matthew replaced the binoculars, hefted the

satchel back up onto his shoulder, and squinted into the dusk. He stared at the asylum, rejecting his father's euphemisms: this psychiatric facility, sanitarium, shelter for the distressed. Matthew glared at the stone building.

He'd been away too long.

Back in the late sixties, the overcrowded Panecraft housed thirty-one thousand patients. Now there were fewer than fourteen hundred up there behind the leveled rows of cube windows. Most of the current denizens were hospitalized by their own hand on a voluntary admittance basis, or came for group drug or alcohol counseling. Of the five buildings only one maintained a full staff and was kept in continuous use. Three others were in major disrepair and, except for the lowest floors, were shut down. The last was nothing more than a burned-out gutted frame that had been condemned years before.

Epiphanies awaited him. Matthew regarded the series of interconnected buildings and thought of when he and A.G. had ridden their bicycles through the echoing hallways. A.G., to his embarrassment, had still needed training wheels at the age of seven. They'd read comic books and crossed wooden swords and flipped baseball cards against the walls, while floors above people lay strapped to their beds for trying to gouge their own eyes out. Once it had been their fun house, before they'd had to find new names for the appetite of Panecraft. He'd finally settled on calling it the mother murderer.

Before Debbi's death.

On certain nights, you could head down these back roads surrounding the hospital and watch the twining shadows of the complex cut into the skyline and carve down alongside the moon; it got you somewhere deep. You could feel the haunted shells of these tens of thousands of men and women who once dwelled here, curled in its corners. Insanity crept toward tangibility, and if possession had any truth, you could believe this darkness could take over the unwary. High school kids performed primitive rites of passage, knocking down the barbed-wire fences in order to tear the lawns in pickup trucks, swigging Jack Daniel's and heaving in the bushes, sometimes using the condoms they brought, sometimes not buying into the facts.

His father had been the architect of that monstrosity. On the night Matthew's mother was taken away, he and A.G. had watched the trees rustling outside the half-opened windows of his bedroom, her lovely muffled songs and terrified squeals changing to even uglier sounds, his father's soft voice failing to appease her at all as men filled the house and the screaming started.

Oh Christ . . .

Now A.G., too, had been imprisoned behind Panecraft's walls.

. . . give me strength.
And Matthew could hear him calling.

One of the worst realties about a small town like Summerfell was that you were just as likely to be friends with the killers as you were with the victims.

Sweat slid down Matthew's sideburns as Dr. Henry Charters silently ushered him through one of the decrepit tunnels that connected the sites of the facility. Leaves, candy wrappers, tenth-grade geometry notes scrawled in a dyslexic hand, and kindergarten coloring book pages carpeted the cracked tile floor. Dragged in by the wind through the splintered planks that haphazardly covered the broken windows, the litter beneath his feet told him more tales of life than he'd witnessed so far today. Stepping on the trash was like stepping on his own past.

Matthew had a hard time stifling the memories; even more disturbing were the sounds of his childhood assaulting him now, snapping like his steps. If he shut his eyes he could fall back to being seven years old and hear A.G. flopping sideways off his bike, hitting the ground with a squeaky cuss.

"I apologize, Mattie, but I'm still kind of shocked to hell at seeing you again," Hank Charters said. "I'm glad, you understand, and certainly relieved, believe me, but surprised. I wasn't sure if you'd heard or even cared anymore." That last bit proved nothing more than a baited taunt, but Matthew let it slide. Charters dropped a loose, consoling hand on Matthew's shoulder and let it slip away quickly. "I can imagine how difficult this is for you, to return now to face this. If you feel ill I have some tablets upstairs that will help." Charters kept trying to be nice, oppressively so, going too far out of his way.

They walked the complex for nearly twenty minutes while Charters vacillated between acting as if he truly cared and being too damn pushy, hoping to ferret out information. So far as Matthew knew, the apprehension he felt hadn't been betrayed by either his face or voice, though the calm look he worked hard to keep might be a betrayal in itself. Charters enjoyed piercing veils. He'd been the proverbial uncle to Matthew for most of his life, and though they hadn't seen each other in five years they'd both naturally fallen back into their roles.

"I tried getting in touch with you," Charters said, "as soon as it happened." He stuffed his hands into his sweater pockets and the massive ring of keys chimed feebly on his belt. "When this mayhem first occurred, there was no way to contact you. No one had an address or phone number where you might be reached."

"Yes," Matthew said. He hoped it would be enough of an answer.

It wasn't. The doctor paused and measured

Tom Piccirilli

his words carefully, scratching and stroking at his wiry broad mustache as if it were a beloved terrier curled under his nose. Matthew wondered what other psychiatrists saw in that repetitive gesture—masturbation? obsession for a long-gone pet? A hurt look flashed over his face. "I'm sorry. I hadn't realized you'd cut your native cords so effectively. Even Helen—"

"Please don't talk about her." The familiar rage coiled around him, so close and intimate as always. Matthew kicked broken glass aside, enjoying the feel of garbage here. "This is bad enough for the moment."

"Yes, of course. I'm sorry."

"Stop apologizing, Hank. Has he said anything?"

It took the doctor back. "No."

"Not even to himself? Muttering, whispering?"

"On occasion. But nothing of real consequence."

If you only knew. "Anything on tape? For me to listen to?"

"No."

Charters cleared his throat and swallowed thickly. As an uncle figure, he should have known better than to push the wrong buttons, much less attempt to initiate conversation by pressing them; as a psychiatrist, Charters had failed to take into account the Galen temper—being too close tended to warp the analytical view, as Matthew had learned of his father. He'd

18

written two plays about crazy psychiatrists.

"Any visitors?"

"No."

Charters went back to petting his terrier. Clearly he was torn, unsure of which tack to pursue: to follow his line of questioning of Matthew, or answer Matthew's queries about A.G. Everyone had control and power here in Panecraft, and it switched hands from moment to moment. Matthew sensed Charters backing off, trying to regain control. Amazing how clearly a counselor could be read.

"All I knew about your current whereabouts was what I'd stumbled across in the papers these past few years. It was a wonderful surprise to learn you'd so quickly become a successful playwright." The doctor gave a tight brisk laugh, humorless yet nearly a giggle; Matthew had forced his director to replace lead actors because they'd given performances bad as this. "I even went to Manhattan in the hopes of tracking you down, if you can imagine that."

"No." Matthew allowed himself a momentary grin. He could just see Charters stalking down Times Square, mentally configuring notes and papers on sexual mores, looking for the twenty-five-cent peep shows and brazen transvestite prostitutes and finding only the Disney Store, Japanese tourists, guys trying to sell him watches, and scattered homeless.

"After two train connections and getting lost

for an hour on the wrong subway line heading into the Bronx, I finally made my way to the theater where *Epitaphs* was being presented, only to be told by the manager that he didn't have any idea how to get in touch with you."

"I recently moved to a new apartment."

"I tried, Mattie, I wanted you to understand that."

"I do, Hank, and I appreciate it as well."

They moved into another tunnel, this one winding toward Tower C, the only section of Panecraft he hadn't been allowed to freely roam and explore as a child. It still felt like forbidden ground, perhaps of a holy kind. Here they kept those patients his father had called the "highly disturbed" and the "deeply troubled." His dad could make it all sound so loving and caring, so profound in the light of reason. He could never say the "criminally insane." Perhaps he'd never even thought it.

"How long has A.G. been here?"

"Twelve days. How did you finally learn about it?"

Matthew didn't answer, scanning the cracked plaster and spiraling water stains, seeing the various signs and portents in the walls.

The heavy ring of keys at Charters's belt jangled a tone-deaf tune. "I suppose it doesn't matter."

"No, it doesn't."

Anguish and fear snapped together like

20

shears closing shut. He would have asked Charters to give him the tranquilizers if he'd believed they might actually work. He might've asked anyway in order to hold the moment at bay, to keep from seeing another of his loved ones in a cell, but if he stopped now he'd never be able to start on this walk again. His fingernails were weak from a lifetime of nail-biting, and they bent where they dug in against the strap of the satchel.

Corridors revived sounds, scents, and images without form, not even recollections anymore, just kid stuff making no sense now—the migraine came swiftly and he chewed his lips to keep from grunting, ancient languages rising from the silt of memory. *This can't be happening*, he thought, knowing the truth, *not again*. And with startling clarity: *I'm going to die here*.

"Tell me about it," Matthew said.

Hank Charters sighed and held his hands open in front of himself, a meaningless gesture, looking for a way to grasp a greater design. He rubbed at the corners of his eyes, tired, with his voice drained of its usual critical energy. Jesus, this place killed everybody. "From the sheriff's point of view there's not much to tell."

There wouldn't be. There never had been much to say, not even when they were dragging Matthew's mother out of the living room on her belly. "The sheriff's point of view is usually quite narrow and unperceptive."

"Are you aware that over the past six months six people have vanished?"

"Yes."

"Four women and two men . . . my God, men, women, actually most of them are only teen-agers. Talk has gone around about a serial killer, and the police issued a curfew to keep children off the streets."

"I heard."

Charters stopped abruptly and turned, a little heat in his glare now, the bad acting over; mustache disheveled, steel-wool corner hairs curving down into his mouth, the doctor stroked it some more. "Yes, well, did you also know that one of the women was Ruth Cahill?"

Matthew cringed.

In an instant, the scars on his chest began their hideous whispering, voices filling his head.

For a moment he almost lost his balance in the tunnel, feeling the blood drain from his face. The arcane chattering continued, laughter so loud. Charters watched him closely as Matthew went through the motions. "No, I didn't know that." *Walk, make your goddamn feet move forward.*

"She's A.G.'s fiancée now, but no one has seen her for almost six months."

Six months. The Goat had been planning well in advance for Matthew's return. "What happened? Why do they suspect him now?"

"Ten days ago the mother of a newspaper boy named Richie Hastings called the police on the verge of hysteria. He hadn't returned home from school and was already several hours late. Earlier that afternoon, he was supposed to be collecting money owed him by customers on his paper route. It usually only took thirty minutes or so—"

Matthew's pinkie nail split against the leather strap. *It used to take us all afternoon, all night if we wanted it to, cutting through back yards, chasing Lilith's children.* Banal and transparent symbolism, though, the Goat using another paperboy to make a point.

"—but Richie was now very late. The police proceeded with a door-to-door search of Richie's customers, knowing how adolescents, however responsible, don't tend to let their mothers know their whereabouts all the time."

"But they found him."

"Yes." Charters stopped and looked into Matthew's eyes, going for the direct approach now, on the level and man-to-man, though of all places he shouldn't have looked there. You could see how it affected the doctor, made him take a step backward to withdraw from what he'd found in this gaze, but discovering that it was too late to let go. Charters turned again. "They discovered him semicomatose sitting on A.G.'s porch, seated beside A.G. on the verandah swing." Strange to know what was about to

23

Tom Piccirilli

be said, regardless of how much no one wanted
to hear it. Matthew quickly pinched his throat
to keep the nausea from rising any farther, the
doctor paling to another shade. "In his lap A.G.
cradled the mud-covered osseous framework of
a child."

It took effort not to say, "I know," and to keep
the scars from shrieking, and to not punch
Charters in the mouth for being so pretentious
as to say "osseous framework." Three fingernails were bleeding where they'd ripped at the
cuticles. Bones, the inherent power in those
bones. A.G. had gone back for her skeleton. "My
Christ."

They came to the elevator, and as Charters
reached to touch the up button, the car arrived
as if expecting them. They entered and the doctor pressed fourteen, the top floor.

"Even upon initial examination it proved evident the skeleton was too small and much
more aged than could possibly be matched to
any of the other missing people. We turned it
over to the county officials, who reported that
the body was of a Caucasian girl about twelve
years old who'd died at least a decade ago from
extreme trauma to the midsection, according to
the forensic anthropologist. Dental records are
being checked." Strictly professional, without
giving Matthew time enough to ask just when a
small town like Summerfell might need to know
anything about forensic anthropology.

Charters laid it out without a hint of emotion, though he must have been well aware who the victim was—only problem was that Dr. Williamson, their dentist, had long since died and his obsolete records tossed. Her braces had turned to dust in the wet caves. "The police are checking cemeteries in the county to see if any graves have been recently disturbed; they're also backtracking missing-persons reports from that time. They searched A.G's home thoroughly and found the partial remains of another skeleton, of an infant also many years dead, as well as several preserved animal carcasses."

"Any physical proof indicating he'd murdered someone?"

"No, not as of yet, but . . ."

"Nothing besides the fact that his fiancée is missing to directly tie him to these other disappearances?"

"No, but you see what must be inferred . . ."

The ride took too long; he looked at the lit numbers overhead and saw they'd only just passed the ninth floor. "Yes." What was happening? Panecraft had captured him again.

"The curfew is supposedly still in effect," Charters said. "The police stated they haven't concluded their investigation yet, but you know this town. A.G.'s capture relieved most of the tension. No one feels they have anything to be frightened of now that A.G. is imprisoned—they simply couldn't stand being terrified any longer. Everyone believes A.G. killed them all and hid their bodies elsewhere."

"Nothing else in his house or yard?"

"It was completely torn apart, lawns dug up, walls smashed, wood of the floors cut through and broken away, and they're still looking. No, nothing else. The papers have taken to calling him a ghoul."

He is, Matthew thought. *We all are*. "Has he confessed?"

With that annoying kick-back lurching the elevator slowed as they arrived at the fourteenth floor. The doors opened on brightly lit hallways of institutional gray-green, a softened but somber color Matthew had painted his apartment because he'd grown so used to it. Two men in impeccable security uniforms waited to one side. They were either orderlies or guards, he didn't know the current nomenclature, but they wore side arms.

The first guard sat behind a half-moon desk watching several small video monitors, and the other stood with his right hand resting on his gun belt, fingers edging sideways, gently slapping against the handcuffs. Matthew wondered how long it would take before the guy shot himself or his partner in the foot.

Now it made sense why the elevator had taken so long; he glanced back into the car before the doors shut and saw what he'd missed while listening to Charters: mini vidcams hidden high in the corners. He was unfamiliar with these procedures of Tower C, where he'd never been above ground level. It was like finding a hidden room in your own house.

The guards' routine remained thorough, though Hank Charters was the director of Panecraft. He had to display two ID badges and sign in; Matthew assumed they were going through the inspection so they could check him carefully, hoping to gain something conclusive from him to pin on A.G. The questioning would begin soon. They put on little white gloves, and Matthew wondered if he'd have to break somebody's jaw. He had to hand over the contents of his pockets, and submit to a frisking and a search through his satchel, the contents of which they scattered on the desk and poked through. They took his belt, watch, the silver chain he wore at his throat, and they still looked as though they really wanted to draw their guns, practice their karate kicks, put on the rubber gloves.

"Everything all right, Dr. Charters?" the first man asked, and Charters nodded impassively.

A third guard stood stolidly at the other end of the lengthy hall in front of heavy steel secondary gates; following Charters, Matthew observed that this man didn't carry a gun. He was more like a sentry, standing watch, poised for anything. A calm and dangerous self-assurance radiated from him. There was absolutely no doubt he could efficiently protect and murder. The scars chattered and argued. Whoever the guy was, he was gifted, and possibly would play a role. He stood at least six four, and the corded muscles of his arms, neck, and shoulders appeared thick enough to seize up a miner's drill.

"Matt, this is Roger Wakowski. He's in charge of security in this wing."

They were allowed to walk through the electrically unbolted gates. Charters exchanged a few more clipped words with Wakowski, who in turn gave Matthew a lecture on what not to do while in A.G.'s cell. Despite the formality, there was a certain playfulness to it all, as if Matthew were being toyed with to an extent, and it didn't matter that he knew it. "You probably already know these maneuvers from the movies. There's a painted line on the floor you are not to step beyond. If you do I'll have to drag you out. Do not hand him anything; do not accept anything he might attempt to pass through the bars."

"That's stupid. Maybe he'd hand me a note, his signed confession. Wouldn't you like to get your hands on that?"

Wakowski ignored the comment, both of them realizing the high theatrics of the moment, drama compounded by the spilling of blood. "Simply remain seated on the far bench

and talk quietly. Don't rile him. He's not catatonic but does seem to know a great deal about
meditation, so he might not be receptive to your
visit. Any problems and just tap on the door. I'll
be directly outside."

"Watching?"

"Certainly."

A buzzer sounded and the gates slid open.

Wakowski continued. "There's a video camera in his cell, but it's not working properly."
Matthew saw the guy's lips flatten almost im-
perceptibly, the scars also alerting him to the
first lie. "Mechanical malfunction, they told me,
but I've seen some of these men sabotage
hundred-thousand-dollar equipment with their
own feces and regurgitated digestive juices,
which make for nice acids in the long run."
Wakowski's speech pattern seemed to shift
slightly from sentence to sentence, high New
York intellect in there as well as some southern
farmboy. Matthew had the underlying feeling
that the guard found his lies a dishonor to bear.

Yeah, this guy would be along for the ride.

"There's a camera on him all the time?"

"Until yesterday, yes. As well as every other
patient in this wing. I don't know much about
constitutional law, but the state rules are that
we can watch a patient's personal meeting on
the cameras but aren't allowed to be present inside the cell during the visit unless requested by
the visitor himself. It sounds hypocritical to me

too, but those are the rules we follow."

He knows plenty about constitutional law, Matthew thought. He could see a wavering afterimage about Wakowski, a conglomerate of past lives still hovering, almost all of them soldiers and warriors, a few lawyers.

"It's not hypocritical, but it is deceptive," Charters said. "Federal rules."

Wakowski nodded. "Do you wish for me to accompany you?"

Matthew shook his head; he didn't want all those warriors around A.G. "Thanks anyway."

"Would you like a bandage?"

"A bandage? I don't get you."

"For your fingers, Mr. Galen. You're bleeding."

Sticky and dried blood almost to the second knuckle. He made a fist and held it against his thigh. "No, I'm okay."

"Blood excites some patients."

"Not A.G.," Matthew said, and stepped into the other corridor, shoulder to shoulder with Charters as they were led through. He heard the resonant roar of the gates shutting behind him— and it was a roar . . . powerful and full, crying in a way that could shrivel your scrotum. An animal grunting from somewhere out of the depths of this castle as it worked its way toward you, leaving scratch marks every step of the way, and you could smell the wet fur too, once you were within, *the stinking raw meat breath*.

Grating metal doors scraped sidelong in their greased but dirty tracks, clickity-clicking as they slithered and thrummed, and a full three seconds later finally clamped across the width of the hall like a hand over a mouth ready to shriek. Slamming as they shut home with a thunderous concussion of huge bolts being automatically refitted into place, they locked with an endless sound of finality.

His father had made this hell called Panecraft.

Someone shouted obscenities in the distance.

Ghosts walked and spun. He caught vague shades and figures in his peripheral vision, hands waving, an occasional mouth silently speaking.

He clenched his fist tighter, aware that he was scowling, squinting into the recesses of this mother murderer. At twenty-four he had the same crow's feet around his eyes that his mother had at the very end, though even insane she hadn't been sad. "You didn't answer me, Hank. Has he confessed?"

"He hasn't said a word to anyone since his incarceration. That's why I wanted you here, Mattie. I'm hoping you can get him to talk. Either he's guilty or he isn't, but obviously he's had a hideous breakdown." Charters was no longer simply the doctor stating facts; his voice sounded ready to crack. Where was all the medical terminology? He really did love A.G.

"I understand."

Matthew's father couldn't speak in the vernacular if the Second Coming depended upon it. Matthew couldn't imagine anyone finding any peace or reformation here. Redemption remained out of grasp, even for those in charge.

"You don't need a Ph.D. in abnormal psychology to know cradling skeletons is horrifying in its implications." Charters gave a noncommittal shrug. "I can't get through. I've known the two of you since you were infants, and I can't imagine what could have happened to twist him like this. If he's not the one responsible for these missing persons, then there's still someone out there in my town who likes to kidnap kids, and, God help us, who no doubt enjoys killing them as well." The doctor took a breath, this kind of emotional outpouring so unlike him that both Matthew and Wakowski gazed at him apprehensively. "If it is him, I want to know why. Help us to find out the truth."

They came to A.G.'s cell.

"You haven't seen him in five years," Charters said. "That's a long time, and there might be awful feelings between the two of you, a sense of abandonment on either side. Don't be too startled by what you see. He's changed."

"We all have."

Wakowski unlocked the door to the cell and said, "Just tap, I'll hear you. Don't forget what you were told."

No, he never did. Matthew felt nervous energy breaking like surf through his muscles, the same way the newspapers they'd thrown had roiled through the air to break windows and flowerpots, sent frightened cats up telephone poles, and, once, flung from seventy feet with great precision, had struck old Mrs. Grossnet, who never even gave a nickel tip, in the barn-fat ass. He never forgot anything, and that's why they were here.

He knew A.G. and recognized the exemplar of evil coming back for them. His eyebrows hurt him, his forehead having been furrowed for so long it seared. He closed his eyes trying to loosen up and heard A.G. falling off his bike, listened again to their discussions on comic book characters and science fiction stories. Matthew understood there was one more question but was reluctant to ask it.

"What happened to the boy sitting on the swing?"

Without a sound, Wakowski, passive and in control, glanced left, as if hearing the sudden outburst of laughter from Matthew's scars. So that was an answer. Charters stared at the floor, reflexively stroking his mustache again, weighing consequences perhaps, or simply unable to trust Matthew enough.

After a few more seconds the doctor put his hands in his pockets and took them out again. "Richie Hastings is in Tower A. He's been kept sedated because of violent muscular spasms he's been experiencing. He has screaming fits. When he's fully conscious we often can't get him to close his eyes, and he shows no reaction, not even to his family. He's suffering most symptoms associated with narcolepsy, as well. He hasn't spoken since that day either."

"He'll be all right," Matthew said.

"You sound sure about that," Wakowski said.

"I am."

Charters moved in without warning, unashamed, at the point of sobbing, suddenly trying to hug him warmly as if Matthew were the son he never had nor wanted. Jesus, this place could shred you to confetti and throw you anywhere it wanted. Tears welled as he attempted to apologize for the unforgivable horrors of all the insane dead Galens. "Your father was a good man, Mattie. He loved both you and your mother very, very much. Believe me, he . . ."

Matthew broke away gently. He turned to face his past, the present, and discover if there was any future left, surrounded by the presence of his parents, the demented spirits still wandering here, and the Goat.

Give me strength.

Thinking of Debbi, he threw open the door and entered A.G.'s cell, completing the circle he only now realized his life had become. Whispers followed.

Chapter Two

Smiling as she walked down the street behind him, Debbi snatched the newspaper out of his hand and smacked him lightly in the head with it. "That's for the old dog," she said. Vengeance for the arthritic German shepherd he'd frightened into crawling off the McCalisters' porch with his poorly aimed Sunday supplement. Debbi had a thing for animals and always kept an eye on her neighbors' pets.

She whapped him again across the bridge of his nose, laughed and tickled him under the chin until he blushed—it took only a second—then stuck the *Summerfell Daily Gazette* back with the others stuffed in the burlap bag hanging over his shoulder. "C'mon, give me a ride. And don't ask where we're going, let's just go."

Proving deaf to his halfhearted protests that he had to finish his route, she *poo-poo*ed him in a perfect imitation of her mother—nose poised, hands thrown out as if fending off a mosquito, eyes sort of rolling. She climbed up onto his handlebars and scrunched uncomfortably into the space. Debbi was always smiling, never embarrassed about her braces like so many of the other kids were, like he would've been; she pulled his hands farther down the black grips so that his forearms were around her waist. He became heady with her scent and intimacy.

"C'mon, finish later, like anyone's really gonna care." Legs dangling on either side of his front wheel, her new sneakers occasionally bounced off the spokes as they rode, *ka-tink*ing.

A hot day with an intense glare. When the thicker wisps of clouds passed against the sun, shadows fell like cool wash towels pressed against his skin. Her long black hair blew back into his face, fascinating him just as much as her hands and smile, making him dizzy, and he knew he was alive.

"Let's go to the lighthouse," she said.

Chapter Three

The room turned out to be two cells, one nestled within the other. A bench jutted from the far wall for psychiatrists, police, or personal visitors to sit on while talking with the patient. Twelve feet from there was the inner cage, filling the opposite side of the room, spaces between the bars too small to even slip an arm through. On the floor, bisecting the outer cell, lay the black line Wakowski had spoken about. Bright fluorescent bulbs in the ceiling gave an odd tapering effect to the chamber, making it appear that the light was being siphoned off toward one corner. In the darkest section of the cage rested a sheetless bed bolted to the floor. Presumably, the graduated lighting had been determined to quiet the prisoner and allow him to sleep even with the fluorescents burning. Sixteen feet overhead roosted the broken video camera.

A.G. sat in the center of the bed with his eyes closed. He was seated in a modified lotus position as taught by the works of the great Abra Melin, for greatest focus of astral energy: legs tightly crossed and feet pulled up so that they touched opposite thighs, spine straight and head back, hands in his lap with fingers interlaced into specific placement. Pinkies, thumbs, and index fingers steepled, and these three steeples each pointing back at himself—thumbs aimed at the heart, pointers at his throat, pinkies at the forehead. It was also a way to catch passing lower-caste dybbuks that might harass and tempt, and bind them into service.

He'd kept in great shape. A.G.'s biceps strained against the long sleeves of the white jumpsuit, his perfect laterals outlined under the contours of Panecraft fatigues. His hair was much longer, flowing past his shoulders, with his face now framed by a reddish-brown beard that had been peach fuzz only five years earlier.

Matthew concentrated on the floor, watching the line.

Spheres converging, once again crossing.

Like so many other black designs and depictions he'd seen carved into the stones.

A.G. didn't seem aware that Matthew stood in the room with him. For several minutes, as

A.G. continued meditating, the density of the cloying air slowed the momentum of this home-coming. Wards had been set in the cage, but not particularly powerful ones; A.G. never had the patience to fine-tune each incantation, or to train his tongue to accept unpronounceable words.

Silence snared memories and kept them in private places: sound, motion, sight, cogni-zance. Everything proved acceptable while they waited, children still trapped inside the house on a rainy day with nothing good on television, rereading old comic books. Discussing the Fan-tastic Four, Daredevil, and Conan the Barbar-ian—entranced by those voluptuous barmaids Conan always saved, who deceived him in the end. Waiting quietly in the asylum, amiable, as if nothing had changed between them. Who would say "Let's get a Krunchburger" first?

Suddenly there was a sharp twitch in A.G.'s upper lip, an incisor momentarily displayed. A slight flutter in the left eyelid. Coming out of it now. His nerves seemed to be returning one by one, flesh becoming more pliant, relaxing with beads of sweat and deposits of salt dappling his hairline.

The inertia of the minute broke. Inhaling deeply, A.G. moved his hands down and out-ward until the steeples of his fingers were po-sitioned somewhat differently—thumbnails touching his chest, pointers shoved toward heaven, pinkies stiffly directed at Matthew. They both grunted. A.G.'s breathing grew regular, and at last he opened his eyes.

Still hurts a little, doesn't it?

Fighting the urge to mirror A.G.'s posture, Matthew remained seated on the bench, silent, wishing the wards were stronger. *Yes.*

It was a much simpler process once, but in the last couple of years it's gotten tougher for me . . . why do you think that is? Bulging veins in his neck pulsed as the sweat dripped down A.G.'s cheek and wove through his beard. The lingering stink of urine worked from the open toilet under the heavy smell of pine disinfectant. There were the barest tinges of winterfresh toothpaste and mint mouthwash. Screeched obscenities continued, only slightly stifled by the walls. This stagnant atmosphere of Panecraft was concrete slowly drying around them. *Don't you remember, Mattie?*

Of course I do. I taught you.

A.G. smiled. *Nice talking to you again.*

What's happened? Why are you still here?

You recognize the handiwork.

Stop this, A.G. I need you on the outside. I know you haven't killed anyone.

No, you don't. The smile broadened. *You only hope I haven't.*

Why haven't you spoken to them? You're being stupid.

Giles Corey never gave a plea in Salem, not

40

even when they put enough rocks on him to crush him to death. He wouldn't give them the satisfaction of accepting or denying that he was a witch. But we know he was.

Giles Corey, was that his new idol? Matthew unconsciously clasped his hands and pressed his fingers together. It was much tougher than before. *What do you want me to do?*

Nothing you can do. We both know that.

The Goat had told them so back then, and the scars repeated it now, growling with A.G.'s voice, rehashing conversations from the catacombs. Matthew performed a simple evocation, calling forward a sample of spirit to quiet the dead past. The room grew cooler.

You're famous around here now, Mattie, sort of a hometown golden boy. Our English teacher, Mr. Kroft, is going to direct the drama club in their presentation of your The Gift of Nightmares. *They think it's a wonderful play, full of innovation and heartwarming humor. Even the second act, which I think could use another pass, to tell you the truth. Hey, Jazz teaches there too.*

Thank God that Jazz was all right. A migraine wrenched Matthew's skull. *Answer me, what do I have to do? What do you think I should do?*

My advice, you want my advice? Is that what I'm hearing? I had a vision of Father Urbain Grandier not too long ago, rather weak-kneed for a guy who possessed so many nymphos. I suppose being burned at the stake takes something

Tom Piccirilli

out of a man. Jeanne of the Angels showed up too. Not a very pretty woman, though Vanessa Redgrave did manage to capture her nutty side in the Ken Russell film.

More games. What the hell was he talking about? Father Grandier had been sacrificed in Loudon for his political misdeeds. His bureaucratic enemies approached Mother Superior Jeanne des Anges and the repressed Ursuline nuns, who feigned possession, swearing they'd been bewitched by him. A.G. was saying what? At Grandier's trial, Jeanne des Agnes appeared in court with a noose around her neck, threatening to hang herself if she could not expiate her lies, and of course she was ignored. An innocent man was tortured and murdered, and the public so appreciated the exorcism and sudden fame that the convent became a tourist attraction and continued its jesting performances, nuns running around naked, crying about the Devil pinching their asses.

So you're a martyr like Grandier?

No, he was guilty. He made a deal with Zabulon in the order of Seraphims, didn't you know?

Matthew scowled. Who cared, either way? It had nothing to do with Summerfell. *Forget about that shit and be straight with me, damn it. I've come back to pay for my mistakes. I need information. What's happened while I was gone? How were you using the bones?*

(Debbi was dead.)

42

Yes, A.G. said, *you did teach me the lessons, but I won't hold that against you. Not that. Well . . . maybe . . .*

And the black line began scuttling forward, clawing at Matthew's feet.

Paperboys. Christ on the cross, they'd witnessed everything afterward; it was as if the neighborhood needed someone to record its slow crucifixion after the release of their harvested sins, after the shapes of these iniquities had been set free.

(Debbi was dead.)

Matthew had desperately needed to see his mother. At the time he hadn't located her grave yet, and his father wouldn't tell him her Social Security number or why she'd been buried in Potter's Field with the unrevealed dead. His father caught him going through the tax returns and sealed all her papers—why? Just because she'd gone mad, if in fact she had? And why couldn't the great psychiatrist save her, of all people? Matthew prayed that her soul might find a way back to him, if only for a little while. Just to talk. He couldn't have imagined how much he would miss her voice. A.G. sat under the elms and wished his own alcoholic mother would croak, or else leave to make someone else sick with her crappy cooking; she did, soon enough, running off that autumn with a redneck trucker in a rusty Freightliner, packing out sides of beef from the slaughterhouse. A.G.'s dad hadn't cared much.

These nightmares could kill.

Glow-in-the-dark Aurora models of movie monsters shuffled across their desks and climbed the covers, green fangs of Bela leered against starlight while the Wolfman's mangy paws pulled back their sheets. It happened until they came up with the correct incantations to keep their dreams from running wild. Every night for a month Matthew and A.G. sneaked out of their houses after their fathers had gone to bed, met in the park, and practiced the proper gestures. Patterns were crucial and so complex.

They tried their hardest to keep from falling asleep. Dreams infected their consciences. Ruth managed to meet them by the lake. She'd somehow learned to handle it better than they by not remembering anything. Slapping their cheeks and sniffing pepper, they shivered in the cold, sneezing and drinking from a thermos filled with poorly made coffee. Their spells took on a new reality. Matthew cursed and cultivated his raw desire for retribution. The atonement. He had a nice feel for it even at thirteen. How his face had burned with it, his hands like white-hot metal when the hexes were good.

The daemons and djinn came anyway.

Formless in the beginning in their way, sometimes only visions, sometimes not. Watching the sky, Matthew would see a deeper darkness tacked to the rest of the universe, figures dancing up there on rooftops, dipping into open windows and ducking behind dormers. Handfuls of brief, vicious laughter hovered in the treetops.

And through those nights A.G. shared the responsibility and never tried to make Matthew feel guilty about any of it.

Paperboys gone collecting.

They'd been on Cedar Road when Cherry Laudley dug beneath the walnut tree in her backyard, giggling cruelly and occasionally chewing on something. Only two grades ahead of them, at fifteen she'd already been raped by her own cousin and three of his friends. Rumors spread, and the gossip never let up the entire time she was pregnant. Cherry dropped out of school and moved to the other end of town, where the shacks swayed in the wind and old men sat waiting with their shotguns, hoping to spot rabid dogs. Buck Laudley had skipped all inquiries and supposedly left for a job waiting for him on an oil rig.

They'd seen Cherry carefully toss Buck's teeth into the pit.

Matthew and A.G. had skulked along the streets through the following months, smelling the sweet and sickening scent in the breeze blowing through town. They were doing their jobs: collecting.

They'd gone to see what they could see, capture what couldn't escape, and hide from what hunted them. Getting around Summerfell at all hours on their bikes, honing their *Summerfell Gazette* underhand tosses, perfecting the boomerang curve. They'd slunk around Cherry's yard and picked up some of Buck's teeth. There was power in bone. They'd peered into her bedroom window, the two of them listening to her talk to the deformed stillborn child, watching her trying to breast-feed it.

And they had understood something more about the Goat when they heard the dead newborn cry back, *"You had to do it, Momma . . ."* Later, after the cops had found what she'd done with Buck's body, each piece wrapped separately in a garbage bag, buried beneath the walnut tree, organs in the freezer and the skillet, Charters claimed she was schizophrenic.

She was the first they knew about.

They'd noticed the shift of seasons. Folks who enjoyed painting were inspired by the drowning crimson of sunsets. There was less fun to be found. (Debbi was dead.) They dreamed of the druids and pagans who had lived here before them, Batman and Robin, Mork and Mindy. Matthew read the Bible continuously and started frequenting the shops in the slim alleyways of Gallows. Despite the New Age contrivances placed upon the old orders, he recognized the real grimoires when he saw them, having studied and knowing what to look for. Several of the gibbering women of Pane-craft were pagans, and he listened to their warnings, learning what was madness and what was hysterical presentation, sifting through their babble to discover what lay at the honest heart of their beliefs. The elderly bibliophiles in the bookstores patted his shoulder as he dug for pamphlets and texts no one else would care about; even the rickety and myopic could feel and see signs in this boy, and everyone knew his father.

He learned about what he hated, staring up at the lighthouse. (He held pillows over his head, trying to stifle his mother's cries in his mind, Debbi's whimpers in the blood.) Concentrating on the occult as if it hadn't already stolen too much of his soul, chest always burning beneath the cold cream, the scars occasionally murmuring his name.

Seeing Mrs. Gaddis trotting on the road in the drizzle with her overstuffed pocketbook swinging, a kerchief around her head and ankles so thin it was a wonder she could stand at all, feeding the squirrels that would not come to her, three weeks after she was dead.

Seeing heartwrecked Mr. Gaddis eating the terrified squirrels in the park, in his right hand the pocketknife and in his left the trip wire to his squirrel trap, his wife's kerchief tied tightly around his head as if to keep his brain from pouring out his ears, still crying and gagging on animal fur as Sheriff Hodges forced the knife out of his hand.

Jesus, shut up already, Matthew begged.

Hey, but listen . . .

Telephones rang on Pond Boulevard—Judy Ann Culthbert calling him and A.G. inside for a piece of homemade apple pie. Hmm, wouldn't you boys like some of that? . . . How about a five-dollar tip for two hardworking, financially conscious young men delivering those heavy papers out in the sun? . . . Then pleading with Matthew to answer the phone, just to pick up the goddamn thing, it won't hurt you, see? . . . It's only a telephone, but please pick it up for me. A five-dollar tip for both of you, ten dollars, twenty. The wall vibrated with the rage of the ringing. Judy Ann Culthbert reclined on the couch, lifting her skirt and parting her legs now, opening her blouse button by button, finger-nails playing across her nipples as something like a grotesque four-legged fish wriggled out from behind the refrigerator, clambered atop her, and began to grunt, mewling without lips as she groaned in response.

Matthew answered the phone.

A voice called him by name and told him to come across to the beach (it wasn't Debbi, it only sounded like her, oh God), to play in the foam and carry away uncommon seashells to impress the prettiest girl in his class (Debbi was, and Debbi was dead). Bring A.G., come back for me. He stuck the receiver in the micro-wave and watched as it sparked and melted. He and A.G. attacked the fish creature with a couple of yard-sale lamps Judy Ann had on top of the television. It was the first time Matthew ever attempted an invocation, but the words wouldn't come correctly, thank Christ, and he utterly failed. The fishboy bled blue ooze, got mad, and crawled out the bay window.

Judy Ann Culthbert scratched her belly open with a pair of dull scissors, never thanked them, never talked to anyone again. Later, Matthew learned the fishboy's name was Elemi, from a midlevel circle.

They collected and found that six more houses on that block were the same. Ruth Cahill lived on Pond Boulevard, and she swore her grandmother would never be her grandmother anymore, the old lady just standing there doing nothing. Ruth kept an awl in her back pocket. Despite her self-imposed amnesia—she didn't remember the cave, almost didn't recall Debbi at all—Ruth had unconsciously learned one hex, and she threw it again and again. "Get her away, A.G., please, get her away!"

I thought the madness was over, Matthew said, the migraine building.

No, you didn't. Now the first real thrust of fury, all of the smarm gone. *That's why you left.*

I thought it would come with me.

We've been together forever.

49

Yes.

Soon will be Year One, Anno Satanas, said A.G., really meaning it, as if he truly believed nothing could stop the different dawn. *You can't save them, you can't even save yourself. I know, I've tried. You've started to repay your debt too late. I don't hold you responsible, the disease was loose before it found us, but you should have stayed. You should have watched out for us. For Helen. Jazz. Joey and Jane. Ruth. And me, Mattie. And for me.*

Biting his tongue, Matthew said, *Where's Ruth? Do you have any idea where she or the others might be?*

No, I searched and found nothing. My baby's gone, Mattie, the bastard finally took her! Such intense hatred, exploding from his depths, both of them lost for a moment in a swill of rancor before reining in the rage. *I was never as adept as you, never had the real power, and now she's gone. Show me the mark.*

No.

Show me.

A.G. unclasped his hands and rubbed his legs, carefully easing them out of the lotus position. The pressure abated. *If you stay, those scars of the pentagram will be completed, and Year One will begin. That's the real reason the Goat has brought you home. It's always loved you best above all others. I tried my hardest and failed. It's your turn to fight, Mattie.*

You're right.

A.G. stood and stretched. He came to the bars and pressed his palms against them. Spheres uncrossing, drifting back into their own realms. *If you lose we're all going to spend an eternity in torment together.* The black line shimmied into the cage and spiraled against A.G.'s ankle, a beloved pet returned.

"Let the kid go," Matthew said.

Chapter Four

From the darkness, into the dim light and silence, the mighty mouse came around again.

It crawled from the rotted half-inch space between two baseboards that didn't meet together properly by the heating vent. Brown and sleek, meandering across the rug, the mouse seemed more like a gregarious kitten.

Staring at the quivering whiskers, Henry Charters couldn't decide whether to throw his worn copy of Freud's *Dora: An Analysis of a Case of Hysteria* or the unfinished tuna fish sandwich that had been lying on his desk all afternoon. The tuna would probably hurt the thing more than the heavy-handedness of Freud, so Charters tossed the thin book. The mighty mouse dodged with a brisk four-paw sidestep and continued to ease its way through the rug.

I lied and I am getting old, he thought.

Charters moved his reading lamp aside and picked up the largest of several picture frames sitting on the shelves behind him. When was the last time he'd actually welled up, much less nearly blubbered as he'd done on Mattie Galen's shoulder? And when had he ever been so nostalgic, feeling the incessant urge to stare at these photographs?

It took him by surprise. Undoubtedly, hell, any day now his old forty-five records would bring about another round of wistfulness, as well as his school medals and yearbooks. Soon he'd have to curl up with his bowling trophies to go to sleep. It made him ashamed that he could not face these emotions head-on. He could remember his grandparents sitting back in their verandah rocking chairs on Sundays, telling stories of the European villages, perusing captured fractions of a past destroyed by war, turning the pages of their scraps of memory.

He wiped a hand over the dirty glass of the frame, revealing a collage of snipped photos: faces, frowns, ball games and costume parties, barbecues, baby smiles and wedding marches, none of them his own. They were pressed together and fitted in no pattern, without any method. Seeing the pictures of his convoluted life was like watching television with a broken remote, continuously changing channels.

Switching, hopping. Here his first wife, Sophie, and here his third, Maureen. And with a blue sailor's cap tugged down over her eyes appeared his second wife, Melissa. So close together here as if they were great friends, though they'd never met. Divorced twice and a widower once: It took him three seconds to remember who had died. Melissa. He shook his head.

His wristwatch beeped twice, signaling the hour, and he nearly screamed.

"Jesus!" he breathed, stroking his mustache.

In the four corners of the collage a man drank a beer at four different Fourth of July picnics, toasting the camera each time. Matthew Galen had either never seen, or couldn't recall, this side to his father. Seventeen-year-old Matthew making his famous ninety-nine-yard run in the championship game, the day he broke his ankle and met Helen. All of their lives laid bared before one another, so why didn't Matthew know his father? Ten-year-old Mattie grinning into the camera just above a toothless baby Mattie goo-gooing in a hard pine crib. Sophie sat on the white steps waving, hair swept into a thousand auburn streamers by the wind. A.G. in wrestler's gear, pinning an opponent on the mat, A.G. in the hospital hallway, crying after falling off his bike and skinning his knee.

Charters picked up the phone and, out of sheer frustration, toyed with the dial and started to call a number that belonged to no one he knew. He dropped it back into the cradle and checked his watch again: 9:05 P.M. He turned back to the frame and used his handkerchief to clean the remaining dust from the glass.

He found Matthew's mother and father sitting on a hammock at the bottom of the collage. She had a smile that brightened every facet of her face, freckles lightly sprinkled in a straight line down her tan nose, eyes slanted with a camera-shy glint of amusement; incredibly beautiful. God, it could get him, it could always get him. Her husband's arm around her shoulder, her fingers reaching up to touch his but not quite meeting, with his other hand resting possessively on her knee. Look at how Galen stared at his wife's face. Anyone could tell he was eager to kiss her at every instant. Both of them smiling and perfect together, so that their deaths, which had come and gone long ago, felt as if they'd never actually arrived. These people seemed like fabrications—he could imagine too clearly that they'd never truly existed except in his most humble, human fantasies.

A knock at the door.

"Come in," he said, grateful for the interruption.

Roger Wakowski entered.

Standing six feet five, the ex-marine filled the doorway, and Charters could sense the disapprobation in the air. He continued to be amazed at how the guard's intimidation factor could make a swing from zero to one-eighty if the situation called for it. In Tower C, where men could make razors from their own toenail clippings and made themselves throw up into a security guard's eyes, there was no one Charters would rather be standing beside if a patient went manic. He had yet to see Wakowski in anything less than total control of circumstances.

Seven or eight months back a weight lifter on LSD—which appeared to be making a comeback as drug of choice in the area—had undergone a whack attack and become psychotic in a bar in Gallows, and had later been wrestled into the hospital cuffed and escorted by two police officers who didn't want him in their jail. By the time they got him to Panecraft he appeared docile and nearly coherent.

You heard about men who could snap handcuffs when they were on PCP, but Charters never imagined seeing it like this, the links of the cuffs twisting apart as if in frighteningly slow motion, the weight lifter showing no sign of effort at all, just a dazed frown on his face as the bones in his wrists snapped along with the cuffs. He didn't know he was in agony. Hands held together double-fisted like lumps of iron, the weight lifter swung his massive arms around violently in two sweeping motions, knocking the officers to the ground where he kneeled and began strangling the men despite his broken wrists, one throttled in each hand. Calmly, with great indifference.

And with an equal amount of indifference, and three unimaginably forceful, quick, effective blows, Wakowski battered the man unconscious.

With his self-indulgent grin—when he grinned at all—Roger Wakowski proved to be a hell of a nice guy when you got around to it, and considering the figure he cut when he stood in your doorway, you always got around to it fast. He proved himself quite an actor, as well, when ordered to be. Without question, Wakowski performed the part he'd been assigned. He, too, could lie.

"I have the tape, sir."

Charters pointed to the television console and replaced the picture frame on his shelf. "Put it in the VCR, please. How long did Galen stay?"

"Nineteen minutes."

"That's all?"

"Yes."

"That was simply rhetorical, Roger. Did he say anything to anyone as he left?"

"No."

"Did you view the visit?"

"As instructed, I merely taped the meeting." Only the barest hint of unsettling anger in that voice as Wakowski shoved the tape into the VCR.

In an attempt to alleviate tension, Charters

briefly considered using his smooth, calming doctor's voice to speak with subtle professionalism, but was afraid that Wakowski might smash in his trachea. "I'm more sorry about this than you'll ever know, Roger, so please don't add to the burden by giving me the cold shoulder. I apologize that you were forced to become part of this charade, but it was necessary, and it's your job. It's my job. And you of all people know how difficult it is to get to the truth of these matters when we're not sure of all factors involved."

Wakowski stood at attention now, hands behind his back, eyes averted and gaze resting on a spot somewhere off to the left of Charters's ear. Was he looking at the collage?

"Sir, may I . . . ?"

"For Christ's sake, you're not in the Marines anymore, Roger, though you might wish you were. You can say whatever the hell you like. And I would appreciate your honest opinion here."

"I think it's wrong."

Charters waited. He hung forward in his chair, stroking his mustache. Wakowski said nothing more. "That's it? You think it's wrong?"

Wakowski's voice changed, loosening, as if each portion of himself were just another role, as if another man entirely were talking now. "I think you're handling it badly. This wasn't advised by the police. It wasn't a part of our normal procedure. We either watch a visit for its duration on the closed-circuit monitors or we don't. You're too immediate and confined to this case."

"There may be some validity to that."

"This is too covert without any reason. If you suspect that Galen is a part of this crime, then he ought to be under investigation as well. You should have informed the police of his arrival. By attempting to protect him you've already implicated him. If Galen knows anything he'll still have to cover for his friend, and I doubt that either of them is stupid enough to talk freely when they know they're being monitored. I can see nothing useful in any of this."

Glad that Wakowski wasn't staring directly at him, Charters wondered about Roger's past for the first time in a long while. Men always in strife are accustomed to strife. Charters could only guess Wakowski's age to be between forty-five and fifty, and wherever he'd been had apparently been bad enough. Yet his distinct code did not allow him to question his superiors. He'd been perfectly trained, and you had to be curious about a man who ever grasped perfection in any form.

Charters felt as though he were working a CIA mission in the night deserts of Tehran. "I agree, believe it or not. But unfortunately I have no other choice." The tuna felt like rubber cement as he brought his fist down on it. "Do you think

I enjoy playing these games on men I've known since they were children? These boys are family to me, but even if there is the slightest chance that A.G. might open to Matthew, and that Matt Galen himself might speak freely, then I have an obligation to this town and to six families to learn as much about this case as possible."

"You're working blind, and under misconceptions. You're nearsighted because you knew them as children, and you've lost the ability to discriminate. You know little about the patient himself, and less about Galen. You're baiting them with each other, and that's simply foolhardy, and probably worthless."

"Something's brought on A.G.'s collapse, and Matthew is my best chance at discovering the impetus. There's an incredible bond between them. They're the two most stubborn young men I've ever met, and if I have to use Matt to gain the truth then I am prepared to do that." Charters realized he had begun repeating himself.

"So am I, but I wanted to state my position clearly," Wakowski said, his tone switching again, "that I have my reservations about you being able to handle this case efficiently due to its personal nature."

"What else can be done? I'm the most qualified doctor to handle this case. Moser and Cohen have never dealt with an aberrant psychosis like A.G.'s. My Christ, they heard about him sitting with a skeleton and started quoting the Chianti and fava bean scene from *Silence of the Lambs*. And Patterford, Peale, and Willits have enough to do running the group therapy sessions and the alcohol and drug rehabs. I can't just pull them and walk away."

"Let him be taken out of state to Stanfield, or up to Corzone Sanitarium."

"If he is criminally insane, they won't be able to handle him. It hasn't even been proven that A.G. is guilty of these crimes. I won't commit him to that without more evidence."

Wakowski crossed his arms and leaned forward slightly, voice controlled and focused. "He's already been committed in one sense, sir. He's guilty of exhuming the bones of children, and though the police haven't formally charged him in this case, you know they will. You talk as though he's a little boy playing in a sandbox, riding his bicycle with a skinned knee."

So Wakowski had been looking at the collage. "Be that as it may, Sheriff Hodges is still trying to find solid evidence. He's hoping to make an open-and-shut murder case out of this, and I'm afraid there's more to be learned, good and bad. He wants to keep A.G. within his jurisdiction, and I want to keep the boy within arm's length in case he needs me. Now, if you don't mind, Roger, I'd like to be left alone."

"No," Wakowski said, turning, looking as

Tom Piccirilli

though he might maim someone as he left. "No, you don't. You're so lonely it's warping your perspective." His nostrils flared as if a noxious and overpowering odor had suddenly invaded the room. "It bleeds from you."

Charters grimaced as he viewed the flare of black snow and realized there had been some kind of camera malfunction after all. Such pure irony wasn't lost on him. "Beautiful, this is just so goddamn beautiful." Disgusted, he kneaded his temples. "Maybe I should've been a shoemaker like you, Grandpa." The mighty mouse gazed up at him until he threw *Man and His Symbols* at it.

A.G. and Matthew could hardly be seen through the crackling interference. The entire bottom third of the picture fluctuated fiercely, filled with scrambled static and jumping billows of color, creases, and strange aftershadows. He tried adjusting the tracking, but nothing helped.

"Beautiful. Wonderful, just fucking great. And just how in the hell did this happen?"

Bulging silhouettes swung across the screen, superimposing the outline of A.G. so that others appeared to be sitting on his bed beside him, moving in tandem. Video figments concealed the shifting remnant figure of Matthew entering the room, eclipsed by the gray dead area of tape. Charters wondered if A.G. could have smeared his own feces on the camera somehow.

The doctor pulled his chair to within inches of the set but could make out little of what was actually happening in there, who was doing what, if anything at all, but the sound seemed unaffected as Matthew's footsteps rang through the cell, the snap of the bench as he sat. The sound must be working, yes, but even now, after three, four, then five minutes more, no one had said anything. Why wasn't he saying anything? Sign language, speech through gestures, lip-reading? What was going on in their heads? "Damn these machines!"

Now only a low, vague, indefinable noise beginning to hiss over the speaker: whistles, tickings, like the rush of breeze through a wood. Frenzied images changed, looming larger, stretching over the blurred, shady forms like swaying dancers. He could almost see Melissa there, twirling.

Matthew moved, perhaps, but still said nothing.

"What is he doing? Why isn't he talking?" Whistles grew much louder. Snippets of faraway chattering faded in and out. The picture jumped erratically, and flickered. "Why?"

His eyes ached terribly, but Charters couldn't keep himself from watching the screen, couldn't hold back this attack of anxiety that gripped him as he waited for something to happen, anything that might give him a hint as to what caused the breakdown, his own or anyone else's, a clue to the missing children.

For nineteen minutes he waited for a word, stroking his mustache, staring into the storm. He sat back in his chair and regarded the collage, the mighty mouse nibbling on *Dora*.

Matthew said, "Let the kid go."

The VCR vomited the tape.

Chapter Five

If it was a dog, it was the ugliest one he'd ever seen.

Evening porch bug-lights gave off barely enough yellow illumination for Matthew to notice the heap lying on the sidewalk in front of him. Despite the jutting pink tab that might possibly be a tongue, he couldn't be certain it wasn't a worn-out living room carpet, a mohair beanbag chair, or a Hefty bag put out in the trash. Dangling fur puffed out at intervals, as if from an exhaling snout. In the darkness of Manor Lane's canopy trees he found himself wondering.

Leaves whipped before his face, falling from high branches. His legs were tightening up on him, sore after the lengthy walk across town.

His bad ankle throbbed, and he needed more time—he hoped there was time left—to scope the situation, to plan and rest. To relearn some of the more difficult disciplines.

Fatigue pervaded his mind and body. He had to get some sleep before he crashed so hard he wasted tomorrow slumbering. There weren't any hotels in Summerfell. There was no need for them in a town without a tourist attraction, unlike Loudon, where people came to see nuns cavort and kiss in the moonlight, though Matthew's mother, too, had danced naked in the dark streets.

The only motel in town, The Outside Inn, was actually a run-down bar with a few extra rooms for rent upstairs, where you'd have to sleep on sheets you wouldn't touch even if knotting them together was your only escape from a fire. Sheriff Hodges constantly raided the place for any number of justified reasons. Matthew elected to try to get a room over at the Carmichaels' boardinghouse, if it still existed.

The ugly dog didn't stir.

Luna moths fluttered in the glow of the streetlamps, casting shadows onto the curb. The satchel strap cut into his shoulder, so he unbuckled it and let it slip into his hand. From an open window of the house behind him, a stereo played loudly. The moon lay submerged in clouds, and he chastised himself for not having the foresight to check and find out exactly what phase it was in. That would make a great difference.

The reunion with A.G. had proven more taxing and less worthwhile than he'd been praying for. It had been exhilarating and god-awful to see him again, inside each other's heads, even with the bars and spilled blood between them—merely being in the same room was a reaffirmation of their friendship.

Their castle had swelled and accompanied them; come to life, the insanity followed them everywhere. It was true. They *had* been together forever, just as A.G. said, perhaps even entwined in an earlier incarnation. That counted for more and less than Matthew could understand. He knew whose bones had been unearthed and what they were being used for.

A.G. had returned to the altar and carried Debbi up the stone stairs. Then he must've gone to the sunken meadow beside Potter's Field, and—in accordance with the rituals—using only his hands to yank clumps of sod and dirt, he dug until his hands bled, making damn sure that his hands bled, until he'd burrowed far enough to smash his fists through the rotted orange crates that the hospital had once used to bury the aborted and stillborn. The remains of the unblessed.

He's using them as locks, to keep out the Goat.

It wouldn't be enough.

Headlights flashed down the length of the

cross street and a '69 Mustang—the kind Jazz used to drive—full of teenagers, made a wildly sharp left around the corner, tires screeching. One of the kids lobbed a half-full can of beer at him and a couple of girls in the backseat laughed and waved; the driver blared his horn twice. Screw the curfew, everybody had to buck the decree.

Matthew caught the can with an athlete's graceful ease and flipped it behind him into the grate of a sewer drain. Summerfell at night appeared to be no different than before, except the neighborhood seemed less full of motion. Old ladies weren't out in the park walking their poodles one last time before bed. He saw no couples sitting on their verandah love seats.

He wondered who would deliver Richie Hastings's papers. Who would go collecting.

It surprised him that he felt so certain the people and places of town had not changed—could not have changed—in his absence. He remained the catalyst. He'd even thought of the dead past in the present tense, as though only a few drunken days had been skipped instead of five years. You can never leave home, no matter how hard you tried. You were nailed to the life you once led. He'd passed ten thousand unaltered sites. Like pulling snapshots out of his wallet. The houses were painted the identical color year in and out, rock gardens with the same rocks, seashells highlighting the brickwork. So many lawns mowed in long-established patterns, Mr. Shelard's going east to west and curving eights around the trees, the duckbill weathervane twirling in the breeze.

Above the town floated Matthew's own past, the eerie bane of children. Night wings flitted.

Whatever the thing was that lay on the Carmichaels' walk, as Matthew approached it finally lifted that part of the body it probably considered its head, then gradually raised the rest of its sizable bulk off the ground and began to shamble down the driveway toward him. Gravel crunched beneath its slow, plodding steps. Perhaps they were paws. Perhaps it had a face hidden somewhere in that densely matted fur that barricaded what might be its head. Or possibly not.

Matthew leaned against the street sign and tried to see if it had a tail or any other canine features he could discern. The closer it got, the less certain he became. Drooping fur continued to puff up every now and then, so at least it breathed, producing a kind of wheezing, gurgling sound that your lawn mower would make if tipped into your Jacuzzi.

"Jesus, pal, you are a walking stretch of similes," Matthew said as the dog tripped and fell over the curb like a gutter ball, sniffed at his sneakers, and hunkered down next to his knees. "I can't help myself." The dog shoved something round and wet and hopefully nonsexual against his hand; Matthew at last recognized a nose, and there, below it, the slobbering indent of a mouth. He petted its head, trying to part the fur so that he could see eyes. He found a collar with two tags buried within layers of black knots and fat.

One read:

Remember that the most beautiful things
in the world are the most useless;
peacocks and lilies, for example.
—John Ruskin, *The Stones of Venice, I*

The other read: *Disgusto*.

He patted it some more. "Disgusto? Pretty rude, but man, you ain't kidding."

Curious if the Carmichaels would remember him, Matthew started up the walk to the house. Disgusto joggled beside him, wheezing and coughing.

Knocking on the screen door, Matthew squinted into the glare of the bug light. He shielded his eyes and pressed his face close to the screen. Strange that the door should be open in the October chill, but on occasion somebody would start a blazing fire in the fireplace and still leave the windows open. "Hello?" he called. A water tap ran in the distance, pots banging together, and a television muttered canned sound-track laughter. Someone humming, snoring lightly.

Eugene Carmichael's gruff voice cut through the undercurrent sounds. "Come on in! Hold on just a sec!"

Confused by that, Matthew grabbed the latch and started to enter, shrugged, and decided to stay put until being formally invited in; again he realized that the old habits had not died easily (they hadn't died). His mother's lessons had been with him too long, and to this day he couldn't put his elbows on the table even if he wanted to, or drink straight from the milk carton.

Disgusto wagged his flank without any visible tail, then stood on his hind legs, scratched at the faded white shingles, and wailed a unique dog bark.

In a way, it sounded like the bleating of a goat.

Mr. Carmichael came to the door, wiping soapy hands on an apron. "Somebody been teachin' you how to knock, Gus?" He addressed the dog standing stretched on its hind legs before him, and said, "Now, you know better than that, get down this second or I'm taking you for booster shots, and you know what a pain that can be, the vet havin' to hunt around lookin' for your ass all day." Gus dropped to the ground. Eugene Carmichael opened the screen door, and the dog cantered inside.

Whiffs of lemon-scented dishwashing liquid drifted by. Mr. Carmichael had not aged a great

71

deal, though the last time Matthew had seen him it didn't appear that the man could age much more anyway: Eugene Carmichael remained one of those eternally enduring people who never look older or younger than sixty. Bald except for the same few silver wisps that stuck like lint to the top of his narrow head, with shaggy tufts of white hair springing from behind his ears, his beard trimmed and still containing some brown patches. Spry and wiry, he had a pair of arms that looked as though he could heft a cannonball across a football field.

Mr. Carmichael always spoke to the kids as though he were a kid himself, which proved better than having him talk to them as if they were adults. He'd often played two-hand touch with them; Manor Lane was the widest road within several blocks, and all the kids that didn't take it to the park played their street games here. The Carmichaels never shouted if you ran to the side of their house and drank from their hose, or climbed their trellis to get a Frisbee off the gabled roof. He couldn't recall anyone ever having spoken a bad word about them.

Carmichael stared for a moment with some glint of recognition, a thoughtful grimace curving his mouth. "I know you, son? I know you." He glanced around like a contestant on *The Price is Right* searching the audience for answers.

"I'm Matthew Galen. I used to deliver your paper."

"That's what you say? That you used to deliver the paper? You don't say that you're a big playwright in New York, got all kinds of awards and news clippings in the town hall? You say you used to deliver that gazette?" Carmichael laughed, stepped outside smiling broadly, and lifted his arms to clap Matthew on his shoulders. "Mattie Galen, come home after all this time only to catch a henpecked man like me dressed in an apron. Damn! It ain't fair, I believe, but there's nothing I can do about it. I'm forgetting my manners; come on inside."

Ushered through the foyer, Matthew stepped into the large house, recollecting how they'd chase Ruth under the sprinkler, how Emma Carmichael would bring them lemonade. He noticed the historical decorations the instant he came through the door; Carmichael was a Civil War buff, and on the hallway walls were paintings of Lincoln, Lee, Grant, John Pope, and Jeb Stuart. Positioned around them were the different versions of the American flag in its various stages. Emma preferred a more European flavor to the decor—a French-styled writing desk, Victorian rosewood furniture set under the shelves where Swiss clocks sat beside reproductions of *La Pietà* and Rodin's *The Kiss*.

Gusto pranced, and Carmichael shooed the dog off. Gus lay in the middle of the hall, so they had to step over him. "Damn nuisance, watch yourself, 'cause he can't see nothing." The smell of lemon became stronger. "You planning on staying long, Mattie? I suspect you're here about getting a room, not that I wouldn't have enjoyed a visit from you just to shoot the baloney and such."

"I'll be in town for a few weeks."

"Heck, you know this place, always a bed here for most souls who needs one, long as he ain't drunk or on the lam or got too much of a dirty mouth, which seems to be the case more and more lately. Must be that you've been gone some, what, four, five years since you left town?"

"That's about right."

"Glad you're doing so well for yourself in New York City. I went there once, long time ago, and a man nearly pissed on my shoe, a Wall Street type too, damned uncivilized bastard. Had a hell of a time getting out damn Grand Central Station too. Should've just gotten back on the train. Here, let me introduce you to the other guests. My Emma doesn't believe that calling them boarders is friendly enough, and I think I agree. You look bushed, Mattie, but it's a matter of course I let the others get a glimpse of you so they don't think they're being burgled if they spot you wandering around."

Matthew swallowed a groan and ventured a weak grin. His ankle could hold him up a little while longer, but the migraine had worsened and the edges of his vision pulsed with white light. Wards had to be set soon, or he'd foul them in his fatigue. He touched the walls, searching for the Goat, and came away with a gritty feeling he couldn't explain.

They passed the empty kitchen, and Carmichael tossed his apron onto a Formica countertop. "Doing the dishes makes me feel like a suffragette. I have more respect for my mother the longer I live."

They came to the den, faintly lit and paneled in dark brown grain, cooler than the rest of the house. He touched the wall again and felt the same corporeal oddness. Matthew licked his finger when Carmichael turned, and tasted a stew of death, revenants, and anguish: A house this old would have a cryptic history, but something didn't sit flush.

At a small mahogany table, two elderly men faced each other, playing chess; both had their elbows propped, resting their chins in their hands and smothering gray beards, sharply regarding the board. Neither spoke nor looked up as Matthew and Carmichael entered. Determination and near-fanatical intensity creased their wrinkled brows. *Anything can take you over.* Foreheads mottled from the strain, mustaches wet with nervous spit. Except for their alert eyes, they didn't move at all.

Carmichael leaned over and whispered,

"These two are the Happy Boys. Hoffman and Kessner. They ain't much in the conversing department, so don't feel obligated to sit and chat. They play a lot of chess, so if you ain't that whasisname Bobby Fischer, I suspect you won't have a lot to talk to them about anyway. Besides, neither one speaks a heckuva lot of English. Don't ask me what they do speak in, all those foreign accents curl my ears, but I'm stupid that way. I don't mind, 'cept Emma keeps bustin' my chops about being neighborly. I try my best, but they don't care. That's all right by me."

Matthew gave a brief wave of his hand, waiting for Kessner or Hoffman to respond or at least move a piece. They did nothing. "Hello."

Through the den and down another short hall Carmichael walked him into an immense, old-fashioned, deeply centered living room. A woman a few years younger than Matthew lay on the couch napping, arms splayed over her belly. Jodi, having become so lovely. Petite with rich curling black hair and small attractive features that some might have called 'elfin.' She actually *zzzz*ed in a cute way when she exhaled through her partially opened lips. Carmichael took a red and black crocheted blanket and covered her with it.

"This sleeping vision of beauty is my daughter, Jodi, who had knock-knees and braces the last time you probably laid eyes on her. She used to be scared to hand you the paper money when you came collecting."

"Not anymore, I shouldn't think."

"No, nowadays I have to keep a shotgun around to chase off all them hormonally imbalanced little pukes in their sports cars. Like that Jello Joe character." He tucked the blanket over her shoulder so she wouldn't throw it off. "She's a fine lady now, but I suggest you don't ever wake her if you catch her snoozing like this—not that much wakes her, you understand, the crazy hours she's keeping—but she's mean as a wolverine in a kettle drum. Needs her coffee. Takes after my mother-in-law. In character, not looks." He held his palms together in prayer. "Thank you, Lord, not in looks. My hand to God, I once seen my wife's mother get into such a frenzy she bit into a telephone when some fool put her on hold. Gusto witnessed it, though I don't suppose he seen much, him being without a face and all." He flicked off the television, shut the overhead light, and left a reading lamp on. "Jodi'll remember you, so that's okay. C'mon, I'll show you to your room. You look halfway beaten into the ground."

Funny way to put it, here in a house where the flavor was like freshly turned graveyard earth. "I am."

"I'm getting there myself."

Gusto stood and followed them up the stairwell, pacing along beside Matthew, licking his hand with an unseen tongue. "You might want to take him to the dog groomer, get a bit of a trim."

"Who?" Carmichael said, stopped at a door, opened it, and flicked on a light switch. "This'll be your room if you find it to your liking. Sorry to say it'll be your room even if you don't."

A fragrance of illicit behavior, scarlet past, and subterfuge, a good deal of lust and not necessarily a little madness.

"It's fine," Matthew said.

"Okay, then, let me see if there's anything else I might be forgetting. The bathroom's down the hall, and there's a clean towel on your bed. We got a giant water heater, so there's still plenty of hot water for all of us who take showers before Jodi, otherwise you're out of luck. Breakfast is at nine, and she does a terrific job, me a bit less so if I'm needed. Don't worry about the rent yet, we'll work something out at the end of your stay. And now, after saying that, I'll wish you a fine good night, Matt."

Emma Carmichael's whereabouts hadn't been referred to directly—had she died? For the past hour he'd been caught up in the sense of how Summerfell hadn't changed after he abandoned it. He didn't know the names of the dead yet, he hadn't even asked. His chest grew warm. "Where's Emma? I haven't said hello to her yet."

"She's down state visiting her sister Martha, who doesn't chew through telephones, though she looks like she could with them dentures. Emma will be back in a couple of days, and everyone'll be right glad when she is. Her cooking's a lot better than mine, and Jodi's too. Have a good night."

"Thank you." He watched the man descend the stairs. Gusto tripped and slid down the carpet on his haunches, moving with almost human intent, flopping when he hit the bottom and barking that sort of weird billy goat cry again.

He shut the door and fell back against it, the migraine now unbearable. Alone again, he was abruptly struck with more nausea, the dry heaves clawing at his belly. *How can I possibly win?* He couldn't, but perhaps the stalemate could be extended another few years. Perhaps he and A.G. could find help, or teach others how to defend themselves and hold the malignancy at bay.

No, that was a stupid way to think. He couldn't shirk his responsibility any longer. Already too many people had paid his dues for him. He slumped and sat on the floor, hands in the air drawing arcane symbols, the heat of fever clawing at the back of his neck. When he finished the preliminary rites he closed the blinds and curtains.

From his satchel he pulled out the gris-gris pouch containing significant but mostly ineffective elements of arcana: a pair of bone dice with

hand-etched Roman numerals; preserved cat-
gut thread from the stitches of a Wiccan priest-
ess whose drunken husband had slashed her
with a shattered beer mug; a stone chip from
one of the rocks that had crushed Giles Corey
to death in Salem; copper bands twisted seven
times around a ball of wax. The wax contained
the tears of his father. A handful of other ingredients and tools he tossed on the nightstand.

He ground the dice in his fist until he drew
blood from the heel of his palm, then released
them gently on the floor. Instead of rolling
smoothly they bounced and spun with vicious
energy, clattering together like teeth biting, until settling one atop the other. He knelt and retrieved them: a IV and a I, signifying the
northeast. Not much, but it would give him a
place to start tomorrow.

Matthew knew he should place the seals and
sigils around the windows and across the center
of the door, however little protection it might
prove, as well as commit himself to the speaking of the prayers, but was too tired to care
about safety anymore. He hadn't come back to
be safe.

The Goat would approach; it always did. But
it wouldn't attack tonight—there was still too
much blood to be let.

Compelled to perform at least one ritual of
defense, he drew a piece of twine from his back
pocket and tied it quickly and precisely into an

elaborate series of knots, spiraling them together until they became like beads, forming a Litany Web. Then he put it in his mouth and spoke his name, then placed it on the bedpost. It resembled a luna moth.

He lay on the bed.

Chapter Six

Debbi told him to pedal faster as they laughed and rode down the sand-swept shore roads.

"C'mon! . . . Watch the gravel over there. . . . Faster!"

His legs were already hurting him, and his face dripped sweat, red from the summer sun and the exertion of pumping up the rolling curves of these streets. Her giggles spurred him until he felt light-headed.

Jutting wooden mailboxes planted along the curbs made him swerve out of the shoulder. Cars hitching trailered boats sped by. Trucks occasionally blared their horns, and a surfboard hanging from a luggage rack nearly knocked Debbi off the handlebars.

"Hey, creep, give me a break!" Her weight

threw the bike off balance, and he feared they might fall over into the path of the Freight-liners. She kicked out a Top Forty tune on his front spokes—*ka-tinka-tinka ka-tinka ka*—sing-ing along with the melody. "C'mon, you know the words," she said, genuinely wanting him to join in. He tried staying attentive, but the ab-rasive burlap bag dug into his neck and collar-bone, and it hurt like hell.

After nearly four miles of riding he was tired, and he strained to keep from losing control; twice during the spring, they'd both skinned their hands, knees and elbows from skidding and somersaulting head over ass into the road after losing traction in the sandy gravel. Already the front tire rubbed against the inside fender, and the chain was beginning to slip.

She grabbed his wrist suddenly and yelled, "Watch it!" He shifted hard and narrowly missed a scattered six-pack of bottles lying in the thick weeds on the shoulder. She giggled and gave two triumphant claps over her head. He couldn't keep from chuckling as they veered and maneuvered downhill between scattered glass.

*Caw-caww*s of hungry seagulls and the smell of the ocean brought on strong thoughts of other summers and other sunburns. He didn't really like when it happened; it made him help-less somehow, as if he had no control over where his mind went. He vividly recalled coming to the beach with his parents: too distinctly, though he used to love it.

His dad would make shadow animals against the walls of the snack shack, and his mother would slowly eat a cherry ice as she strolled along the boardwalk, her sandals snapping against the soles of her feet like firecrackers popping. She used to wear black bathing suits even when they weren't in style, looking like sealskin when wet. How she loved old-fashioned wide-brim hats with silk scarves that trailed around her neck like smoke. At the end of the day she'd sit by the wishing well where the goldfish swam among shining coins, while his father took him to the showers to rinse the salt off, getting the sand and seaweed out of their shorts.

Afterward, as the crowds left and the vendors shut down their stands and closed their umbrellas, his dad would sit beside his mother and rub the dried grains of sand from her legs with slow, sweeping strokes that made her hum. Then the two of them would flick their change into the fountain, laughing quietly about nothing in particular, watching the fish dart into the reflections of the sun.

Seagulls dove and picked at debris around them. Debbi's billowing hair clung to his sweaty forehead, and he wished that she would be with him like this forever. *Ka-tina-tink tinka-ka-tink*. He thought about dumping the rest of the *Sum-*

*merfell Gazette*s in the sewer, but knew he wouldn't be able to do it. Later this afternoon he'd finish delivering them and apologize to his customers for being so late. Spiteful old man Owsley would throw another fit, his only tip this week a sermon against sloth, which sounded like some of the greenish stuff Owsley hacked up and spit on the lawn.

In the distance, looking west toward Etcher's Point, the lighthouse loomed over the ocean, silhouetted in the haze of sunlight. He understood why she needed to come here so often, and was content to do whatever would please her. Sitting together in the surf and feeling the tug of the tide, watching the sandpipers, collecting seashells she kept on a shelf beneath her ballet trophies, putting the lotion on her burned back until his fingertips quivered—and it made him special when she called and asked him to come here with her. A.G. laughed sometimes and made fun, but he didn't care much. Besides, nowadays A.G. acted the same way where Ruth Cahill was concerned, though nobody else would admit it yet.

The lighthouse had always been off-limits. Several of the older kids had spent anywhere from a couple of hours to a few days in county lockup because they'd been too drunk or high to notice the cops coming up behind them as they tried to break through the chains on the door. Wanting to get in to go even higher, climb the catwalks naked, dare each other to walk the rim wasted.

It wasn't the same with Debbi. When she spoke about the ocean he saw how her blue eyes dimmed, hardening and dampening until they turned a shade of gray, then grew brighter. Her voice rose when she talked, words rattling. Like now, going, "Wheeeeee! Hey, hey, you think we can get our own boat soon? You know, a small one, like that one. . . ." She gestured fiercely with her hands in the air, pointing—"Over there, there, look there, there!"—out at the rippling water.

He was entranced, realizing how alike they were in these instances. How they could both crack through the bone-wearying boredom at the same time, when you couldn't take the routine any longer, even at thirteen. You would just sit, and maybe—if the day hit you wrong—let just one or two gasps escape you like a geriatric's sighs. His father would walk by his door and say nothing.

Debbi's own father had been a fisherman who went out on his trawler on a clear morning and never returned. That frustration left her stuffed with questions she never talked about with anyone except him—so he chose to believe.

And yet everyone could tell that it still slashed at her whenever she came in view of the harbor. Their other friends thought she was stupid to spend so much time at the beach when it brought on dark thoughts and made her cry, but she could always hope her father would come back. And wasn't that why she wanted to be here? He could understand how she'd been driven to keep watch over what the lighthouse watches.

He was thirteen years old and his mother had been dead for less than a year.

"I want you to do something," Debbi said, and he was already nodding. "I'm going to show you what I've found. It's pretty weird. Don't bother asking me what, because I don't know. But if anyone can find out about it, you can, right? Say right, I know you can. I want you to go to the library and study and learn whatever you can, you're good at that. Will you do it for me?"

He sighed a long breath.

She already knew he would do anything for her.

"Almost there," she said.

Chapter Seven

Sipping coffee, Roger Wakowski reviewed this week's stack of files.

He drew a small piece of metal from his shirt pocket and rolled it between thumb and forefinger, caressing its dents and creases, hardly aware that he held the fragment. The action proved a conditioned response, as much as any well-learned lesson. While studying the reports, he made notes of his own. Interesting to see how the doctors described certain patients' activities here: *Over the past fifteen weeks he's made a great deal of progress facing his own physical and sexual inadequacies and the corollary rage exhibited towards women who make him uncomfortable*—that from Dr. Patterford, referencing materials on a twenty-year-old kid who raped and scarred four nurses because he was striking back at his mother, who had hurt his feelings when she made him wear a jacket and tie for his second-grade class photo. Insanity could be that simple; you could trace it almost to the instant.

Patterford lacked even the properly balanced semantics, wording the paragraph to make it appear that the attacks had been provoked by the women, that they acted without discretion and "made him uncomfortable." That's all it took to beat somebody so out of shape, the moral structure so terrifyingly weak. Psychiatrists would look for other causes, try to unwrap the melted fusion of feeling, and never be able to get it done. Insanity came in a ketchup bottle. In a murmured insult, perhaps spontaneously generated.

The kid had kept one of the nurses for half a week while he systematically cut her fingers off. To this day he wrote letters to her family, asking her sisters to forgive him and come for a weekend visit. Roger had all the letters and love notes stacked in the bottom drawer of his desk.

He intently read on, file after file, signing his name at the bottom of the review sheets.

After a while the twisted bit of metal began to feel like silk—though he did not consciously feel it at all—and then like warm flesh, and then like nothing that had a name.

Twenty-eight years earlier the fragment had

been a bullet fired from an AK-47 at a distance of no more than a hundred yards into the brush line. The damage it caused had almost forced the surgeons to amputate his left leg and right arm—the vicious angle proving the sniper was in the treetops to the west, not even facing into the sun and still nobody could cap him—in the hopes of getting to a more seriously wounded soldier first. No time or facilities for meticulous microsurgery or resewing of minuscule arteries, not when you'd stamped on fléchette mines and had beehive rounds slicing chunks out of anyone standing over two feet high, and the Fucking New Guys were setting off trip wires all day long. If the doctors were going to take precious minutes saving his arm and leg, then the other soldier there painting the walls with arterial spray, trying to plug his holes with his own fingers, was going to do more than just weep and growl his wife's name; he'd flop off the stretcher and die in a pool under their feet, and the bad juju would grow on Wakowski like moss.

The other guy was a hard-stripe sergeant named Kevin Brooks U.S.M.C., and he did First Lieutenant Roger Wakowski the favor of dying quickly so that the surgeons could save his arm and leg.

He shut the files and finished his coffee.

Heated by the friction of his constant rubbing, the metal grew extremely hot now. The calluses and scars on his fingertips kept them from blistering.

Over the years he'd held on to the fragment as a talisman of sorts; the bullet had failed in its duty to murder him, and now that he owned the round he'd stolen its power, and to this day possessed a piece of the sniper who'd fired at him from the treetop bush. Wakowski had been superstitious before East Asia, growing up in the backwoods where men and myth met in the swamps. Afterward, he'd returned even more animistic than he could understand, carrying with him revenants he usually only saw in nightmares, in walls, and staring out certain windows. They crept on him through the fire-fights like smiling children screaming banshee suicide prayers, wired with explosives that made C4 charges look like sparklers.

Rolling the bullet under his knuckles, staring at the steel mesh over the windows, he waited for the end of his shift so he could go and grab something to eat at the all-night diner, hoping he'd be able to get into bed and not look at the ceiling for six hours straight. Maybe this would be the end of his insomnia. It felt like tonight could be the end.

After twenty-eight years and a dozen wars—only five of which had made the U.S. papers—he still hadn't gotten used to the faces of his dead friends gazing down at him from the walls.

He signed the sheets and put the fragment back in his pocket.

And then pulled it out again.

Trapped, as always, or at least feeling that way, now on her stomach the way they make you when they're about to rape you or shoot you in the head. With feet entangled, a hand on her ankle and screams edging up her throat, Jodi spun over in her sleep.

She kicked and shifted, sank into darkness, nearly shrieking if she hadn't been suffocated by the crocheted blanket. She awoke floundering and flung her arms out to keep from dropping to the floor, uttering pleas. These sounds snapped the room's utter silence, and because her throat was so dry and raspy, so hideously masculine in the middle of the night, the husky and unfamiliar voice terrified her.

Pressing her palms over her eyes, Jodi flipped the curls of her disheveled hair out of her face, coughed cotton from her mouth. Disoriented, she looked around, with only the orange glow of the small night-light from the kitchen to focus on. *Oh yeah, what a wild life I lead*. She'd fallen asleep in front of the TV again, in the middle of a stale rerun of a desperately unfunny sitcom. There'd been nothing better to do. How could there have been nothing better to do? *Action-packed chills, spills, and thrilling adventures . . .* It was becoming a habit, this napping, and tomorrow she'd pay for it once more with a spineload of aches and cramps.

"Where do you go from here?" she whispered.

Leaning forward, she stretched and whirled her arms, tilted her neck back and forth, shrugging out the kinks. She felt more tired than when she'd drifted off earlier, and the now dark bags under her eyes would blacken further. Great, this was just great, all right.

She'd awakened with a brush-stroked face painted heavily in her mind. Jeez, her erotic pubescent fantasies rising to the surface after all this time? Having a dream of their old paperboy. Where in the hell had he come from? Jodi couldn't guess why, after all this time, she'd envisioned him of all people. So she'd read a couple of his plays and occasionally looked at the oil painting of him in the Town Hall. She hadn't thought about Mattie Galen since that heart-pounding crush on him had been transposed to Gigantor Davidson the basketball star, in the ninth grade.

Strange, side effects of too much radiation from the television. She had tumors, she knew she had tumors. *I'm just horny.*

Sitting in darkness, she wished for a cigarette, and promised herself not to wind up a couch potato yet another night. It started screwing with her head, all this lying around the house with nothing to do—except helping Dad out every now and again when he'd allow it, while Mom visited Aunt Martha.

Three days before, Jodi had come downstairs smelling smoke and discovered her mother gone, her father in the kitchen surrounded by splashes of flame. He stood like a performance artist, making some incomprehensible point on the stage. Burning black lumpy pancakes on the grill, waffles smoking in the toaster, hash browns in the microwave, a grease fire in the frying pan, as if hoping to burn himself to death in the center of the conflagration. This was his first attempt at cooking on his own in thirty years. He smiled through it all, even as the flames came for him. If she hadn't found two full boxes of baking soda and been able to put out all the burning breakfasts with them, there would have been serious trouble. He'd only grinned at her and said, "I suspect you may have to help me here until your mother gets back."

After cleaning the place and serving corn-flakes and muffins to Mr. Hoffman and Mr. Kessner—they didn't seem to mind, not that or anything else—her father explained that Aunt Martha was ill and Mom, despite not having seen her for more than a year, went home again. Grandma's phone chewing was another matter.

We're all getting weird.

Jodi had no choice but to face the truly awful facts at hand: Shit, it was time to get a job.

"Ba-lech," she said, and tossed the pillow to

the other side of the couch. She hadn't been able to wait any longer for a DJ slot to open at the radio station; a friend of a friend had promised her the next available position, but she'd heard the station's plans to expand had fallen through. Now she had to get any lousy job she could grab onto, even if she had to work checkout or shelve books at the library. Or, hell, maybe go back to that bastard Farlessi and serve up another million overcooked Krunchburgers to snotty asswipes who thought they were tough. Keep on Krunching until she was too fat and old to escape Farlessi's groping, sweaty meat-hook hands. Since she'd quit four weeks ago she'd made the rounds to all the other diners and restaurants, only to go through the endless repetition of leaving her application in bins overflowing with similar applications of similar girls hoping to get out from under their parents who threw blankets over them on the couch, and trying to make the very same buck she was trying to make.

The radiator clinked with rushing water as Jodi cursed Frank Farlessi's greasy ways, his total lack of manners, tasteless speech and food, and the slimy come-ons. You could forgive him some of the time and handle a lot more, but not all of it. In the year she'd worked at the Krunch she'd seen at least six girls quit because of the vile things he'd implored them to do in the back of his '61 pickup. Some had left because of the

95

snaking fashion his hands reached out to touch those glorified G-strings he made them wear as uniforms.

She was amazed at how few of their fathers ever came back looking for a fight. But it was well-known that Farlessi was loud and obnoxious, but otherwise harmless. Her own daddy, though, yeesh, if he'd only known about half the crap she'd gone through, Daddy would have stuck his shotgun in Frankie's face and reprimanded him for his vulgar ways. Double click. Boom. That was her dad—always quiet and considerate, but damn, oh so pernicious when you got him riled.

Jodi stood, folded the blanket, and laid it over the back of the couch. Whatever happened tomorrow she'd have to worry about it in the morning, after she got through covering the bags under her eyes. Maybe Mom would call, give her a pep talk. She turned off the outside light and sleepily headed off to get a glass of water before going to bed.

She hadn't taken three steps before tripping over Gus and kneecapping herself on the recliner. "Jeez, Gus."

Gusto came over, rose, and ploomped his front paws onto her belly. His breath brought tears. He followed beside her as she stumbled into the kitchen, got a glass of milk, and refilled his water bowl. Passing the den, she saw that Kessner and Hoffman were still playing chess.

"Good night," she said, walking by without waiting to see if they would respond, knowing they wouldn't.

Gusto curled into a lump at the back door.

The clock in the hallway read five to midnight.

The radiator rumbled off.

Jodi went upstairs and hit the bathroom, brushed her teeth quickly, and went to her room. She set the alarm for eight o'clock. Thinking of the pale empty stares of the cashiers in supermarkets, she said, "Uh, I can't believe this, I just can't." She wondered once again where in hell her thoughts of Matthew Galen had come from.

She shut the drapes but didn't notice the roiling cloud above parting to show the moon, surging silver-tipped and tacked on black, a mutating shape with ten thousand rushing wings, heading for a window.

Chapter Eight

A dream could kill. He opened his eyes inside the nightmare and realized he'd been invaded.

"Idiot," he said.

An obscenity in the sky, the sun rose bloated and plague-ridden. Birds fell from the air with their feathers burning, eyes bursting, screeching as they plummeted around him, striking the sand like dying streamers.

The book writhed in his hands.

Flames spelled out his name, GALEN, in blue-flame script, charred through the cover. Rain sizzled where it touched the binding, hissed and smoked as it pounded against his skin.

Throbbing methodically, the book shuddered and quickened its pace to match his racing pulse, beating steadfastly to the rhythm of his heart. GALEN bulged, a growing cancer. Its cover stretched toward him, laced with barely distinguishable veins like those at the edge of Helen's jawline, weaving up to her ear. He gritted his teeth and the pages erupted, throwing blood into his face.

He wiped his eyes. Crouched before the boulders that rimmed the area north of Etcher's Point, he looked at the lighthouse. The rocks cracked in the heat. The diseased sun sagged. Waves struggled forward, tide rising with the flaming rainfall.

"Subtle," Matthew said. "Very sophisticated."

From the center of the nightmare he watched Helen seated and crying offshore, a symbol of his redemption. Damn it, now that he was home the evil could slither through his mind and touch others. Pressured by longing and fear, his throat closed when he saw the silver cord at the base of her neck whipping fiercely in the wind. They were still tied. *Thank God, she still loves me.*

The scene receded, and he made a stab at the cord. It squirmed before his face, thrashing so wildly it threatened to rip free from her neck; he got his hands around the line and struggled to control it. If the cord snapped she'd die in her sleep.

He'd done this to her, *my baby*, allowed the Goat access through his affection; just for being devoted and dreaming about Helen now, the beast might reach into her.

"Like hell."

She seemed to stand in a whole other nightmare. It proved to be difficult for him to grasp her. Matthew doubled over, straining to keep the astral line affixed to Helen, the cold sweat dappling him now. He had to hold on. The cord was freezing. Ice rimmed the ethereal silver. In the winter she sat with snow sprinkling her upswept auburn hair, snowflakes thickening on her lengthy eyelashes. Her coat was open; she'd always hated the confined feeling of anything too near her neck, and she'd gripe whenever he nibbled her throat.

Helen remained as beautiful as ever. Another aching skewer shoved into his heart, turning there. *How could I have ever left her?* He mouthed his father's name, and his scars rasped out a pledge to Beli'ya'al, Aztorath, and Mammon.

Her tears dappled her lovely face, nose running.

The crimson-tinged pages of his life and death twirled and spun in the clawing winds. Nah, this game wasn't going to work. He saw only Helen, kept his focus on her, where it always belonged. Rain scoured blood from the beach. He got as close to Helen's dream as possible, but couldn't breach her sad winter thoughts. It made him grin, that red Rudolph nose of hers. This game played him. Matthew pulled until the slack in the silver thread was taken up, and the cord stabilized and straightened. He let it go safely as her astral self sniffled on the shore.

Gritting his teeth, he abruptly felt drunk, and laughed once, a short bark of madness. He could accept death, guilt and loss, loneliness, and even damnation, but not a cheap insult like this, a little trick meant to chip at his resolve. Helen stared through him as he stepped away from the book in order to break through the scorched walls of his vision. "Idiot," he chastised himself. "This is what you get for not putting up the protective sigils." In a way it was true, he might have been able to fend off this initial brush with the Goat.

But perhaps it would work in his favor, the beast needing and wanting him to such an extent that it came to him even in these droll dreams. It was getting too eager for his love, and that could work to his advantage.

Kneeling in the sand, his hands out in front of him, moving into position, Matthew concentrated beyond the illusory rain. Tightening his muscles, he attempted to vanish behind these false eyes he saw with now, created from the fiber of phantasm. The sun sank in thirty seconds and the sky blackened. Silly, he thought, he and his enemy were both making the wrong moves, too hungry. He dealt with the deceiver.

The beacon of the lighthouse came on, and the cruel ambience of the world grew worse as the thrum of the signal's generator became louder.

The lighthouse was alive, and it hated.

It stooped to one side like an old man asking a scared girl to come closer, its flecked paint stripped in long jagged strips, the rails rusted.

If you knew what to listen for, you could put an ear to its weather-beaten wood and hear the loathsome murmuring. You'd learn the hard way that it was built over another temple, one meant to sacrifice whatever innocence was left in you, counting on rape and rage, insecurity and humiliation. These winds grew worse as it waited; it had great faith in the keels of ship-wrecks to crush their drowning captains and crews against the rocks, and for the undertow to gather and sweep the mangled remains into the caves below.

Footsteps striking the rickety metal stairs inside resounded in the surf.

Who?

This Helen chimera peered at nothing, forever weeping. The beacon revolved and shone down upon Matthew. An intense whiteness brightened the beach, sparkling like the sneer of fangs. At his knees, the book of his life and death crawled in the sand and rubbed against his leg.

The light filled Etcher's Point with grandeur,

a scalpel ripping the sea wide open. Everything it touched became reality, as the sense of his childhood overshadowed his adult life. He shut his eyes and sought the prayers, muttering the words, but his concentration kept snapping further and further apart.

More burning birds fell toward the boulders, cawing pitifully as he attempted to back out of this double-helix snarl of nightmares. The beam of light swung and fell on the seething ocean, chewing through the surface and dragging dead fish up from the bottom. The generator squealed painfully, its motor on the verge of seizing.

He saw Debbi on the lighthouse platform, her black hair billowing, arms outstretched to him, features twisted into an inhuman scowl.

(Debbi was dead.)

Oh no.

She giggled and disappeared down the stairs, coming for him.

She's calling, she's coughing. Red strings of spittle hung off her chin. Blood filled the marble canals chiseled into the cave floor. The Goat's face was painted over the carved pentagram, and he backed away. She weakly touched his ankle and he flinched from her hand, too stunned to do anything else. Her mouth was crimson and drooling; the stalagmite lifted the back of her dress like a tent, but it hadn't torn through yet. She blinked and tried to speak.

He could hear the pounding of the ocean behind the cave walls. A.G. and Ruth were
screaming for more than their lives, running up
the tunnel as the cave began to glow with life,
lost, searching for the stone stairs, demented
with horror now. There was laughter.

Debbi reached out and clung to the cuff of his
pants with one hand, stroking his ankle with a
feeble back-and-forth motion with the other,
her eyes pleading with him to help her, save her,
to do something, but there was so much blood
he could only watch it dripping off her braces,
thick and syrupy, trickling from her nose. There
was no time for it to well or pool beneath her
as it was siphoned off into the thin trenches,
flowing down the rock. Her tented dress ripped
apart and the red was beginning to show
through as she groaned and her body roughly
slipped another inch down the sharp stalagmite. The pretty dress tore in half and he saw
the rock gouging up through her stomach, her
insides sticking to the tip of the point, and she
wanted him to help her, her fingernails catching
in his sneaker laces.

The catacombs echoed with A.G.'s cries,
Ruth's screams, and now the insane animal tittering rose up from the edges of the altar, and
from elsewhere in the catacombs. He clamped
a hand over his mouth in case it was he. Some
of the laughter stopped. With her eyes, Debbi
pinned him to the pentagram he was standing

over, his feet on either side of a stone channel running with her blood. They were both there in the center of the Goat's face, with the red streaming in little rivers along the carved outline of the five-pointed star. The pentagram filled with the fluid of Debbi's warm smile. The Goat grinned at him.

When at last her hand fell away and the wet lines met, Debbi was dead (Debbi was dead), but her eyes pursued him. There was a rush of force, energy like a shotgun blast, a blazing hand that picked him up and swept him up high into a whirlwind of pain and malevolent joy as he shrieked. It reached from the altar and struck him hard in that same place in his soul, slamming him backward into the cave wall, where the stone crackled and he crumpled facedown in her gore. His shirt was on fire and his chest burned. The mark was seared upon him.

Debbi was dead. And now the door to the lighthouse opened in slow motion with an unseen, yet somehow definitive, feminine touch.

A shape filled the doorway.

Matthew managed to remain calm for all of two seconds before he broke and whirled. The abomination he could face. Anything.

But not her.

A once pretty dress was now torn and bathed in malignant light, smeared with a dead girl's dying, and his past.

Oh Christ.

Debbi came rushing out the door, running over seashells and down the scrub grass toward him, eye sockets empty, tongue lolling, upper lip raised in a snarl that showed the dried blood on her braces.

"No!" What did that mean, who was he crying to, who did he pay for these offenses? Her, of course, always her.

A.G. had been using her bones, and still it wasn't enough. Raised jagged fingernails were aimed at his heart. "Deb . . . !"

And he'd actually believed he could endure damnation.

Bracing himself as Debbi leaped the distance between them, Matthew whimpered, "Deb . . ." as she dove onto his chest, shrieking without any humanity left. Teeth hunted for his throat, those claws scratching down his chest. He caught her wrists, touching her again, too late, and she was too strong, and he just couldn't hurt her again, no more, no more. He'd loved her, he had, and hadn't been able to do anything but pull his foot away from her hand. She caught his hair and jerked his head back, exposing the jugular. He heard her incisors clack together loudly when they met through his flesh; she tore into him. Through him, and from him, finally ripping out.

The beam of light swung and engulfed them both in a tidal wave of white-hot ice.

*   *   *

When he awoke to life he was standing in front of the mirror, fingers tracing the contours of the scars on his chest on their own accord.

The twine of the Litany Web had been unraveled and retied in the shape of Debbi's profile.

In a wet and sticky carpet of weak flutters, a thousand dying moths lay strewn about his feet.

Chapter Nine

"C'mon, Ibsen, rise and shine," Jazz said.

The window shade rolled up with a loud *thwack*. Outside, dogs barked excitedly down the block.

Matthew bit hard on his tongue, where a killing hex had been poised ready to be spoken, the spells already in his hands. Sweat dripped down the side of his face. His eyes focused. He relaxed and loosened his fists, swallowing the blood in his mouth, then cautiously looked over. Christ, it had been close. The bedsheets were scorched at his fingertips. He'd nearly murdered Jazz.

"Hey, you don't want to sleep through your first beautiful day back home, do you?" Jazz asked. "There are quests to be pursued, legends to be made, songs to be sung. So get the hell out of bed, let's get moving. Up, slug! It is I, Jasper William Metzner, your comrade in literary arms. He—"

"No, stop," Matthew said, knowing what was coming, and knowing it would be impossible to brake, now that Jazz was on a roll.

". . . he who is . . ."

Bright sunlight crowded the room, the dogs finally quieting, and the hearty smell of breakfast floating up from the kitchen.

". . . defender of the crown, and sinner, of course. Rogue, conqueror, quarterback extraordinaire as you well know, yes, me, slayer of more bluefish than most men who sail these waters. Tactless and brazen braggart. Obtainer of a 1260 on those damnable SATs God be praised . . ."

1090.

". . . yes, I, lover, poet, master of fine and not so fine arts, watcher of grade b-c-d horror flicks. Possessor of the sensitive heart, son of Dancing Lord Metzner the hippity-hop king, gnasher of teeth, rogue . . . damn, said that already, didn't I? . . . buckler of swashes, husband of Jenny May Fernhold-Metzner and now divorcée . . . divorcer? . . . of Jenny May 'thank you very much but I've now dropped the damn hyphen that I never truly wanted anyway' Fernhold some seventeen weeks ago."

"Oh my boy."

"Yes, fair Ibsen, it is I, derring-doer Jazz, now

109

turned English teacher to a gaggle of students far hipper than I am and, sadly, ever was." Jazz bowed theatrically with a two-step shuffle. "Ta-da."

"Not possible."

"And how are you doin', Mattie old son?"

It took a moment to realize that the unfamiliar, startling feeling in his throat was a deep laughter, the kind only Jazz could bring up. Downstairs in the living room a vacuum roared. Jazz always entered a room like a billow of nitrous oxide, ranting and canting. Matthew reached for his T-shirt on the bedpost and quickly put it on. "You mean you actually went and married Jenny May?"

"Keep in mind this was after her skin cleared up."

Matthew smiled and snickered. It felt good but sounded low and demented, like his father's. "Of course." He stood and faced his friend.

"Mattie, you're looking good."

Jasper Metzner, besides being rogue and poet, had been a part of Matthew's life almost as long as A.G., cutting at least a small swath through much of the anguish. Jazz remained outside the facts, beyond the truth of the veil. He'd been the quarterback on their varsity team when they'd forgone their coach's order to punt and Matthew made his ninety-nine-yard run, the day he'd broken his ankle on Jello Joe's helmet and met Helen. With his cast propped on the dashboard of Jazz's Mustang, Matthew and Helen had made love for the first time.

But what did it matter then, if he'd had to squeeze himself backward into the driver's seat because he'd already been enraptured from only a glance at her photograph shown to him by Jenny May; Helen had been cheering for the opposing team's players, and Christ on the cross how that had enraged him, so insanely jealous after only one glimpse that he would have run the ball over the line even if it had cost him his arms and legs, the rest of his soul, he just had to do it, in love with her already, until he couldn't contain all the ardor he had for her. Knowing they were already connected. At that moment of their first touching he didn't even flinch as he'd done with so many girls before her. (Debbi was dead.)

That first kiss—he recalled the heat that had come over him. . . . After the game he'd hopped on crutches with the fracture, heading back from the clinic across the field, to the parking lot where Jazz's car waited like a honeymoon suite. Afterward he'd escorted Helen home, and when finally he fell into bed he didn't even hear his father's snores or drunken cries, the vomiting and muttering. It was the first time in years he'd been able to sleep through the entire night.

"Ah . . . hey, just 'cause I said you look good doesn't mean I want to kiss you."

Jazz smirked, aware of exactly which memory was being reviewed in Matthew's mind; Jazz had an intuition about such things, the guy could read your eyes like few else could. He was famous for his sarcasm, wit, and dramatics, as well as for holding tightly to a world record for coitus interruptus. He'd been found on floors and rooftops, in taco stands, ladies' shoes and underwear departments, the DMV—he'd been found by UPS drivers, cops in the park, beach patrol, meter readers, meter maids, meter maids' boyfriends while on rooftops with the meter maids, National Guardsmen out on maneuvers. It had the touch of the Goat to it, though Matthew could never be sure.

Jazz searched for a cigarette, gesturing hand to lip to see if Matthew had any. Jazz patted his pockets. His hair was pulled into a tight ponytail, his already wide eyes magnified by a pair of octagonal glasses. That perpetual trademark smirk soldered to his mouth, off kilter. He had a way of talking that made you forget the fact half of what he said just didn't make sense. His voice remained sedate and composed, each word carefully enunciated—not at all how you expected him to talk when you realized how rapid-fire, manic, and nonsensical his shtick truly was.

Left hand emerging from his jacket and holding a pack of cigarettes, Jazz said, "You've got wrinkles and gray streaks that would impress my lonely grandmother, you know. She's still pretty spry, and she's got some bucks laid away in real estate."

"How did you find out I was back?"

"How do you think? You've been gone so long you forget how it works? Summerfell isn't exactly Staten Island, nobody sneaks in or out without being seen by some blue-haired biddy." Despite the grin, Jazz couldn't keep the accent off the word "sneak," and Matthew's stomach clenched. "Would Eugene be mad if I smoked in here?"

"Beats me."

"Better not risk it. I hear he's getting friendlier with his shotguns." He shoved the butt back into the pack and breathed out slowly, staring into Matthew's eyes. The moment kept lengthening. His smile uncurled. "Mattie, kid, I should give you a lecture on undying friendship and keeping in touch, and how you're not supposed to bug out on your buddies for five years without so much as a goddamn phone call." He was really putting the bite into it now, but then letting it roll. "And all the rest of the heartwrenching stuff . . . but right now, I'm so glad to see you that I'll forgo chewing you out until another time. Of course, then I might just have to kick your ass up and down the street."

"I'd appreciate it."

"Give me a hug, brother."

The growls of the vacuum cleaner ground to

a halt as Jazz embraced him, patting him gently on the back. Matthew swallowed a groan as his chest tightened. Except for when he was with Helen, he couldn't stand to be touched like this. The scars always reacted violently, crawling over him and biting deeper. Being tackled on the field was different, the vehemence and brutality working for him.

He squirmed as Jazz hugged him more firmly, the damnable crying growing louder in his skull. Once, in the Outside Inn, Jello Joe's sister Jelly Jane had drunkenly stumbled forward hoping to hug Matthew, and he'd instinctively sidestepped her open arms and sent her sprawling with an explosive huff across a booth full of beer, the legs of the table snapping sharply as all two hundred and eighty pounds of her rebounded and rolled to the floor, covered in buffalo wing dip.

The look on her face humiliated him more than she could have been by the incident. Flushing and glaring, cheeks burning so violently, she'd simply sat there watching him until he'd backed out the door and fled.

He shoved Jazz out to arm's length. "Good to see you, too."

"You've got to remember that these types of close, peaceful communities flip sideways when the town hero returns home," Jazz said.

"Don't call me that."

"What? A hero?" Jazz kind of wavered, seeing

the chance to slip in another knife, but not wanting to do so. "But it's true in a way, you oversensitive pup. There's even a framed oil painting of you hanging in the entrance of Town Hall."

That took him aback. "There is?"

"You should check it out for yourself, sort of impressionistic, but still done in meticulous detail. Weird. You'll have to excuse me if I wax poetic here for a minute, but when the light strikes that painting just right, I got to tell you—"

"Shut the hell up, Jazz."

"No, I'm serious, man, hear me out. Sometimes that painting reminds me of our yearbook pictures. It captures the feeling of that final year, Mattie, really, listen to me!" Anxiety in his voice, stressing the point. "You must know what I mean, because you write about it all the time, about how it was back then. The painting's got you with your eyes gazing solemnly through your windblown mess of curls. . . . It's goddamn spooky, you've got to listen . . . but do you remember how on that day we had our senior pictures taken and we had to rush to the photographer's after practice? And Helen and Jenny May were waiting for us up behind the bleachers . . . and we went to the gym and met A.G., Ruth, Jello Joe, and Jelly Jane over in the wrestling room, and we hung out in the park for most of the night, playing sex charades and fuckin' around until the sheriff broke it up?"

"Yes," Matthew said. Of course he remembered.

"And I sneaked into Jenny's house and fell asleep in her bed, and in the morning her mother caught us and the old bat starting beating the shit out of me with my own belt . . . cripes, a turquoise buckle, big like this, it was scary and terrific, and almost too real to be happening. Somehow, I'm not kidding, that's what that painting reminds me of, even now." Jazz shrugged tightly, like he'd been winding up instead of winding down. "Ah shit, all right, maybe I am being just a bit too nostalgic. It's no sin, right?"

Yes, it was—everything was a sin in Summerfell, because everything could be turned into a transgression by Beli ya'al and Azmodeus and the Goat, and the others, all of them waiting for you to feel open and warm before taking the world apart one bitter bite at a time. "No, I'm glad, actually."

"I just missed you, man." Jazz sought more words but came up empty, gesturing with his open hands a moment longer. "I'll bet the mayor asks you for a public speech, you better get ready for that. Copies of your plays are selling well, and the library has a whole shelf reserved for your work, I swear."

"What time is it?"

"Nine-thirty. C'mon, I'll buy you lunch and

you can tell me about your life on off-Broadway." He spun. "Heya, by the way, what the heck is that thing lying on the carpet downstairs?"

"That's Gus."

Jazz was simply nervous, even more frenetic than usual, searching out the jokes and the sentimentality, whether he genuinely felt it or not. "Oh yeah yeah, right."

"Who did it?" Matthew asked. "The oil painting in Town Hall." As if he didn't already know; he'd seen a dozen such works hanging on the walls beside the trophy cases at school, a glut of plaques above them, *Winner of the S.H.S. scholarship for Excellence and Outstanding Ability in the field of Creative Arts*.

Clearly uncomfortable, Jazz crossed the room, leaned against the windowsill, and scrutinized his feet. "Ruth did." No more shtick, his tone straight as a razor. "You heard about her, right?"

Matthew dressed, nodding. He reached into the satchel and chose a black cotton sweater, and felt something cold and soft press against the back of his neck.

"It's that kind of shit that's been making me so sentimental, Mattie." His left hand returned to his pocket and he retrieved the cigarettes again, lit one, and blew smoke forcefully through his nostrils, keying himself up now. Matthew wondered how the Goat had touched

Jazz, what had been twisted up inside him, or would be over the next few days. "Ah, look, I'm really sorry about A.G. and all that, I know he's like a brother to you. I used to like the guy myself sort of, but don't expect me to—"

"I don't."

"I mean, he was a nice guy and everything, but always a little off, you know, especially after you left. I think he did it. Just so long as you and I have that straight."

"We do."

Clearing his throat, Jazz smirked once again, putting on the second act of his performance, getting back into character. Matthew didn't hold it against him and wished he could do the same, but had no time or talent for it. Not for that. "Friends change, yes, true . . . as in my case, where I've become even more incredibly handsome. You remember Spinetti?"

"Our old English teacher."

"Yeah, I work with him now. The senior class truly digs your work, and living in the same town where you grew up gives them another tie to the writing. A lot of kids would love the chance to put one of your plays together if you're willing to let them, now that you're back. A couple of them are outstanding talents, kids that can grab your guts and make you take notice. Maybe you could use them in New York, or at least get us some tickets. I don't remember our drama club being that dedicated, but I suppose we had our moments, too."

"You were great in *Marat/Sade*."

"Yeah, I was, wasn't I? Right up until Mothers against Porn came in and stopped the show. Those ladies were tough." Smoke wavered between them until a breeze from the cracked window blew it back into Jazz's face. He smoothed a hand over his ponytail. "Hey, have you noticed how Jodi Carmichael has filled out? Her tits, brother, whoo boy. Perfecto. I think you're going to like living here for the time being." Again, the tone straightened, seeking to slice. "I won't bother to ask about how long you'll be staying, because I know how recalcitrant you can be when you're feeling cornered, which is usually always for a paranoid like you. Besides, I know you won't be going anywhere until you see this thing through to the end. So how about you and me grab some lunch at the diner, where I can try and coerce you into lecturing to a few of my English classes and telling them what a great guy I really am."

Finding a balance. Up on the stage, both of them in their own fashions. "Sorry, Jazz, I can't today. I've got things to take care of."

"What have you got there?"

"What?"

"This." Jazz pointed to the back of Matthew's neck. "Looks like a hickey. You get a tattoo of a moth?"

"Nothing." Reaching up, Matthew ran his hand over his neck, his fingers at once languid and fleeting, flickering in a sense with a strange motion. When he straightened his collar, the thing was gone.

"Oh, I thought you really did get a tattoo. I forgot how good you were at sleight of hand. Hey, you pierced at all? I hear it's big in the theater district, getting needles in your eyebrows and stapling your tits."

"I'll see you later."

"Yeah, okay," Jazz said. "Hey, maybe tonight. Bosco Bob is having a party. As usual, everyone is invited out to their place."

That surprised him, that the gatherings should be allowed to continue, when strength of friendship and family were so reprehensible to the Goat. "Jello's dad still throwing bashes?"

"Always. Never a particular reason needed for the richest folks in the country to party. I just thought it might be nice if you stopped in for a drink or ten and said hi to the neighbors."

"Maybe I'll show," Matthew said, liking it less and less. Everyone congregated together, all their vices centered, like prisoners corralled. He saw the danger in it now, and wondered if the morality and malfeasance would balance out.

"Have you seen Helen?" Jazz asked.

"No."

"All right, I won't break your arm about any

of it. But hey, just remember one thing, brother."

Matthew turned.

Jazz ground out his cigarette against the window screen and smiled. "Never fucking punt."

Chapter Ten

He got out of the boardinghouse without talking to anyone else, slipping past Jodi and her father, who were both in the kitchen cleaning the breakfast table. His stomach grumbled at the smell of ham and eggs, and he couldn't recall how long it had been since he'd last eaten. Along with the aroma of bacon and hash browns came the fragrances of winter mint air freshener, lemon furniture polish, and pine disinfectant following him out onto the porch.

Jazz's '71 Mustang was backed into the driveway, and Matthew could see it had had plenty of additional body work done in the last few years. He stared at the seat where he and Helen had first made love, and thought of what it had meant then, and now. A pang of remorse knifed him in the midriff, and he nearly groaned in pain. So much he'd given up, too much, and still Jazz and A.G. had forgiven him, and he remained tied to Helen.

With the chilling October wind blowing in roughly from the east, the day grew colder than he expected. Matthew jogged down the sidewalk, occasionally ducking tree branches, past acquaintances raking and bagging leaves on their sloping lawns. Those who glimpsed and recognized him smiled in surprise, waved. Pumpkins and lopsided scarecrows were propped on porches. Nobody realized just what the holiday meant. He waved back but wouldn't stop.

Up ahead, on one side of Manor Lane, crows rested on telephone wires, fluttering wings in the winds, waiting and resolute, definitive in their mastery of the moment, with the sharp noise of feathers riffling in the cold.

There should have been a rule book, or a special illustration, or a specific play that Matthew could run, a certain way for him to act—there should have been someone to confide in besides A.G., a relative or a priest, or a teacher, someone other than the crows who could understand what lay at the heart of their home.

The week before, by way of fending off the paralyzing dread, he'd tried to restore his belief in himself and in his God, using what little faith remained to reinforce his flagging will. He prayed the Christian prayers his mother had taught him, then recited the black incantations to see if the power still dwelled within him, the angels Azriel and Gabriel perched outside his door. He reread the high school love notes from Helen that he still kept as bookmarks in the Bible, going out of his mind in the late hours of night, as shadows and scars ceaselessly whispered about death and A.G.

I'm not a poet, don't forget (I know you won't). Hey, I like the loose rhymes all right, but listen to what I have to say to you:

I take from you the strength of your grin
the love of your lips
now the tip of your tongue
while down below me your hair
tickles my belly
and I cry into the character of your eyes
as we fold into moonlight

ocean ears
a sand dune smile
nuzzling my neck
licking dimples and you call me Darla
as I reach over these sheets
to the rhymes of the lapped beat
of our whitecap water madness might

teeth
at the edge of a tasty lace throat

you're touching the pulse
so you're nibbling on my chin
and I am lower and higher
in your hot hand of fire
throwing ourselves all over the night

I love you! (Yes I do!) xxxxxxxxxxxx

He had awakened in the warm light of dawn, lying on the living room floor, curled under an end table with grit stuck to his teeth and empty tequila bottles scattered, his plays torn from the bookshelves. He rolled onto his back, once again scared enough to call random phone numbers and murmur into the receiver, begging help and weeping without humility, thinking that he, Matthew Galen . . . he could redeem himself, he could recover what had been lost . . . he could be the scalpel that made the incision to cut out this cancer of hell.

He made phone call after phone call, mixing the beer with tequila and vodka and rolls of antacids, babbling into the receiver about Thoth and Amon, and the gris-gris pouch of power, how the Kaballah made perfect sense if you only thought about it, and the lower hierarchies of Pandemonium where the daemons weren't nearly as evil as men, but inflicted themselves upon you just the same. Women cursed him, you rotten lunatic, and don't ever call back or else . . . Matthew played with the cord, wrapping it between his fists, winding it tighter and tighter. It was a perfect garrote. Some lady told him that if he wasn't even going to at least breathe heavy or moan or make obscene suggestions that might actually help her through her sexually repressed upbringing by strict Catholic parents, giving her the freedom to fantasize, then why bother, didn't he know it was much healthier to use fantasy to lead a more productive sex life, and that if he wasn't going to at least offer the chance to mutually masturbate then he wasn't worth talking to in the first place, and she'd join a guy name HardOn-Freddy in a private chat room on the net and do a little cyber instead.

He redialed. His vision kept unfocusing, eyes swiveling, and he spit into an ashtray with the burning bile seeping down his chin and saturating his shirt, while he called number after number.

Until one lovely-voiced girl spoke in his ear, telling him to be honest, to speak his mind, everyone needs a friend, she would help him, yes, and she would listen to him—You're not all alone, do you hear, do you understand?—and she breathed into the line, breathing for him, taking his breaths the way Helen used to do, and he couldn't say anything more beyond that point because the scars were screaming. He couldn't even plead his case and offer up his terror. He'd slipped and fallen on his face and the scars laughed out loud, and she asked if there was somebody there with him. He didn't want to hang up on her, so beautiful, that voice, so needing and wanting in her own way, but he had no other choice. She might've been crying by then. He hung up.

Matthew ran past the crows.

Pacing a six-minute mile, he decided he had to get more information before he'd have an adequate plan of action. He didn't know enough about the movements of the Goat in the five years he'd been away.

Start back where it all began.

He'd return to the library where he'd first studied his craft, searching for the names of the people who'd vanished, their ages, where they'd most likely been abducted. See if he could find the pattern.

After fifteen minutes he came to the intersection of South Windsor and Metacomet Roads, slipped between parked cars, and took a diagonal shortcut behind Mrs. Friendwald's large greenhouse, hopping fences and sprinting by a spinning clothesline that flapped girdles in his face.

Which brought him, sweating, to the library. Scanning the faces of librarians, he walked past the reference section and made his way to the microfiche, coming full circle again, as he always had and always would.

When he was thirteen and he'd begun his research he'd found books here not always in the card catalogues, *The Complete Encyclopedia of Satanism* opening before him on the shelf, others waiting for his arrival: *Dissecting Demons, Witchcraft and Idolatry, Europe's Inner Demons*, and *Mystification and Enrichment in the Black Day*. The librarians were the same, barely appearing any older, as if they'd been placed here for only this purpose. He could remember further back to when he came in with his mother and took out *The Five Hundred Hats of Bartholomew Cubbins* and *Green Eggs and Ham*.

The computerized magazine and newspaper index showed him what he needed to know, and he loaded the machine with spools of microfiche containing those issues of the *Gazette* that he required.

The resonant background noise distracted him from reading. Years ago, you couldn't even sneeze without getting dirty looks from the ladies, their fingers pointing at you like claw hammers, myopic eyes staring as mean as a pig's. Only Millie, the head reference librarian, ever smiled, looking at him now but too blind at that distance to see him. He squinted at the screen.

For the next three hours he read everything he could find pertaining to the missing victims and A.G.'s subsequent breakdown and arrest; he searched for any other news between Summerfell and Gallows that seemed out of the ordinary.

Jesus, there was a lot.

He came away with facts, but no design.

At five in the afternoon on April 30, Ruth Cahill left her job as advertising consultant to meet her fiancé for dinner at a recently opened restaurant downtown. Six hours later, A.G. himself put in the missing-persons call to Sheriff Hodges after finding her condo empty and phoning all mutual friends; the sheriff put out the word to deputies and highway patrol despite the twenty-four-hour required waiting period. No suicide note was found, no ransom letter ever sent. Search parties combed the woods, beach, inlets, lake, and other secluded areas where a body might have been disposed. "We are following several promising leads at this time," Hodges boasted. "We're certain we'll soon discover the whereabouts of Miss Cahill."

April 30.

Matthew sat back in the chair. He stared into his palm, and could see the subtle wrinkle at that day, reading the flow and ebb of murder, though his lifeline occasionally shifted.

April 30, Beltane, one of the great Celtic solar and fertility festivals, symbolized by bonfires in the preparing for Maypole. People danced *deosil*, clockwise in turn with the natural order, around the fires. Eventually Christianity absorbed the festival, and church services replaced the pagan rites. A priest would lead the congregation to the fields and light the fire himself.

Why would the Goat choose such a benevolent, though powerful, sabbat to begin the madness again?

On June 3 Tina Barnett, twenty, disappeared while walking to the Head Shop Hairstylists, where she worked part-time in the afternoons. Having recently relocated from Los Angeles, she had no family and few friends in the area. Several of those interviewed spoke of her with a general sense of distaste, even contempt. Tina Barnett was a young woman with a history of alcohol and cocaine addiction who'd voluntarily admitted herself into the Panecraft drug rehab program. Some believed she'd simply fallen off the wagon and returned to L.A., bored with the slower pace of a small town. Most of her few belongings were gone. Because of that, it took months before a possible connection was made between the two women. Symbolically, she was buried in the back pages until the next woman vanished.

No corresponding sabbat.

Person or persons unknown set fire to ten neighborhood house cats.

Swastikas were drawn in lipstick on the faces of seventeen newborns in the viewing nursery of the maternity ward of Summerfell General.

Joanne Sadler was sixteen, attractive, and wanted to be a poet able to make a living from her work, which she realized was nearly impossible. She was an honors student. Her poetry had already been published in numerous literary magazines, journals that had rejected Matthew when he was her age, and several times since. She vanished from the high school on the morning of July 28, after attending the first half of her Advanced English summer class. At 10:30 there was a twenty-five-minute break for lunch, during which some students went outside and relaxed from the intensive writing course. When class resumed Joanne's seat remained empty and Mr. Spinetti questioned her friends, all of whom believed her to be in the bathroom. She never returned, and wasn't the type of girl to cut school at all, much less a summer class three hours long that counted for three times as much at the end of the session.

By two A.M. the following morning Joanne's hysterical mother lay tranquilized in Panecraft. The newspaper photograph showed her husband beside a hospital bed, his wrung hands knotted atop his wife's sleeping form, hollowed eyes nothing but two charcoal slashes.

Only three days from Lughnasadh—Lammas—on July 31, a holiday celebrating the ripening of apples, and more important that of winter wheat, which was made into loaves and then blessed in church. It was also a day of accounts, when Scottish farmers took their first grain harvest to pay the rent.

A day of collecting.

Still, such a nurturing sabbat. Why take her then?

In church, one out of every ten missals was inexplicably replaced with a copy of Anton LaVey's miserably self-indulgent *The Satanic Bible*.

August 3. With the worst thunderstorm the county had seen in five years uprooting trees and sinking boats in the harbor, Steve Callaghan and Dominic Lowe decided to rob the local Stop-'n'-Shop. Their faces and voices were recorded clearly on the store video camera— Steve taking a bite out of a fruit pie as he shot the night clerk in the face, and Dom's moronic giggling loud and much less than human as he vaulted the counter, kicked the dead clerk in the head, and poured half his stolen beer over the body. Their car was found the next day, less than a mile away, in an empty patch of scrub wood, the gun on the floor of the passenger side. The five remaining bullets had been fired into the dashboard and windshield, splayed as if fending off multiple attackers—the stolen $64.43 lay scattered on the front seat. There was no blood of any type.

They were two seventeen-year-old cracker thugs who never came back and would never be missed, not by the elderly neighbors they tormented or even their own white trash families. Police were hesitant to add this case to the others, but it appeared, for the time being, that no other scenario could be worked out. Hodges refused to give comment, but the questions were obvious.

Only three days after Lammas—balancing out the murder of Joanne Sadler? The account paid?

The front door of the Sauter house was equipped with three interior locks that Mr. and Mrs. Eric Sauter heard snapped in place behind them by the baby-sitter as they left their home on the evening of September 21. Their next-door neighbor, eighteen-year-old Donna Maybanks, was a thoroughly amiable, somewhat neurotic girl who constantly complained about her cheekbones and fat thighs, but proved especially capable of taking charge of their sleeping four-year-old daughter Sarah while the Sauters attended a real estate business seminar. "She never thought she was pretty enough," Mrs. Sauter told the *Gazette*. Donna had begun her freshman year at Gallows Community College, her major being oceanography. When the Sauters returned at ten that night they found their daughter on the couch with her I Love You Truly Trudy doll sitting upright beside her, the child eating potato chips and melted ice cream, watching the most visceral scenes of a slasher flick on cable television. Donna's tattered copy of Jackie Collins's *Rock Star* lay beside Sarah on the sofa. When questioned, the child told her

133

parents that she'd been awakened by extremely loud laughter, and came downstairs to find Donna gone. The front and back doors remained locked from the inside. None of the windows appeared to have been tampered with.

A keen-eyed deputy found that I Love You Truly Trudy had been smeared with a dab of blood between its plastic legs, as if signifying menstruation.

The autumnal equinox, September 21, when day and night, male and female forces are equal, a time of second harvests when the Eleusinian rites are performed in the name of Demeter and Persephone. Why wasn't the child harmed, if the Goat was taking blood? Why the little gibe with the doll? Matthew thought that Donna being a student of oceanography might have something to do with her being chosen; perhaps she'd strayed into the caves, studying the tides. Perhaps Elemi the fishboy was still around.

He added up the days, seeking another cycle, checking meteorological reports to see if lunar phases were catalysts. He sought out distances between events, looked for angles, degrees. A.G. was altogether separate.

As he rose from the microfiche table Matthew turned and saw Jazz standing behind him, reading the articles over his shoulder.

"Jazz?"

Pale and looking spaced, Jazz nodded as if hearing him from a distance. "Hey."

"What's the matter?"

"I checked some of your old haunts and figured you'd be here," Jazz said quietly, motionless and paling even more. "You've been busy, Mattie? Think you're going to help your old buddy." His voice warbled. "I thought you'd want to know that they just found one of those missing kids." Trembling, sweating now and looking sicker, Jazz fell into the chair. He glanced at the screen, and looked up at Matthew as if seeing him for the first time. "My girlfriend works the switchboard. Cindy Banks, captain of the debate team, remember her? She gave me a call." Jazz bent forward. "A.G. should die, you know. Mattie, it's all become such a fuckin' mess."

Chapter Eleven

Carried by the wind, the ugly sounds of retching extended beyond the abandoned train station, wafted along the trail to those hidden burial grounds of babies, and drifted past Potter's Field and the strewn dread roses lying on a nameless grave.

Wildflowers shook and sprang back and forth in the grass. The woods captured and returned a sense of menace, the flashing lights brushing against bark, melding with the sun. Vomit puddled in the weeds.

Car radios buzzed static and crackled barely distinguishable orders and responses: "Hey, Sheriff, what the hell's happening up there?" The M.E. coughed through his scarf and shook his head in the direction of the deputy throwing up against a sugar maple. It could happen like that sometimes, but he hadn't witnessed it for a long time. You could see it day in and day out, never letting it affect you, and all of a sudden it would catch you deep in the gut and make your legs weak as if you'd never been around it before; or you could be a rookie on your first assignment and handle it as if you'd been on the job twenty years. You never knew quite how it would affect you, no matter how often you grinned in the face of it.

And murder had never been like this in Summerfell before.

Feet tramped over the meadow heading for the platform while indifferent ambulance attendants parked out front looked over the rest of the hillside with impassive eyes. They knew they were on the scene strictly as a formality and hated every minute of it. Bored and cold, they would rather have been scraping the body up and bagging the little pieces. There was nothing to do now but wait for the word to go, running their heater in the shadows of the wrecked buildings of the asylum.

They hadn't been inside.

Marty Cruthers, the rookie retching in the weeds, wiped his mouth with the back of his hand, face ashen and wet as one of the other deputies tried and failed to speak words that could seem consoling.

"I knew her," Cruthers said. "She lived only a

few blocks from me, been there for years, I'm telling you. We even went on a few dates, before I met Janice." He slid and leaned back against the side of the tree. "I'm only a couple of years older than her." His eyes flitted, catching bits and pieces here and there. "I liked her, I really liked her. I mean, she's young, it's not like we ever did anything, nothing in the sack, you know, but that was okay. Like we were friendly." He was having trouble breathing. "When, Russ, come on, come on. For Christ's sake, Russ, come on . . . when are they going to take her down?"

She remained hanging in the station.

Swinging slowly, gradually spinning in the air by leisurely degrees.

Upside down.

With arms outstretched below her head, throat precisely cut in order to avoid, it seemed, any arterial spray. The carefully drained blood had flowed out in two steady streams that ran off behind her ears, a great deal of the fluid had been absorbed into her long thick hair, turning blond curls crimson and coiling them into tightly matted knots. The rest of the blood had dripped into the perfectly circular pool drying beneath.

Naked young girl with alabaster skin, belly smooth and beautiful as marble glistening with condensation, so thin and papery because it was empty. Camera flashes exposed every act inflicted upon her, from a hundred varying angles, veering position and points of view, passionately igniting the blue of her open eyes.

Her countenance glowed in the sunlight arcing through the broken windows, face untouched; no bruise, slice, no welt of any kind. They were thankful for that, and curious as well. Her tongue had been torn out and the mouth wiped clean after.

The wire used to string her up was hitched to a rafter and tied around the left ankle, cutting into her foot so deeply as she spun that it couldn't be seen inside the wound anymore. The other leg had been shattered and bent, forced back and down so that she looked as if she'd been snapped in two like a wishbone. After she had been bled, the toes of her left foot had been jammed into her mouth and her jaw worked violently enough to bite them off herself. In the coagulating pool her toes lay atop her broken ribs, heart, and lungs; the contents of her abdominal cavity had unfurled into her chest, which hung with intestines. Until the coroner cleaned up, they wouldn't know if anything had been taken.

White.

White, so intensely white, her stomach hadn't been damaged at all, and you could look at that part of her and think of the days when you dated teenage girls, and how amazing it was to stroke a belly like that, soft line of blond fuzz traveling her midriff. The rookie outside kept mumbling for them to take her down, to please take her down now, please.

Her hands brushed the station floor, jagged fingernails scraping the freezing cement. *Tik*. The carcass, which nobody with any mercy would call Joanne Sadler any longer, continued being played upon the breezes. *Tik*, like a swimmer diving naked into darkness, half turning now in midair to look at you, turquoise nails still sweeping the ground, *tik*. Her body had been swung through the blood in a particular manner, those dripping hands used to draw out a circle and spell two words along its circumference.

Written in her blood, with her own hands, facing to the north: YHWH.

And to the south: BAPHOMET.

As she kept scratching at the floor.

Webs cross-hatched the ceiling and spiders made their way out to the wire. More flashes from the camera drove the dead girl's stare across the room.

"That's enough of the fucking pictures, Benny," Sheriff Hodges said. "I want those rolls developed and sealed. I ain't kidding. Everything, including the negatives, all of it sent back to me by five tonight."

"Five?"

"And no help on this one, Ben, I want you to

do it all yourself. None of the kids work on it. None of them can keep their mouths shut about it."

"Can you blame 'em?" Benny Turnball said, knowing better than to whine or argue, and not feeling strong enough to contest such demands. He unsteadily hefted his camera bag onto his shoulder, fighting to keep his breakfast from rising any farther up his throat, relieved to be getting the hell out of this place. He refused to think about how at the age of forty-eight he could conclude, without any satisfaction at all, that he'd been right his entire life for being a bitterly cynical bastard. "You're going to piss off the press."

"Yeah, and won't that keep me up at night, knowing them vultures can't eat this one up?" Hodges's barrel chest heaved, taking it all in, letting it all out, with that one breath. "Why don't you just let me worry about that, all right, Benny? Hey, didn't I just tell you to do something?"

Hodges turned away then, his face never anything but caustic, glad that he'd made it without smashing the little shit of a photographer's teeth down his throat. He could rein in the rage, sometimes; not always, but sometimes. Every vein crawled in his neck, threatening to burst. Still, he wouldn't let this wrath pull him too far along, though he wanted to go. He hadn't shed a tear in forty years, not even when his son died of leukemia while Hodges fought a war to make it safe for other little boys instead, and especially not when his wife had been run down by a drunk driver. Drunk—the guy had shot back only two Lite beers, but just couldn't hold it.

Most people mistook his apparent lack of emotion for apathy; he heard it all, and noticed the glances, but didn't care much as long as it all worked out. If you really knew him—and only one man could claim to—or had an eye for watching such men, you could see the murder eating into and out of him every damn day, like some unlucky suicide who couldn't quite manage to kill himself off.

Hodges pivoted and called, "Don."

"Yes, sir?"

"Where the hell is Russell?"

"Outside with Marty," Donald O'Malley said. His gun was very light at his side, it did not feel as if it had enough power to hurt the person who'd left the girl like that. "He needed some calming down. I think he used to date the girl. They knew each other pretty good."

"Go and get them. And while you're out there send off those assholes in the ambulance. They haven't seen anything, and I don't want them to have any part of this. None of their goddamn EMS interference, and no stupid conjectures either. Tell them to keep their mouths shut or I'll rip their lips off and nail them to my desk. Get on it. I'm serious."

"I know. But, Sheriff—?"

"Would you please fucking go already?"

Hodges put his fists in his pockets and waited until O'Malley did as he was told and returned a minute later with the grim-faced Russell Stockton and the bleary-eyed Marty. One crime, Hodges thought, a thing like this and my force is torn wide apart. We're supposed to be the tough ones, and look at this. Why in the hell did I hire any of them? They milled around him, his three deputies, and the coroner and his two assistants, all staring at him now, waiting for him to speak.

The floor wasn't firm enough under his feet, not sufficiently stable to bear up under the hate. It was like that, when the pain and anger grew too wide, and you could feel just how useless you were. As always, his voice remained flat, without any of the inflection you might expect from a man with those types of eyes and wrinkles and sneer. "No one says anything. Not to your wives, not to your friends, and for Christ's sake, not to any reporters. Nobody." He stressed it, and it came out *"No body,"* as if they couldn't still see her swinging there. "If any of you has too much to drink and leaks what you've seen here today you will answer to me, on a personal level, and believe me, I will cause you great damage."

"We ought to call in the state," Marty Cruthers said.

143

"You dated her?"

"Yes, but only a couple of times. I'm only two years older than her, she lived—"

"You love her?"

It took Marty back a step, and he wiped sweat from his puzzled face. "She—"

"Did you love her?" Hodges repeated. "Deeply? You feel like you want to kill yourself now that she's gone?"

Marty's mouth moved for a while without sound, until he finally said, "No, I mean, I just . . . I thought we caught the bastard, so how . . . ?"

"You ever see someone you love strung up like that?"

"No, of course not." Marty's eyes widened and his voice slipped again like gears shifting poorly, until only a whispery hiss escaped him.

"Then be thankful, and if you ever throw up at a crime scene again I'm going to toss you in jail for corrupting an official investigation. You think I'm kidding? You think I'm exaggerating? Fuck the state and fuck the rest of the county. This is our job. If this hits our streets we're going to cause an even more awful panic than we're already in, and we can't afford to have every idiot with a shotgun shooting up the town. I don't feel like arresting any of our neighbors for killing his friend or wife or kid or even a goddamn dog. Until we can figure this out I want total silence."

"What about her parents?" Russell Stockton asked. He brushed a hand through his thinning hair, his gaze a little far off but not glassy, wondering how he would feel if he found out his own daughter had ever come to this. With A.G. in Panecraft, this should have been over, they had capped the lunacy. But now, with her body dancing, he realized what a fool he'd been not to believe in the urgent alarm that had been gnawing within him this last half year. He actually wanted to get out of Summerfell with his family, maybe see the folks in Montana, or head up to Canada if that was far enough away, though he knew it wasn't. "Will you tell them?"

Hodges replied without hesitation. He'd been working that question from the moment they'd walked into this corner of hell. "No, not yet. Not until we have some answers. Maybe in the morning. Tomorrow."

"That's not going to go over well."

"No," Hodges said. "It won't."

Marty couldn't quite keep the pleading from his voice, his face dropping inch by inch like melting wax, thinking now that maybe he did love her, a little, maybe more, seeing her hanging up there. She'd written poems to him. "Can't we at least take her down?"

"Everything's going to be okay, Marty."

Moving to the other side of the station, Hodges and Russell continued searching for evidence in the wall, on the wire, standing over the puddle as the M.E. coughed and picked about the pile of viscera, and his assistants finished their initial study of the corpse. Hodges grabbed O'Malley by shoulder. "Don, I want you to take Marty home. He lives alone, right?"

"Yes, just moved out into his first apartment. Kid's only eighteen, nineteen."

"Stay with him for a while. Make him a couple of drinks. Make sure he either passes out or gets some of his shit back together before you leave."

"All right. What have we got here, Sheriff?"

"I don't know," Hodges said. "But I'm going to kill it."

Richard Karragan, the medical examiner, stepped from the dangling body. He sounded nearly dead himself, coughing in the same deep wheeze that split through the police chatter coming in over the radio. When he caught his breath, he spoke softly to Hodges. "I'm not sure if I agree with your not telling the press."

The sheriff wiped his face with both hands and said, "I don't much give a shit if you agree or not, Rich, so just do me a favor and don't piss me off more. Tell me what you know, is that so goddamn much to ask? How long has she been dead?"

Karragan knew how Hodges reacted in extreme situations like this, the man being pulled internally as much as externally, as much wire inside as out here. The sheriff wouldn't give him enough time to simply provide a full report, instead interrupting and asking questions that would be answered soon enough if only Hodges didn't keep cutting him off. But it's the way they went about their jobs; the sheriff quizzing and thereby accepting, one step at a time, more and more personal responsibility for these death watches. Karragan knew it all, because it had been this way since they'd served together in the war, and even longer than that, since they were boys living across the street from one another, best friends. "Six hours."

"Can't be. This place is full of rats. They would've been all over her."

"I'm telling you. Six hours." Carefully snapping off his plastic gloves, Karragan added, "She doesn't seem to have been malnourished. What was the exact date of her abduction?"

"July twenty-eighth."

"And it appears that her captor kept her comfortable for all this time. From what I can see she doesn't have any semihealed ligatures or recently acquired scars, no rope burns or handcuff welts. I'm giving you the short form, of course, it's far too early to tell."

"I know it. Could she have been with this guy willingly? Faked her own kidnapping for whatever reason? She tan? Maybe they headed off someplace, to the Keys. The guy got sick of her, she wouldn't back off, so he killed her?"

Karragan shrugged. "She's very young and attractive, there are men who would take her anywhere, wouldn't they? She's not tan, but all the rest is certainly possible, isn't it?"

"No." It had just been a shot, nothing real. "No, not if what I understand about this girl is true. If we go with the idea that she was abducted, where could she have been kept hidden for these months?"

"No apparent evidence without an extensive autopsy. Nothing under her fingernails, and we'll have to search through the viscera to check on what she's been eating. I don't think we'll find anything. I believe her abdominal cavity was emptied so that the killer could remove the stomach itself. We'll do blood work."

"What kind of weapon was used?"

"A number of knives, ranging, I would think, from scalpels to kitchenware. The incisions are of various sizes, types, and sharpness. This guy was packing a butcher shop under his shirt."

"Raped?"

"Give me a fuckin' break," Karragan said, the cough and wheeze coming together just right to form a nice, low growl, showing exactly how he felt. "Most of her respiratory system and half her intestinal tract is on the floor. I need to get her out of here before I can give you anything more."

"Then go and do it, but I want to know everything."

"Of course. What the hell is that? What, you think I'd hold back?"

Hodges ignored the remark, trying to throw his chest out more, put as much emphasis into the moment as possible. "You're going to find out what all of this means, Rich. Why you think this maniac did what he did here, how he pulled it off . . . when . . . everything."

Karragan actually felt a little sorry for him. "Yes."

"And one more thing."

"What?"

"Was she alive when it started? Did she live long while he did that to her?"

Karragan weighed his options and found them extremely limited, as usual. He considered two things, both equally out of character: He could lie to the sheriff, but instinctively knew lies wouldn't ease Hodges's quandary any, and that the lie would surely come back to haunt them both, no matter how large or small it might be. The second consideration was to use Hodges's first name, which no one else on the force, possibly in the town, even realized he had anymore.

Karragan knew, though, and when the time came to put aside duty he realized he had to make his friend remember he wasn't entirely alone in this life, and that they were the strongest they had to be, when the world was at its worst. As both of them were and always had been, even as children.

"Yes, Louis," he said tersely, because this was the truth and there couldn't be any other way now, struggling to beat back the pain, all of it coming closer. "She died in agony."

In time, they took her down. As they always took the murdered down, regardless of remorse or hardness of heart, with or without prayers, because she looked so much like your daughter, your girlfriend. It made no difference how tough you believed yourself to be, in the light of this, because they could never take the dead down fast enough.

Finally, they bagged her and put her on the gurney.

"There's no way we're going to be able to keep this under the lid," Russell said. He thought so much about his own daughter that his ears were beginning to hurt from the sounds of her giddy voice so loud in his mind. He'd already called home and told his wife to keep the doors locked, get the spare gun out of the drawer and load it, keep it handy. She knew better than to question him, she'd haul up their little girl from her swing set and stay inside until he got home and told her it was safe, if he could manage that.

"We'll do it."

"What was he waiting for, Sheriff? Why kidnap her so far in advance? Because he wanted to keep her?" He felt wrong, talking about the case out loud like this, but there it was. "This guy's been keeping her a prisoner, hiding, living with her for so long, doing what, making friends? Looking for a lover? All the time knowing that he was going to do this to her?"

"He's kept quiet too long," Hodges said. "Now he's screaming for attention. You can feel it."

"What about A.G.?" Russell said.

"What about him?"

"Does this mean he's innocent? Did—?"

The word "innocent" didn't sound the same in this place anymore. "So he's a lunatic with a partner. Or partners. Does an innocent man sit with a goddamn skeleton and somehow foul up a child's mind so much that the kid goes catatonic?"

"So he was part of something bigger."

"We're missing something, Russell. Something. Someone. And you'd better start helping me to find out who and what it is." Hodges forced himself not to go over and kick Karragan's assistants in their asses, grab somebody by the back of the head, twist, and demand satisfaction. They were already too intimidated to even talk, thank Christ, so he didn't have to hear whatever it was they whispered back and forth while they put the pieces in bags and jars. "And if we give him any attention it'll feed his hunger even more. If we starve him, maybe he'll slip up, maybe we can bait him."

"I hope to Christ you're right."

"Me too."

Russell was surprised to hear that, and wondered if the food metaphor was accurate. He decided to roll with it for one more turn. "And if the others are still alive, won't that mean he'll just gut them even more quickly, trying to feed himself?"

Hodges didn't hear. "If this guy is from town, then I don't want him to be able to get his rocks off every time someone mentions this girl's name. Those other kids might still be alive somewhere, and we have to find them before he decides to . . ."—to do what, how did you put a name to any of this?—". . . to do it again."

"Sure."

"We've got to be tighter than ever before," the sheriff said, more to himself than to Russell or Karragan. When he became this emphatic he began speaking with such a strained focused gaze that you couldn't tell anymore if he was staring at you, into you, or only within himself.

"Tighter than before what?" Russell asked. "What do you compare it to? When the Fredrick brothers knocked over each other's stills? When Henderson's girlfriend found him in bed with his wife?"

"Maybe you should phone Sheriff Bradley," Karragan suggested. "I heard he had some problems like this over in Gallows a few years back."

"No."

"Why not?" Russell knew why not, but had to put the question out in front anyway. "If there's a chance he can help, then let him in on it."

Hodges merely stared at the side of Russell's face until the deputy shook his head and checked the ceiling once more, watching the spiders poised in their nests, examining from a distance the cut wire still hanging from the rafter, detailing the inches, the traces of madness. The sheriff spun and looked at Karragan, who simply stared back at him, the two of them locked alone in this because they understood each other so much better than the rest, and understood at least a part of this new phase of blood. "She's a sign. A note to us."

"Yes, Louis," Karragan said, coughing into his fist.

Russell looked down at the circle on the floor. "What does it mean? Those two words."

"I don't know. After we finish up here I want you to go to the library and check it out. Ask Millie the reference librarian for help if you need it, but only Millie. She's the only one who'll keep her mouth shut." He tried to pronounce the words and couldn't; how did you say *Yhwh*? What kind of clue was he leaving behind? "The bastard left them for us to find, so we know there's a reason. You know how to read."

"What did you mean by saying she was a note?" Russell asked.

"Like in the war," Karragan explained. "You would leave them nailed to a tree and they would leave us signs staked out in the jungle, usually with their eyes and genitalia gone. Just so we would never forget how much hate we could live with. So you remember your foe every minute."

"It's working for me," Russell said.

Stepping on a spider, knowing it bore witness to everything that had happened here six hours before, Hodges told them, "Until I know what it is he thinks he's doing, nobody else gets in on it." You wouldn't think you'd have to repeat yourself so much as this, but Hodges realized how effusive his orders were at the moment, how often death could come between him and his men instead of banding them together.

"Too late," Russell said, gazing beyond Karragan's shoulder out into the field where the leaves kicked up into the rising shadows. "Hey, there's already two guys standing over there watching us."

What had been set in motion continued to move.

Now, Sheriff Hodges saw Matthew Galen reach out, unzip the body bag, and touch the girl's forehead before anyone could stop him, pressing his palm against her tormented flesh and, with two flicks of his fingers, describing a mark on her skin.

Time contracted as forty years and forty pounds disappeared, and with a growl that made them all look up, Hodges rushed over as if sighting the killer and backhanded Matthew with such ferocity that the sound of bone fracturing filled the room.

Matthew's nose shattered instantly as blood spurted and gushed down his face, the cartilage snapping with ease, and the sheriff recalled just how good it felt to let some of the venom escape. Almost crazy enough in this moment of red-trimmed vision to scream his dead son's name, he grabbed Matthew by the shoulders and swung him around, slamming him full force into the station wall where the windows broke like ice crackling. Hodges heard yet another snap, maybe the guy's clavicle or maybe his neck or back, as his hands closed over Galen's throat and tightened, and tightened, and kept tightening.

"Louis!" Karragan bellowed.

"Sheriff!" Jazz yelled.

Neither of them could get ahold of Hodges as Russell shouted into the sheriff's ear and tried to pry his fists loose from throttling Matthew.

"What the fuck is your problem?" Hodges screamed into Matthew's face as the kid coughed, choking, his face mottling, but with a curl of the lip as if he was liking this. "You get your kicks out of touching dead girls, huh? Or maybe you just like making them dead, maybe

155

you know where the rest of them are, eh, Galen? I remember you, you're the fucker who thought he was hot shit just because he ran a football across a field once upon a time. I know you're best friends with that other shithead in your mommy and daddy's bugfuck house on the hill. I wouldn't put it past you being a part of this thing from the beginning. Right? Say it now! Tell it to me now!"

Jazz tried to break Hodges's hold, grabbing at his wrists, but the sheriff shrugged once and elbowed him in the gut. Jazz went down on one knee. Blood spumed from Matthew's nostrils onto the sheriff's fists. "Maybe you thought it was time to leave a body behind, throw off suspicion, make it look like your pal was innocent. But it isn't that simple, fucker. He's not going anywhere except for when I put him and you into the cold ground, you hear me! You're going into the ground! When I find out you had something to do with this girl's murder and those other missing kids I won't waste my time going through the system. Bet on it, just me and my Colt .45 will find you and make you pay. Believe it. You know what those words over there mean, don't you, Galen? I know you do!"

As the blood flowed down his face, his voice became a snarl torn from his throat, more feral than Hodges's, if possible, with the blood filling his mouth. Matthew's eyes deepened with all that dwelled in shadows inside them, and he said, "Take your hands off me."

Heartbeats thudded around the room.

And Hodges released him and backed up a step, bottom lip trembling, the boiling rage turning to fear in an instant, and came this close to letting loose a whimper.

Hodges thought of his son still racked with pain and his wife's mangled face after smashing into the windshield—Jesus no—dropped suddenly into terror as solid as the cement floor but far colder, like nothing he'd ever felt or seen before, there in those eyes, the feeling already passing as he obeyed and Matthew fell backward out of reach and into Jazz's arms.

"This could ruin even one of Bosco Bob's parties," Jazz said.

Matthew staggered from them all, past the girl's body on the gurney, his fists bleeding black hexes as he stumbled outside and down the steps of the abandoned train station. He made it to Potter's Field before dropping to his knees, spitting out precious blood, bracing himself against a crumbling tombstone as he tried to stand and failed.

He staggered to the grave that might be his mother's, dragging his feet through the weeds until at last he sank on top of it. Blood smeared the stone, and somewhere the Goat collected

Tom Piccirilli

more power. He lay against the hard earth and soft crumbling roses.

He stared at Panecraft.

His enemy peered back.

Chapter Twelve

Debbi stood silhouetted on the horizon. She listened without interest as he gestured and drew weird pictures in the sand, talking on and on about stuff that didn't mean anything much, though he really got into it: pagan rites, names of power, scrying, and summer solstices and witchcraft and the differences between Wicca and Satanists, and something called the Inquisition.

She sighed and tossed a handful of broken scallop shells and periwinkles back into the sea. "But what's all that got to do with the lighthouse?" she asked impatiently. "You've been going on about it for a half hour, and I still don't know."

He could only shake his head and shrug. He wasn't altogether sure yet.

She watched the waves. "It's pretty cool, all that. You mean it really drove them underground? Like down in the caves? Or are you just speaking like that, what they say, figuratively? Makes sense, though, if they were being burned and tortured and stuff. Even if most of it was just religious maniacs over in England and Germany, and like what you said, hysteria, fanatic people killing midwives and them herbalist-type folks, what if some of it was true? Don't you think that some of it's got to be true? And what if they came here?"

Over near the reef, a group of little kids flew kites and threw pieces of driftwood to a barking golden retriever, who chased the sticks into the greenish-blue surf and returned to the children with seaweed and bits of kelp clinging tenaciously to its fur.

"You'll keep studying up on it, though, won't you?" Debbi said, putting lotion on his sun-burned shoulders, toppling a large pile of library books and comic books as she slid closer to him. "You're really getting into it. I can see you're having fun, going to those bookstores." He reached out with a beach towel and wiped off the side of her sweaty face. He wanted to ask why she cared so much about this, but the questions lay back in his mouth the same way the two of them lay on the blanket, listening to the

Here's how it works:
Each package will carry a FREE 10-DAY EXAMINATION
privilege. At the end of that time, if you decide
to keep your books, simply pay the low invoice price
of $7.50, no shipping or handling charges added.
HOME DELIVERY IS ALWAYS FREE!
There's no minimum number of books to buy,
and you may cancel at any time.

AND AS A CHARTER MEMBER,
YOUR FIRST TWO-BOOK
SHIPMENT IS TOTALLY FREE!
IT'S A BARGAIN YOU CAN'T BEAT!

✂ CUT HERE

Mail to: Leisure Horror Book Club,
P.O. Box 6613, Edison, NJ 08818-6613

YES! I want to subscribe to the Leisure Horror Book Club. Please send
my 2 FREE BOOKS. Then, every other month I'll receive the two newest
Leisure Horror Selections to preview FREE for 10 days. If I decide to
keep them, I will pay the Special Members Only discounted price of just
$3.75 each, a total of $7.50. This saves me between $2.48 and $4.48 off
the bookstore price. There are no shipping, handling or other charges.
There is no minimum number of books I must buy and I may cancel the
program at any time. In any case, the 2 FREE BOOKS are mine to keep—
at a value of between $9.98 and $11.98. Offer valid only in the USA.

NAME:_____

ADDRESS:_____

CITY:_____ STATE:_____

ZIP:_____ PHONE:_____

LEISURE BOOKS, A Division of Dorchester Publishing Co., Inc.

radio. Baby crabs skittered through their collapsing castle just as the waves came in and filled up the moat. The wet dog ran past, spraying water on their feet. "Uh-huh," she answered for him, tickling his ribs. Her hands were too cold. "You'll keep on studying. Of course you will."

Kites threw shadows across his pictures in the sand.

Yes, of course he would.

He would do anything for her.

Chapter Thirteen.

There were strange sounds on what might be his mother's grave, as if coming from the ground, or somewhere else, distant and yet too close, as farther away the breakers crashed and the ocean continued to croon.

There were smells too, the dead roses so sweet, analgesic, and potent, overpowering the wildflowers no matter where you stood in Potter's Field. These noises, like bones striking together, like shards of mirror drawing back into place, and groans pressed into the dirt, and wind shrieks whistling through the dead trees, both eerie and human, went on like that for only a few seconds more, and then there was nothing left except blood on his jacket and a chiseled social security number behind his back. He sat and waited, feeling the weight of murder on his shoulders, the dead girl's face perfectly alive in his mind. After another two minutes he heard footsteps, and then Jazz hovered over him and helped him to stand.

Jodi Carmichael had not spoken with her ex-boyfriend Jello Joe since the night she'd caught him in the Krunch parking lot with the giggling, squeaking, and, she thought perhaps, meowing Charlene Dorwette, while the two of them made an awkward version of love in the backseat of Jodi's own six-cylinder rust-bucket '79 Duster. He had that kind of audacity.

At the moment, though, Jello Joe stood on the porch with his mouth curved into a grin that was undoubtedly intended to be irresistible, and would have been at one time not so long ago, she supposed. With his eyebrows knitted and hair mussed just enough by the breeze, and jaw dropped with little boy charm, it was exactly the same face that Marlon Brando gives Kim Hunter in *A Streetcar Named Desire*, when he walks in the door after work, seeking forgiveness again.

Stella took Stanley back, and look what she got for it.

Jodi wanted to smash all of Jello Joe's teeth in.

She chewed the inside of her cheek and glared at him so hard that after a second she couldn't even see him.

"I heard Matthew Galen is back in town," Joe said. "Is he staying here?"

"Get the hell away from me."

"Listen, Jodi, can't you give me a polite answer?"

"Fuck you very much," Jodi said. "That polite enough for you?"

"That's nice talk," he said, doing his best to look offended. He was that kind of guy.

"I know you enjoy meowing much better."

"What the hell's that mean?"

"Shut up. It means that I have no idea where Matt Galen is. In fact, I haven't seen him yet. My father told me this morning he spent the night here. He got in late and missed breakfast. Jasper Metzner came for a visit, and I guess they left together, I don't know." The normal talk just about wore her out, holding back so much. "Now I politely request that you drop dead, preferably from a disease of the venereal nature so that poetic justice can be served."

"C'mon, honey, you aren't still made at me, are you, babe? Listen, listen, I . . ."

She wondered what the whine in his voice actually meant; was it just the little boy who'd had his toys taken away or lust because Charlene Dorwette had turned the frosty shoulder to him when she found out she couldn't tweak his bank accounts quite as easily as she could his libido?

Wind blew leaves over the verandah. Jodi

kept the screen door latched. "Cut the crap. If you're not off my porch in five seconds I'll have my dog rip your heart out."

"I don't think Gus could even find the front yard."

A bad bet. Gus, somewhere in the kitchen, rose from beneath the table at the sound of his name. He poked his tongue from with in the mass of knots and licked his front paw, sneezed, and clambered forth. Despite his goofiness, he'd do whatever she commanded him to do, and that included attacking. You couldn't see the fangs, but they were there all right. Gus barked happily and wagged his tail, but when he came to her, he sensed the atmosphere, and, almost inaudibly, began to snarl.

Jodi crossed her arms. "Just as well. You don't have a heart, anyway."

"Let's be adult about this. I know I made a terrible mistake, Jo, but I really want to—"

"Adult?" The word struck her completely wrong. She brought her heel back against the door stop, determined not to cry anymore. Gusto's snarl grew louder. "Adult. Now all of a sudden you want to be adult? After what you did in my car with another woman? What, you think you're going to be clapped on the back in the bars with that kind of story, about how you fucked Charlene in my car?"

"No no, listen, Jo, you've got it wrong—"

"Bullshit, Joey. Tell me the truth, you did it just because it sounded like a real joke you could tell the boys over a few pitchers. Yeah, let's get adult." Amazingly enough, she didn't even feel like sobbing as she regarded him standing outside, all his charm gone, his hair too messy now. The anger in her became fluid, making her mouth water and eyes itch while she watched him.

She smiled. Real fury didn't leave her lacking, and welled, oddly enough, in her fingernails, which she kept digging into her palms. She thought about shredding that mouth she'd kissed so many times, so it would never grin or kiss anyone else like that again, she wanted to kick herself for ever having fallen in love with what stood before her so gracelessly.

Not only had the sight itself been obscene that night—as if finding her car broken into by her own boyfriend and catching him humping another girl hadn't been bad enough—but Joe had actually smiled up at her. Always with the grin. Always with the over-the-edge gall.

"You've got to admit it was kind of a funny situation," he said.

"You stinking son of a bitch," Jodi said. "No, of all the things I've had to do lately, Joey, that's something I don't have to admit."

He stepped forward and grabbed the screen door by its handle, and found it locked. "Look, I really care about you, so please, let's . . ." The whine had turned into a full-fledged snivel of sorrow. Jodi couldn't figure it out, why all of a sudden it should come to this.

"Get out of here, Joey."

"If only you'd listen to me."

"Bug off before I call my father and he comes out here with his shotgun and shoots your undiscriminating balls all over the lawn."

He stepped back. Gus caught the shifting scent of the scene, and growled louder. She put her hand on his back, feeling just how much muscle lay there beneath the shaggy fur.

"Is that how you solve all your troubles all of the time, Jodi? Huh, forever and ever? You let your father make all the moves for you, too?"

"Too?" she repeated. "Make my moves for me? Shut up. You're so caught up in your father's money that you think you can do anything."

Jello Joe didn't hear. "Just let your old man and your mother take care of all the guys who show some interest in you? Scaring them off so you can stay safe from the world?"

"You've really got some set." Of course, he was turning it around. Somehow she'd forced him to screw Charlene, she'd thrown them together, just begged him to cheat on her. Throwing in the other guys, like he felt sorry for her other boyfriends.

"That's always been your problem, Jodi."

"Enough of this shit! My problem!" Jodi

bolted out the door without her coat on, the cold cutting up her arms in a good way, accenting the anger. She grabbed Joe by the wrist and twisted him sideways to face her. She knew the game, and had fallen into it, but wouldn't play this out how he thought they would. Fine, now she's out here, and he's supposed to grab her and kiss her against her will, and after a few seconds of struggling she gives in with a moan and falls into his arms, right? "What's my problem, you conniving bastard!"

"And you can't speak calmly, either," he said. "You're never willing to listen."

"What is there to listen to? You can't apologize enough to me!"

"I never meant to apologize, Jodi. I expected an apology from you."

And there it was, the insolence rising to the top until he smothered in it, like a fog he was trying to hide in. Where was the whine or the charm now? He had a whole list of attitudes he could throw at her at any minute, turning it on high or low like switching a radio dial, everything but an acceptance of responsibility. Jodi stood with her cheeks turning crimson, stuck between a laugh and apoplexy, going "Wha', wha', wha'," until the rest of it broke loose. "What the hell do you mean by that, you lousy shit?"

"Stop calling me names!"

She couldn't take it; a wall in her chest suddenly broke and a giggle crashed through, followed by a deep breath she didn't know she needed to take, and then tears were in her eyes. In a moment she felt completely weak and cold, and her teeth chattered as her nose began to run. She looked around and couldn't quite figure out why she was out here on the lawn at all, why she'd opened the door and chased him.

Joe spun and lifted his hands as if to touch her shoulders, but she shirked backward, repulsed. "I bought dozens of violets for you, because I know they're your favorite flower, and . . ."

Getting her into a conversation was bad enough, but she couldn't seem to stop talking. She tried to keep her teeth from chattering, but words hissed through. "It doesn't mean anything, Joey, certainly not enough—"

"Would you shut up and listen to me a minute." Now, finally, his voice was back on terra firma, was no longer pulled out of shape by these dramatics. He groped, looking genuinely lost for an instant. She'd never seen him like that before. "I was wrong, I know, but there was a reason. You don't listen, you never listen . . ." A little apoplectic himself, now turning in the wind. "I . . . look, I took you to go see lovey-dovey movies because I know they were the type of flicks you wanted to see, because it's what you saw when you dreamed about what you wanted in your own life. I took you to the finest restaurants . . ."

"So it's back to the money."

"It's not back to the money, damn it . . . listen! I took you because you deserved to have the best, and I didn't want to take you anywhere second-rate. It's not the money. It's not my father's money, you understand? I know you sometimes thought that, like it was easy for me to do these things, and so they didn't matter so much, as though they didn't come from the heart. But they did. You shortchanged me." He drew his hands to himself as if to say, *Look at me, look at how I'm dressed*. "The cash doesn't matter to me, it doesn't make me, I do what I want. I'm not flash."

He was, but didn't realize it, simply flash in a different style. "You're not making any sense."

"I would be if you'd listen. I wrote letters to you all the time, called every night, I mean . . . I thought we meant something to each other. I never felt that way about anyone, but then you would only give back so much, Jodi. I didn't want to rush you, didn't want to force you, but . . ." And now he was drained, and standing there looking pale with leaves in his hair, almost sickly as if he hadn't been sleeping well either. She noticed the bags under his eyes matched her own. "And I'm not talking sex, you're just going to harp on that, the sex, as if that's all it mattered. You never said you love

me, like the word was too strong for your taste,
you never even said that you *cared* about
me . . ."

"Of course I—"

"No, no, cut that out, there are no of courses,
Jodi, there's nothing like that. You couldn't look
me in the eye half the time, and you returned
so little affection that sometimes when we were
on the phone together I thought we'd been cut
off. You got a kick out of it, me going 'Hello?'
and you giggling, but it wasn't funny. Like you
weren't even on the other end anymore. For a
while I thought that you weren't receiving my
cards and letters. You so rarely even mentioned
them, never really said thank you, hardly returned anything like that."

Was it possible? Jodi wondered. That he was
the romantic, and she'd failed him in that? *He's
just worming out of it, another example of letting
her shoulder the burden*. But what if he was being honest? Her father occasionally complained
the same thing about her mother. It was true
enough about the letters and cards, she loved
them but didn't return much of those same kind
of sentiments. "I didn't think you cared about
that."

He was working himself up, staring sidelong
at her. "You took my love for granted. All right,
all right, before you shoot me down with Charlene again, I know I was wrong, I've said it. But
it wasn't the sex, it wasn't to tell stories over

beer. It was callous, and rotten, but it came up from where it was real Jodi, from inside. I did it to hurt you, damn it, I wanted to hurt you. Don't be so stupid. When you and I were in bed together it was like I was annoying you or breaking your arm, embarrassing you some-how, making it all vile and terrible, and how is that supposed to make me feel?"

"So you go off with another woman, in my own car?"

He raised his hands, again seeking to put them on her shoulders. Though she didn't move this time, he didn't touch her. "I was in your car waiting for you. You said you'd get off work by nine, and instead you stayed for a double shift without bothering to tell me. I popped your lock with a coat hanger and was waiting for you when I fell asleep. Charlene was going in for a couple of burgers, she spotted me, I started talk-ing, about you, and . . ."

"Yeah," Jodi said. Charlene made no effort to hide the fact that she'd always wanted to jump Joey's bones, either because of his athletic, sleek figure or because of his cash. "And. I know what she is."

The words wouldn't come anymore, and the tears were there where they hadn't been before, and the wind made it much worse. She spun, and he followed her back to the porch. "And now you expect me to apologize to you for being the way I am?"

"No," Joe said. "I just expected you to love me."

Gus barked inside now. And again, and then howling, scratching at the base of the door and driving his head against the screen. She said, "Gus, stop it, calm down. It's over. Quit it." She opened the latch to step inside, and the dog came barreling out in a heap. Jello Joe crossed his arms in case it was true that Gusto might chew his heart out, but instead the dog raced off across the lawn, heading up the street.

"What's the matter with him?"

"Why are you here, Joey?" she asked, her chin jutting. The rage dwindled, though she couldn't quite explain why that should be. It still felt as if he was only manipulating her, throwing everything at her. He was a conniver. There were some things she knew about him that she couldn't pretend she wasn't aware of, and hadn't already accepted long ago: She could pretty much tell when he was lying and when he was too distraught to even try bullshitting her—he could put it all on a stage if he had to, but sincerity wasn't an act, that much was certain. The rest of the relationship might be in the air, but she realized he was honest at this moment.

"Why am I here? You're really asking that?"

But if she believed he loved her, that somehow made the pain worse. "Why are you here?"

She searched his face for that charming grin, and didn't find it.

He put his hands in his pockets. "I came over to talk to Matt. I wanted to invite him to my dad's party tonight. And because I love you."

Jodi rubbed her freezing arms.

Quietly she said, "Oh."

YHWH.
  Blood.
  Spirit.
  Knowledge.
  Witch.
  Ritual.
  Magik.
  Death.
  Frenzy.
  BAPHOMET.
  These words.
  The houses rushed by as Jazz drove on.
  One by one, whirling past Matthew's vision like killers falling on victims for the taking.

He knew almost every one of them, or had known them years before in his childhood: the owners, yards, the cats and dogs that lay curled on the welcome mats or roamed freely up and down the blocks, the special way each of those doors clacked shut with its own unique *whuff* of air, different in the winter than in summer. The *thwack* of rolled-up papers thumped in his thoughts, on top of patio roofs and stuck in rain gutters, until after time and with greater finesse, the newspapers could be shot whipping like boomerangs right into your mailbox from thirty paces away, or left leaning against the door at the perfect angle so that your dog could grip it in his jaws and bring it to you, or you could reach out with your toes and flip the paper up into your hands, if you were inclined to do so. It was funny to watch some of them try in the winter, wearing fuzzy slippers, sliding their toes under the paper and giving a quick knee jerk, kicking up so the *Gazette* spun into their grasp and their slippers landed fifteen feet out in the snow on the blizzard-ridden lawn. Such a small common sound, that thwack, and it had become such an uncommonly large part of his life, like the taunting of the scars.

Jazz took one final drag of his cigarette and threw the butt out the window, reached for another, and found the pack empty. He crumpled it into a ball and bounced it off the dashboard. "Man," he said, making a ridiculously wide turn around the corner. His already erratic driving had grown worse now. "The sheriff sure fucked you up. We're going to the hospital."

"I'm okay."

"There's a gallon of blood on your shirt, Mattie. We should go. You need attention."

"No need. I'm fine."

Jazz shook his head, ponytail bobbing side to side. "I don't see how he didn't break your nose.

What the hell made you go and touch the body, Ibsen, huh? Why'd you do such a god-awful crazy thing like that?"

Matthew said nothing, staring out the car window.

"I just hope Cindy doesn't get into any trouble. Hodges made me a promise that he'd chew on my eyeballs if you or I said anything about what we saw back there. He's got to know she filled me in on the scene. He gets demented like that sometimes." Jazz clicked the heater's fan up another notch. "She didn't tell me what it would be like, though. Jesus, why didn't she warn me?" He gripped the steering wheel so tightly that his fidgety fingers squealed against it. The car zagged, pulling to the left, and he constantly had to fight for control. "I suppose I imagined there'd be cameras and clues and we could watch the cops go to work and maybe even see them capture the son of a bitch, you know? Christ, I'm so limited. I didn't stop to think there might be that in front of me. I teach kids her age all day long." The car crossed the yellow line and the driver of an oncoming pickup swerved and shouted. Jazz gestured obscenely, the car again crossing the line. He reached for a pack of cigarettes he didn't have. "Shit. I was all set to watch them hang him by his nuts, but now . . . now, with him still locked up, I'm not sure what the hell is happening. I thought they'd have to release A.G., or at least consider the possibility of him being framed. Too much freakin' television, I guess. And me, a dramatist. Mattie, you got any ideas?"

"He hasn't even been formally charged. What they're doing is already illegal."

Things would get more insane as the town came out of remission and the cancer attacked once again. *Who are the dead?* he wondered. *Who are the mad? What forms are the daemons taking now?* Some of them were fond of animals, others luxuriated in insects, and still more enjoyed the human form. He watched the houses. His feet beat at the floor mats, and he thought of Helen here in this same car way back then, the first time they'd made love. His leg throbbed as if recalling the break.

There were too many people already involved, and more would become entwined. How many had succumbed and still acted normally? . . . The nosy neighbors and blue-haired biddies and bored housewives, and those with nothing better to do than watch him wherever he went. He had to be careful, especially now that Hodges had come unstuck.

They passed Pond Boulevard, and saw the old house where Judy Ann Culthbert had invited him inside for a fresh piece of apple pie, when he and A.G. had attacked Elemi as the beast had tried to make its love to her. He remembered the familiar voice on the phone.

A few more doors down was the house where

Ruth Cahill had lived, her mother's light always shining on the third floor.

"Who's Aleister Crowley?" Jazz asked, slowing for a stop sign.

STOP: red octagon with white letters, clouds on blood, a symbol inherent with power from several levels. The pole had been bent awkwardly, face of the sign spray-painted with cutting black lines.

Shaping a swastika.

Crowley had claimed the Nazis stole their idea—not from antiquity, but from him.

"Nobody," Matthew said. "A bad showman."

"What, an actor?"

"More like Vaudeville."

Jazz turned, came as close to sneering as he could, and said, "You want to just answer my goddamn question straight, Mattie?"

And in that instant, Matthew had the feeling that he'd jerked in his seat though he hadn't moved; the sensation was like spinning through the air and being dumped from a great height before suddenly being stopped short, the way they'd used the *strappado* on suspected witches, tying their arms behind them and then dropping them from above until their shoulders were yanked out of the sockets. Like when he was drunk and the perfect words to improper spells couldn't be kept under his tongue any longer. "Why do you ask?"

"A.G. mentioned the name once, before the

fans jumped into the shit. I thought it might mean something important, a valid connection. You say an actor, but I was thinking maybe a drug dealer, you know? Somebody like that, or a whole lot worse?"

"No, nothing like that."

"Why do you think he talked about him, then? Who is this guy, for Christ's sake?"

Checking the rearview, Matthew watched the stop sign dwindling in the distance.

He could tell Jazz some more of the truth, but not all of it, never all of it.

He could tell Jazz that—

—Aleister Crowley, fool, idiot, joker of the troupe yet reputed to be a powerful magician, at least until the end when drugs and syphilis had destroyed his garnered reputation, who referred to himself as the Beast 666, born in 1875 and who believed himself to be the reincarnation of Eliphas Levi, the ex-priest who published *Dogma and Ritual in High Magic* in 1856, the second volume of which contained the frontispieces of the famed Black Goat, the Baphomet of Mendes—with its cloven hooves, wings, and goat's head with a pentagram on the brow; the torch of knowledge lying between the horns to represent sin; the twisted twin snakes of the caduceus rising from its lap representing eternal life and sex; and the rounded female breasts representing humanity; Baphomet pointing to two crescent moons at its sides, black and white, one above and the other below, like the sides of two boys' faces.

In 1898 Crowley became a member of a group of occultists known as the Hermetic Order of the Golden Dawn, another member of which was the brilliant poet William Butler Yeats, who put lyrics to the witches' songs, pursuing the study of magiks and mysticism. They used the ancient textbooks, perhaps the same volumes Matthew himself had paged through, the tomes inviting the proper seeker: the *Hermetica, Book of Sacred Magic of Abra-Melin*, and also the ugliest, perhaps, because it was the most enchanting, *Grimoire of Pope Honorius*.

In his arrogance, Crowley sought claim to being the wickedest man in the world. Given the new law by Aiwass, having been worshiped by the Egyptians as Set, he had the pomposity to presume, the entire law being, horrifying in its overt simplicity, "Do what you will." He'd studied the Enochian language, which sounded something like Sanskrit—melodic, nasal, and musical, yet extremely difficult on the throat, disrupting your rhythm of breathing when first making the attempt—and which enabled one to communicate with angels, spirits, and the djinn on the astral planes called Aethyrs. He'd had only nominal success, several daemons had implied to Matthew. Crowley was usually too drunk to focus his *chi* correctly. Attempting to climb the third-highest mountain in the world,

Kanchenjunga of the Himalayas, he'd allowed
the rest of his team to be buried in an avalanche
without making any attempt to help.

Later, when he joined the sexual order of
Ordo Templi Orientis, he renamed himself Baphomet and always kept with him numerous
whores who indulged him with drugs and oral
sex, through which he believed he could work
invincible magiks, attaining new levels of consciousness and enabling him to contact Aiwass.
Both his wives went insane. Years of heroin addiction followed, until Crowley died in 1947,
nothing more than a shade pressed against the
black wall of magus history—

—he could tell Jazz that.

Instead Matthew said, "He was a writer of
horror stories that A.G. and I used to read when
we were kids. He used to host one of the
Saturday-night Monster Features."

"Oh, so that's what you meant. Is he still
alive?"

"No."

"Jesus Christ, Mattie, he was talking about
this guy like he hung out with him every day."

They turned onto the Avenue.

"Do you have a suit I can borrow?" Matthew
asked.

"What?"

"A suit."

"You've got to be kidding me. You mean like

a real suit, you're talking about something nice, a three-piece?" Jazz warbled. "Me?"

"A blazer, a tie, anything."

He shrugged. "Yeah, sure. Somewhere, I guess. How come?"

"For Bosco Bob's party tonight."

Frowning, Jazz went back to playing with the heater, turning it up notches, then down, then flicking it back up again, until the plastic grip of the knob came off in his hand. "You can't be seriously considering going."

"Of course I am."

All the rest of the day fused with the past now, and he saw it as it had been, right here in his own car. "Because of Helen, sure, sorry. But with all of this happening, with A.G., and everybody knowing how tight you two were, and now you're back . . ." And then, breaking through, as much of a non sequitur as possible, because they were just talking here a little bit, about horror movies and so forth, looking around at the town, just a short drive down the Avenue, with no transitions except the blood that came around and around again in his mind: ". . . oh God, she was only sixteen . . ."

Jazz blinked and took another breath, letting it out, and it felt like the first breath he'd had in his entire life. It sort of brought him back to normal. "We're going to swing by my apartment and I'll rummage through the closet for you. Never can tell what might have fallen off one of the hangers and started breeding new forms of life back there. If a battalion of slime creatures hasn't been spontaneously generated by now I'm sure I can find something for you. I wore a tie for our communion, didn't I? Did you?"

"I'll pick it up later. Just take me home."

No, not home, Jazz thought, he couldn't mean home.

"Ah, yes, to Emma and Eugene Carmichael's boardinghouse, shelter from the elements, chateau of the wanderer, residence of one large-breasted Jodi, oh yes, ho, onwards . . ."

"No," Matthew said, shutting off the heat and rolling down the window, letting the chill in where it ought to be. "Take the shortcut through the park." The houses rushed by. "I want you to leave me at my parents' house."

A cat was on fire in the middle of the road.

Chapter Fourteen

In the exact center of the spinning wheel, there is no motion.

Wakowski dove.

He didn't understand why, and didn't stop long enough to think about it or ask questions of himself, unable to feel perplexity or embarrassment. Movement like this is instantaneous, the way moves must be when something dim and cold turned inside his skull, rotating him back into the comfortable state of Grunt.

Throwing himself on the floor, he kicked the door shut with his foot, dropped his shoulder, and rolled until he hit the bedpost. He crawled on his belly until he was in the tight nook between the bed and wall, a perfect vantage point to see the rest of the room. He didn't wish for a gun since he didn't have a gun, and merely hoping would be useless. Wakowski almost expected to feel sharp elephant grass tearing at his skin, and to hear mortar bursts and screams inside the silent hospital.

It didn't matter that this appeared to be foolish—you left all thoughts of appearance way back in the bush, even before the first time you smeared cow shit on your neck to hide your human stink. He did not question his sanity as other veterans might have done; different men might fear flashback, or a loosening of rage or unhinged conscience. He'd only experienced one flashback in his life, coming out of the shower a long time ago, and it had felt less real than this.

His instincts had warned him the second he walked into Richie Hastings's room, feeling the danger around him despite all appearances to the contrary. It happened like that on occasion, if you were lucky enough to learn the lessons. Memories of murder from deserts and forests sped by, and Wakowski was glad he'd never laid any of them to rest. The other wars and skirmishes proved less intrusive than Nam, though Nam hadn't been the worst of them. It had simply been the first.

In some respects, the best.

He lifted his head high enough over the boy's covers to see the rest of the room, and acknowledge what he already knew.

It was empty.

Richie Hastings continued sleeping in his odd catatonia.

Wakowski's reflexes urged him into action. It was mind-boggling, and yet not altogether as bizarre as it may have appeared. Certainly not as strange as returning to the States and seeing the cheering throng with banners at the airport, his wife and two kids smiling and so beautiful, and his intense desire to stay on the plane.

There was a war going on. He crawled, making no sound.

He'd experienced this type of reaction before in the eighteen months he'd been employed at Panecraft. There had been several times over the past twenty years when he'd gotten that feeling Merryman and Anklehumper used to call the grab-your-balls-and-duck reflex. It was a sense that alerted you to the reaping, and told you to drop before you were dead. Maybe you even felt it after you were dead.

In Soc Trang, he'd felt the itch coming on while driving a jeep—the trail ahead looking too safe, the way it did when Merryman had been killed—and without hesitation, perhaps hearing his friend's whisper beforehand, he'd flung himself sideways into the road just as the front tire ran over a mine.

The explosion picked him up like a molten fist and threw him thirty feet backward through the air. He managed not to break any bones when he came down and hit a mud hole, but while spinning ass over elbow in the grass, he touched off a fléchette blast. With his life still welded to him, the angle of the shrapnel from the small mine had hit him flush in the flak jacket. Another few inches and his face would have been torn off.

Anklehumper and Topcat were only a half a click behind him that day and got him the hell out of there, they nicknamed Wakowski "Rabbit's Foot" after the incident, and used it for about a week. But tags like that didn't last long in any platoon, considered signs of the bad juju, like you were tempting karma to get on the rag and fuck you up.

Now Wakowski's chest and abdominal muscles tightened, veins in his neck and biceps bulging. His pulse instantly lowered and he could feel the prickling in his hair and under his arms as his sweat glands turned off—with training, some people could learn to do that so their scent wouldn't give away the position, and you wouldn't have to keep smearing cow shit all over you.

Another layer of calm descended over him. To call the reaction mechanical was to neglect emotion and thought, and the willpower it took for a man not to think, not to feel.

He scanned the room again. There was nothing to see.

The boy had fallen into a psychosomatic

coma somehow induced by the prisoner A.G., Summerfell's resident stalker and graveyard crasher, though they'd never found where he'd lifted the skeleton from. It was all illegal, keeping him here without charging him, but nobody seemed to mind. Drs. Charters, Patterford, and Willits had their own views of the situation, and with all their combined years of psychological study not one of them was smart enough to realize there are some minds that cannot be understood, certain events that can't be explained by either rational or irrational methodology.

Some eyes were death, plain and simple, meant for death, designed for death. Wakowski's innate sense told him that the first time he saw A.G., and it was for that reason alone he wanted the guy in Stanfield Sanitarium or out at the Corzone hospital, or anywhere else so long as he was out of Summerfell. There was something inherently dangerous about A.G. and his friend Galen that prevented them from being fitted into the carefully cut peg-holes these analysts dropped humanity into. Dangerous in the sense of sitting in your car at a railroad crossing—all it took to drive you onto the tracks was some idiot coming up behind you too fast. Even at its most normal and convenient, life could grow more precarious than most could ever believe.

Beaucoup bad juju, Anklehumper would've said.

Wakowski had spent most of the morning re-reading A.G.'s file; he held no false hopes that he might find answers to why the patient had been driven over the edge, but he still wanted to know how come the guy had decided to take the boy with him. That was the key. Find out what makes the boy insane and you discover what lies in the man's insanity.

Richie slept.

An hour before dawn, Wakowski had sneaked into Charters's office and reviewed the video of Galen's visit, only to find that the bad juju had struck there, too. He should have monitored the meeting on screen, but he'd held back, deciding to let the doctor run the show for the moment. He'd lied for Charters, and the fact that the lie had become truth reminded him just how closely fate listens, how it's always waiting to jump into your chest.

Charters's personal involvement with the case made him a poor choice to counsel the patient, though it was true no one could counsel a man who wouldn't talk, who would not confess to either innocence or guilt. Unlike the doctors or the police, Wakowski held off from actual judgment, but that didn't stop the agitation he felt in A.G.'s presence; a long time ago he would have called it fear. Back when he could still become afraid.

As he crawled on his belly under the bed, his guts prodded him farther.

Nerve endings fired. Wakowski rolled again and came up in a crouch-crawl with his back to the windows. Parting the cards and flower-stuffed vases that lined the sill, he glanced outside and saw the red glare of the sky, the shadowy forms of the five o'clock shift getting off work, sweeping across the parking lot as they headed for their cars. Some of them were laughing. Wakowski would never be able to completely comprehend how people could put so much behind them from hour to hour—like Merryman, who had turned the switch on and off, allowing him to separate one life from another.

After returning from Nam Wakowski had been filled with such an exhausting, consuming call to battle that it corrupted his entire life. His wife left him. He would sit in the park and watch men and women falling in love, realizing he was younger than they, and could not associate with it. The civilians and the hard hats and longhairs, the flag wavers and the flag burners—carefree, most of them, even the ones who were screaming in the parks, some of them filled with chic laughter, the women different and the men too unlike himself—imagining how those couples would raise children that would not be wired with C4 charges and sent into bars in Saigon. His own children called him for a few months, she let them do that, but when he didn't visit they left him alone. After a while, a certain pressure built that bore down on him like hooch mud bricks caving in and burying the tunnel rats alive.

He realized his human evil had found a back door, moving in and out of his dreams worse than it had been in that particular green hell. He could not make peace with peace, and found redemption back in the center of other vague wars. The killing kept him sane until the days came when he learned to live with, and accept, what he had become.

Out in the hall there were a number of other guards, orderlies, and doctors. Wakowski could call to any of them now, but what could he possibly say, what good would it do? None of them understood what occurred here either. But to a man who trusted his instincts to such a degree that he didn't question what he didn't understand, it didn't make a difference.

There was a war being fought.

He heard a click and hit the ground again.

The door opened and Henry Charters walked in, holding a coffee cup in one hand and charts and notes in the other. Puzzled, he looked over at Wakowski on the floor in the corner and said, "What the hell are you doing, Roger?"

Wakowski looked up and smiled a perfect smile.

The pause grew thick enough to hang from a noose.

Charters's mustache quivered.

The doctor immediately realized the extent of the situation as he saw the feral, tormented, and yet extremely tranquil look in Wakowski's eyes. He knew the man was in the middle of a severe encounter with Delayed Reaction Syndrome, reexperiencing his part in some long-past battlefield.

So serene and savage. Charters had never maneuvered his way through a mine field or wrestled with a starving animal, but he guessed an equal amount of caution would be required of him to survive this encounter.

The most frightening part of this moment was that Wakowski looked so perfectly in control of himself.

Without losing his pleasant grin, his coffee, his notes or rectal control, Charters carefully closed the door, taking it upon himself not to call anyone else. Wakowski could quite capably kill a great many people in his present state of mind.

When the door latched, he wondered if he'd made a great mistake.

Richie appeared untouched at the moment.

His footsteps resounded off the tile floor. Charters gave no outward signs of the vast fright he felt. His own self-control shocked him. Wakowski's muscles remained corded, veins in his arms, hands, and neck raised like snakes. He looked strong enough to throttle a bull.

Charters walked to his chair beside the bed and sat, gently placing his papers and coffee cup on the table beside him. Those confident eyes of Wakowski's made the doctor more uncomfortable than any convicted killer's stare—that smile, what did that smile mean? And what did it mean in context, when you tried to place it all together with the scene of Wakowski, crouching on the floor?

He ran his fingers over his mustache and fought to remain calm, thinking about what he might say to sound reassuring. He didn't want to fracture the silence in the room, as if afraid to wake the boy. Charters did not want to mutter anything that might make Wakowski punch his jawbone through his brain.

Outside, rubber-soled feet tramped in the corridor.

His coffee mug didn't tremble in his hand, and for that Charters was inordinately thankful. "Roger," he said, taking a swig, the cup in front of his mouth as if to protect his chin from the one well-placed punch that would kill, "this is your day off."

Richie's mouth moved, a slight sigh escaping him, and both men reacted violently. No, there were no days off, for any of them.

Wakowski heard Charters and yet didn't hear; what he heard would not help him to fight or escape. His mantra had shifted many times before—*think like the jungle* had changed to *think like the desert, think like the swamp.* And now, now he had no name for what enveloped them, but he was attempting to think like it.

It was clear that the doctor thought he was having a bout with delayed stress; after a clinical analysis DRS would be the only supposition Charters's limited point of view would allow him to see.

The irony was that Wakowski never delayed at anything.

Topcat would have appreciated the moment; the Cat liked this kind of stink, he would have moaned with pleasure at the heavy scent of fear drifting off the doctor.

Wakowski knew he wouldn't be able to persuade Charters into believing anything different—there could be no way to understand how much discipline and pain and dedication it took for a soldier to crouch on his belly in the corner of an empty room.

Wakowski realized he should say something to break through to Charters, but didn't know what would have the right kind of effect. So, after several more seconds passed and Richie Hastings's bottom lip trembled again, he said, "We're in danger here. Especially the boy." His heartbeat was loud and slow, his words not doing the job he'd hoped they'd do, as Charters looked down, always down, always on the floor wondering how to supplicate this loose cannon. So obvious in his intent and foolhardy in his haughty sense of emotional balance and lordly mental superiority. You found them everywhere you went.

It no longer bothered Wakowski that the doctor did not understand, and so he didn't have to listen to Charters's reply, knowing what it would have to be. "Let me help you, Roger."

Wakowski would use all his training to plan another way to fight an unseen, untouchable enemy, as the enemy was invisible in the jungle, the desert, the swamp, and he could no longer touch Topcat and Anklehumper and Merryman when they pressed their faces down from the ceiling, calling and thrusting their hands out for him.

He would improvise, as he must, and now it would begin. Crouching in the corner did no good. The time for this type of action was past.

In the exact center of the spinning wheel, there is no motion.

He stood.

Startled, Charters leaped out of his seat and dodged to the left, frightened and uncertain, but making a move to the boy. Wakowski straightened the cards and vases he'd disturbed on the windowsill. He had a great deal of respect for Charters, more than the doctor would ever know. "I apologize, Dr. Charters. I didn't mean to alarm you. I assure you I'm fine." The words had a mechanical cadence to them, but at least there was a semblance of meaning. Stilted but reasonably honest, though they held no truth. Still, it would probably be enough.

Charters stared at Wakowski, and down at Richie, and wondered if the three of them were actually going to get out of this room alive. He did not feel particularly reassured. "What happened, Roger? Tell me."

"Nothing to be worried about."

"I . . ." Questions would be useless. Those eyes. Controlled and uncontrollable, wounds opening wider inside the man even as the doctor watched him so casually rearranging the flowers and cards. He'd put a call in to the VA immediately, and see if he could get some people here more experienced in these matters. He backed up and opened the door. "The shift change is over, Roger. Come on. The halls are empty now."

But the echoes told Wakowski differently.

He'd heard something in the tunnels below.

Like the sound of cloven hooves.

Chapter Fifteen

The house hadn't changed much.

His father would kiss his mother in that door-way beneath the mistletoe hanging there at Christmas. It didn't make any difference what they were doing—writing letters, reading med-ical journals—mistletoe seemed to speak to them like music calling dancers, as his father cleared his throat waiting, and his mother came down the stairway laughing. While she cooked, his dad would come up behind her, grab her around the waist, and twirl her into his arms, a little Fred Astaire move thrown in, the only one he'd ever mastered. She'd smile and pretend to protest as he carried her like that to the door-way. When their friends came by, stamping snow off their shoes, his parents would be in

197

the door, already giddy and kissing, until the neighbors threw up their hands.

Darkness descended.

Fading sunlight settled behind the thick branches of the trees that ringed the front yard. Matthew stood watching the remnants of home, grinning in his own fashion as some of the good memories returned and ebbed and flowed, yet keenly aware of worse ones rippling below his present thoughts, waiting to shove through.

It had been like this for nearly fifteen years, since his mother had been brought to Pane-craft.

His grin embarrassed him. His laughter couldn't last, and much of the time he didn't miss it. Seated in the back of the Krunch, looking out at the woodlands, he would sometimes kiss the ketchup out of the corners of Helen's mouth as she ate her curly fries. He liked to listen to her analyzing him; it sounded so harmless the way she did it. She knew his depths, and it irritated her that she couldn't share everything. Her talk went around in circles, and she'd even gone so far as to try to get him high and drunk, shotgunning beer. A simple spell could guard against the liquor when he chose to use it. She'd make exotic love to him, hoping to screw the pain away, believing the scars on his chest were from a childhood accident—he'd forgotten what story he'd told her.

Helen had wanted him to see a psychiatrist,

which was unthinkable—as awful as it was wasteful. His father was a psychiatrist, and all his father's friends who'd filled the house at Christmas. Matthew had listened to dream interpretation throughout his childhood, until the content of dreams no longer mattered.

The men had wrestled with and eventually killed his mother, and his father would not tell him where she was buried.

That resentment would never be resolved. One time, Helen had talked with his father, which Matthew had eventually stopped doing. His dad had listened in silence for a long while, until muttering a few carefully chosen words that caused Helen to sob and flee. She never told him what his father had said.

The house had not changed much, which surprised him. From the outside it looked as though no one had been here since the night he'd left town. Shutters hung askew in the wind, methodically clapping against the battered verandah rails. Hundreds of shingles littered the dead lawn and his mother's forsaken flower garden. The picket fence—Jesus Christ, he'd almost forgotten, they really *had* owned a white picket fence—was stripped of paint, blunt points of splintered wood leaning helter-skelter through the surrounding brush. He tried the front door and found it unlocked but jammed shut. He could see that most of the panes in the windows were cracked but not yet shattered.

He would burn it.

Here at the edge of the park, away from the other houses of Summerfell, his family had been left without a name for their street. There was merely a sharply bent little road of gravel hidden behind a jutting screen of evergreens, virtually invisible and inaccessible except to those who knew of it. His father liked it that way, for reasons never fully explained or discussed. Without any name or number, their mail was addressed to #1 S. Park Road, an address that didn't exist. Now Matthew realized how well all these facts lent themselves to the milieu of the quiet October world.

He braced his shoulder against the front door, shoved it open, and walked in.

The scars tittered.

The furniture had been removed—auctioned off, he supposed, to pay the taxes, or simply stolen. For a moment he wondered who in town had taken which pieces, who was seated tonight at the dining room table that had been in his family for generations, back when there had been a family. A torn and fungus-covered settee and the sticks of a broken wooden chair lying in a heap were all that was left. The floorboards creaked under his weight as he crossed the room. Stale air made him cough as he wandered window to window. Rats scurried in other halls, the attic alive with noise. Walking up the stairs, he listened to the branches scrape the roof like the broken hands of tortured witches.

Matthew stepped into the second-floor corridor and opened a door, his hair whirling into his eyes. The oak tree outside his bedroom window had turned in mid-reach and clawed its way inside, thrusting and crushing the entire window frame.

He grunted and stared down the length of the tree, thinking, *I should've expected this*. Leaves blew everywhere in the room. The boughs wavered.

The scents of fall. This scene brought him back to the days when they would go trick-or-treating in their costumes: Dracula, Superman, Wonder Woman, and Debbi could never decide if she wanted to be Pippi Longstocking or Samantha from *Bewitched*. The wind was always rustling in the trees. Instigating cats and unbemused dogs chased each other across the lawns, yard gates clanking open and shut, and the other kids prowling the area like the goblins they pretended to be. You couldn't get away.

Every hedge hid the ghosts of your friends. Halloween was the only holiday you didn't have your gruesome, unknown relatives grabbing handfuls of your hair to kill you with their tobacco-tasting cow mouths and smear waxy lipstick over your cheeks. The only holiday you were allowed to roam.

Debbi had never been in his bedroom.

There was something ludicrous in that.

Matthew rubbed his nose. The pain was gone. He glanced at the blood on his shirt, knowing it could call the djinn to him and caring little. He'd come so close to murdering Hodges. It disgusted him to know just how natural and good the hate felt to well inside. The sheriff had been fractured a long time ago, and never fully recovered. All he had to do was press a bit harder on the man's mind, the temptation to kill always nibbling at his mercy.

Leaning back against a limb of the intruding oak, he stared at the door to his closet. He closed his eyes, shoved a fist into an open palm. A sign of peace, a show of control and strength, nothing arcane about this particular craft.

But the words were different, rising within him, sentences from a long-dead language. He mouthed extinct phrases and names of power that only a handful of people alive could understand, and even fewer could pronounce correctly. ". . . ezphares irion estyion eryona onera soter Sbaoth Adonay . . ."

Breeze played against his collar, tonguing his neck.

Threads of protection snapped one by one. He heard them audibly breaking, whip-cracking around the room. Rats scrambled and squeaked in the attic, scratching at the corners of the water-stained ceiling.

He visualized his parents' wedding photo—

Dad in the tux, Mother so radiant, the white of the veil so striking against the black of her hair, both of them with so many glowing teeth—woven as a tapestry, blanketing and guarding the closet, now unwinding, faster and faster as he pulled at the image with his mind. It took perhaps five seconds for him to maneuver through his own defenses. Concentrated on their eyes. Their smiles, of course. When the last thread had been lifted, Matthew dropped his hands. Insects buzzed and luna moths fluttered before him.

He opened the closet door.

Inside, packed beneath the carpet, were his old Aurora models. The Wolfman, Dracula, the Phantom of the Opera, Dr. Jekyll in the process of becoming Mr. Hyde, and the Frankenstein Monster (Jesus, you got into more arguments in grade school because you always corrected your peers by never referring to the Monster as Frankenstein, the name of his creator). Certain pieces were luminescent; the gravestone behind the Lord of the Undead glowed green, a rat at the Phantom's feet, Jekyll's spilled chemicals and the test tube he drank from.

Matthew stooped and kicked at the baseboards and the surrounding molding until they slid along carefully filed ruts and came free. It didn't take long for him to remove the slats, revealing a cubbyhole.

Here he'd kept the books that had cost him

more than his paper route money; a dealer in Gallows who asked for three of his pubic hairs—which had to be plucked in the light of a perfect half moon—in exchange for an ancient Latin grimoire transcribed by Pope Sylvester II as dictated by his demon mistress Meridiana, a book that sweats when holy men die. Pubic hair from young boys and girls was sometimes used to make love potions. The notion intrigued him, and he soon came to understand that the bookseller was a fraud more interested in selling talismans and ersatz charms, but who had a glimmer of the arcane affixed to him from generations past.

Touching the smooth wood of his hiding place, he let his hands brush over the leather of the books. Again he was puzzled as to why the Goat or some other agent had not at least tried to take them, after all this time. He lifted the tomes free, centuries-old binding crackling in his hands as he paged through the texts. *The Key of Solomon* and *The Enchiridion* by Pope Leo III, and *The Grand Grimoire* with its instructions for necromancy that Arthur Edward Waite, another member of the Hermetic Order of the Golden Dawn, believed "only a dangerous maniac or irreclaimable criminal" would dare to recite from. A.G. had called Waite a wuss. Matthew agreed.

Off to one side, wrapped several times in soft cloth, lay the mirror in which they'd performed their scrying, divining the future from visions seen inside the glass. It had once been his mother's mirror, given to him by her grandmother, and in age resided power. As a child, Mom had brushed her hair one hundred times each night in long, nonstop movements of elegance, straight through her shifting black tresses, just as her grandmother had been taught as a girl. He used to watch them both when they were children, the memory retained in the scrying glass.

Before his mother had taken to swimming naked in the lake, she used to check herself in the mirror all the time and primp her hair for his father. Matthew looked at his features and couldn't find any resemblance to her, not even in the eyes where a similar insanity reigned.

She'd danced in the storms and vaulted waist-high hedges like a ballerina leaping across the span of a stage, finally hearing something other than the mistletoe urging her on to such grace. Matthew had been proud of her, looking down at night from his bedroom window. His father was openly crying by then, wringing his pale hands and holding his head down between his knees a lot, silhouetted in the light of the reading lamp as he pored over outdated Freud, sitting in his chair without speaking or moving.

Matthew, now possessing two pairs of eyes and twin sets of memories, understood that he'd been an entirely different person before the runes. The same recollections could make him both smile and cry, as when he saw his father falling on the sidewalk, mumbling and giggling. As a child he'd laughed at that, good-naturedly as his father had once laughed, but now understood that the man had been drunk again. His father wept in those days, but dismissed the incidents without word; Matthew followed suit, as you were supposed to follow your father.

He had seen nothing wrong in the way his mother walked the empty streets before dawn with her nightgown flowing behind her like a wedding dress, humming a soft song to herself before shrieking and arching herself against fallen logs, as though being beaten, or loved too much.

The rage rushed up in him. "Why was that so horrible?" he said, calling on his father, seeking to collect. "Couldn't you live with it? Was it so bad compared to what happened?" His fingernails dug into the leather.

Half of him enjoyed the thought of his old man rotting in Hell.

He could afford to condemn his father when the fury swelled and twisted inside his chest. His plays were filled with irresolution; he'd made a career of bitterness and the irredeemable. The myth of his father had been broken beneath the truth of the man, shattered by adolescent preconceptions, and further destroyed by the horror in the caves. Matthew soon lost any sense of his father's authority, realizing the Goat owned everything, and after his mother was put away, he lost all sense of the reality of his father as well.

The oak tree clapped him on the back.

He put the mirror in his jacket pocket and reviewed the texts, finding that he had not forgotten anything of importance. He put the grimoires back in their slots and replaced the boards, shut the closet door, and repeated those steps it took to reweave his parents' tapestry of protection, forging a bond of spirit between himself and the hidden place.

Leaves flitted across the floor, catching at his feet.

He hopped up into the crook of the oak, where it felt natural and somewhat safer to be in physical contact with another living force, especially one that had been with him since birth, guarding the home. Druids had found solace in their gardens and earth gods, and were rewarded for their faith.

Matthew touched the mirror for fortitude and support, letting the heaving branches strike against his arms, slapping his jacket. His breathing quickly became shallow as he set himself to the task, a sickening cold sweat dripping down his back, anxiety and nausea rising.

A cat screeched in the park not too distantly and he wondered if it was being burned alive.

He took off the jacket and hung it on the

branch beside him, pulled out his shirttails and undid the buttons, noticing how much gray now tinged his chest hairs, and him not yet twenty-five. He stared down at the two triangular marks that had been burned into his chest. Two-fifths of the inverted pentagram, the sign of the Goat, upon him.

Centering on the darkness behind his eyes, far off *behind his brain*, in that region of blackness as deep as the range of death's possibilities, he saw the infinite shades that lay across the landscape. The axis of eternity sat at the back of his skull, where the knowledge of necromancy remained—the raising of the dead—power looming large and red, always the same distance from him, *inside the infinity already inside him*. Falling and rising, as the circle of the living revolves once again past the dead. He shivered as the wind blew upon the sheen of his sweat. Words bubbled from his throat. Welts appeared as the boughs continued to lash at him, now like a cat-o'-nine-tails, purging him of sin. This evocation would steal yet another part of his soul, the price he would pay the Goat to kill the Goat.

Matthew wrenched himself sideways, following his father into Hell as he pronounced the ultimate word of power, the Tetragrammaton, YHWH, Yaweh, Jehovah, oh Lord, the most sacred name of God, and the dead girl screamed as the heat hit.

*   *   *

The blacklash of energy—of life, of this death—punched him out of the tree and sent him high up against the far wall, near the ceiling, arms and legs thrown at awful angles as something in his torso ruptured and his mouth filled with blood. He bounced off the wall, leaving an impression of his body outlined in the cracked paneling.

Agony worse than the other two times.

He hit the ground with unimaginable force, the floor's structural beams snapping beneath his weight as he came down. Sawdust fell. The impact shook rats out of the widened seams in the ceiling. They dropped with loud *thunk*s all around him, squealing with broken bones, crawling over him now and run through his blood. His chest was on fire, the smell of his own burning flesh making him choke. He thought he heard barking, or the bleating of a goat. The malevolent laugh returned once again, cackling as the flames seared his skin, scarring him further. A new voice had been added.

The rats writhed, their disgusting bristles burning, as they turned over to thrash and bit at him. He spun and smothered the flames with the crumbling leaves and dust beneath him, hauling himself through the filth.

He raised himself to his knees, and the girl screamed again.

Matthew groaned and slowly turned his head in her direction, attempting to stand.

Joanne Sadler sat shuddering beside the closet door, her arms locked around her calves, moaning, staring at him, the rats dragging themselves across her feet, her eyes murky without pupils. His parents' wedding photo wavered in the background, billowing behind the cringing dead girl, eclipsing the closet. The juxtaposition made it more difficult for him to approach her. These two spheres should never have been moved together, and now never would be separated. He saw his mother behind the murdered child, the girl behind his mother. Passages from the books recited themselves, chanting, *Aieth Gadol Leolam Adonai . . .* His father's gaze followed wherever he walked, so full of mortality, the kind of stare that a man who could hang himself *would* have.

Sobbing, Joanne hid her face against her knees, realizations of life and death fully upon her. Matthew took a step forward but stumbled. The third mark showed that three-fifths of the inverted pentagram had been completed: the Goat's mouth pointing down, and now the left ear and right horn pointing up. Scabs and scar tissue were already forming. He buttoned his torn, singed shirt over it, put the jacket on, trying to layer these disfigurements.

He moved to her.

Telling her, *Forgive me.*

"It hurts," she said, her mouth moving, the voice exactly as it should be, except not a voice at all any longer, though he could hear it. He could imagine her reading her poetry aloud to audiences who could appreciate what she had to offer, soft and humble in the dim lighting. She lifted her chin to face him, those colorless eyes full of pain and contempt. It had been a long time since he'd spoken with the deceased.

After Debbi's death, the catacombs had cracked open and sorrow had poured into town like all the reaped sins of these deserved whirlwinds. Sometimes he couldn't tell the difference between the abominations he'd let loose and the madness that had been here before.

(Debbi was dead.)

I know, he told her. *I'm sorry, but you have to stay with me, Joanne. I need your help*. He traced fiery sigils in the air that blazed and floated for a moment.

"Why?"

Christ, that voice, so lifelike.

I need your help.

"Who are you, Master?"

It's not important. I'm not your master, I won't keep you in service.

"I want to know." Lips set firmly, those empty eyes pinned him, and in her deathless beauty he understood the convictions of the poet. What could he have said to her before the butchering? In the cafés, along the rim of Broadway?

I'm Matthew Galen. His name felt wrong inside his own skull. *I'm a friend*.

She stood, and he almost backed away a step. There was a vacant aura of incompleteness surrounding her, yet for all her weeping Joanne seemed more aware of circumstances than he. "If you're really my friend, Matthew," she said, "you'll let me go."

I will, soon.

"Now, please, please, now."

I can't yet.

Suddenly she was at ease, walking about his room, regarding the empty walls as if remembering his posters and bookshelves. She stooped and peered at the burned rats, grimaced, then grinned as though seeing the wedding photo. It was possible, he thought, connected to him as she was now. "I don't belong here. I'm not Joanne Sadler."

No, you're not, but you are the best lead I've got at the moment.

She stared at him. "Why is it so hard for me to talk?"

Your tongue has been torn out and spell cast to prevent you from speaking to me. But he had touched her corpse, and knew in that instant that she was a virgin, her blood on his fingers, the most powerful of witch's brew. Whoever had kept her all those months before killing her had not raped or maltreated her. What did that say of his foe?

She started to say something, but the doorway abruptly filled with too much noise, a loud wheezing and awful reeking that made him spin with his fists aimed to throw hexes, the first syllables of a killing curse on his tongue. A padding bulk waddled off to one side of the room and awkwardly sidestepped and dipped back, as though drunk or walking aboard a ship.

"Is that a dog?" she asked.

"I don't gaddamn believe this," Matthew said. *That's Gus*.

The girl grinned, her smile lacking human content, a greater caricature for this. Beauty, but no poetry. "Boy, is he ugly." Now sounding more childlike, her front teeth catching at her bottom lip, a nearly come-hither look in those eyes. Soon would come greater seductions.

Gus handled the moment better than any other dog would have, the arcana playing on animal senses—he didn't howl or try to bury his muzzle in the doorjamb, either too stupid to care or too intelligent to argue. Gus sauntered forward to where the dead girl stood and sat near her, panting with his unseen tongue. She put her hands out to pat the dog's head, but Gus turned his face with incredible speed, weaving between her hands so that no ghost could touch him.

Talk to me, Joanne. Who did this to you?

"I don't want to talk to you anymore."

Who did this to you?

213

"Quit it. I have your name now, you're not my master. I want to play with Ugly Gus."

Gusto did not take offense as she tried to pet him but couldn't quite make contact, his slobbering head slipping out of reach, her hands circling his snout. More of the living and dead commingling, their spheres crossing but not meeting. The dog could do what Matthew could not.

Who did this to you, Joanne?

"I don't know! Stop asking me!" She acted as though in pain, but smiled through it. "She didn't see the person. She was on her way to the bathroom and passed by an open door under one of the stairwells, the one that opens up onto the football field."

Yes.

"There was just a whisper that made no sense, a whirl of black cloth. A hand touched the shoulder. That was all. The wire cut into her flesh and her body was being hauled upside down. Two slashes on either side of the throat that would deepen, and the pain began. She didn't know who did it, even when the torture was at its worst. Now, shut up! Shut up! I can't tell you any more than that."

Where was she kept? She was missing for months before she was murdered.

"I don't know!"

You must.

"Leave me alone!"

Tell me, Joanne.

"I'm not Joanne. It was a place, a room. Fevers. Festivities. No more than that, no more memories. She swam. Let me go. I want to go now, I want to be free of you."

The returned dead, so resentful of the living. Her voice, no longer the poet's, bled jealousy and malice. *What is it you want to do?*

"You just watch." She smiled, not even bothering to disguise the malevolence now, eyebrows arching, leering, trying to sex and unsex him with the same lack of subtlety the Goat had shown before. Her hands moved down her chest, as if he did not know what had been done to her, what lay on the floor of the train station. "This dog is so ugly he's beautiful. I love him." And the smile widened further, until he could see every missing piece of her heart. "I enjoy her damnation. Leave her where she is, Galen." Empty eyes watched him. "You'll join her soon enough, you know."

"I know."

There was no proper way to talk to the dead.

With his hand on his blistered chest Matthew made the sign of the cross more for his own benefit than hers; those early religious observances stuck with him much longer than the religion itself had. His hands burned black and flashed, drawing intricate patterns and signs that flamed and rose before her, his voice now

215

rising with ancient words that tightened his lips and bruised his throat.

The wind kicked dust up into Gusto's nose and the dog went into another sneezing fit. Matthew held his hand out to the lie that was no longer Joanne Sadler, vestiges of her blood remaining on his fingers from when he had caressed her corpse.

The ghost sighed, grinning with malice but not quite sure of the evil inside, puzzled as to its own existence. Only in the last instant did she realize he wouldn't release her back into the world as she'd wanted. Unbound, what would she have done out there in the dark beyond the site where she was murdered? She'd probably find and kill the sobbing deputy.

Instead he sent this fragment of the girl back to wherever the remainder of her soul resided.

"No, not this way!" she shrieked. "I said I wanted to be free, Galen! Let me go!" Screeching, she lunged at him, nails aimed to claw his face, opaque eyes blazing with antiquity.

Inches from him the shade of Joanne Sadler faded before the end of her scream as he moved toward her, almost seeking an embrace.

"Damn it," he said.

Festivities? Bosco Bob's parties?

Gusto followed him down the stairs, an urgency and meaning in his presence. The dog had a place here. When they reached the bottom Gusto took off through the front door, sensing what had to happen. Matthew took one last look around the house. He grabbed up a fistful of sticks from the broken chair and faced south, imagining fire, the *athame*, his witch's knife here in his hand, the color orange, fire, representing the metal gold, molten, fire, until the kindling burst into flames.

He threw the burning wood into the four corners of the room and watched the house begin to blaze. He waited a moment longer, staring at the top of the banister, where the varnish of the center rail had been scraped away.

That spot where his father had double-knotted the end of a taut noose before hurling himself over the edge and breaking his neck, just as his nineteen-year-old son stepped into the doorway with hell in his heart and dirt from his mother's grave beneath his fingernails.

Chapter Sixteen

There are minutes when you are out of contact with your skin.

Twilight and the cold breeze further insulated Matthew as he rested on a park bench and watched Gus play at the side of the lake. The faceless dog stuffed his snout under the water, blowing bubbles. A middle-aged couple holding hands strolled along the cobblestone path. The lanterns brightened as darkness settled, and the neon of the Krunch sign flared on the Avenue. From where he was seated, he could look through the far-off brush and make out the corner of the high school and see the sweltering cube of the wrestling room where A.G. had pinned dozens of opponents. Matthew craned his neck farther and sighted the spot where

Joanne Sadler had been attacked, near the only outer door in a stairwell opening onto the football field. The field ran into the knolls and slopes of the park, borders of the school yard determined only by the end of the bleachers.

Behind the bench the couple spoke quietly, and he heard the woman gasp and whisper about the dried blood on him. The man replied, "Shhh, Miranda, don't cause any trouble now." Gus yanked his head out of the water and swung, barking playfully. The man and woman walked away with a brisk stride. Gusto came back dejected and lay at Matthew's feet, dripping and panting, then rose and waddled off again, sniffing at bushes.

A lot had gone on in these fields besides the daily afternoon practices and the famous ninety-nine-yard run. He and Helen had made love in the ravines like a couple of raccoons. Once he'd very nearly wound up atop an entangled Jazz and Bobbi May, all four of them deaf to any noise besides their own, tumbling through the evergreens until Matthew felt a different kind of chill as he looked over his shoulder straight into Jazz's surprised smirk. "Caught me again, huh, Mattie? Hey, at least you're a friendlier face than those uptight National Guardsmen. Hi, Helen. Peace." Bobbi May had hidden her face in the leaves.

On summer mornings they'd played two-hand touch and Frisbee tag, him and the rest of the cast: A.G., Ruth, Helen, Jello Joe and Jelly Jane, Jazz and Bobbi May, and several others who shuffled in and out depending on their patience and tolerance. Helen was fascinated with abnormal psych and played at being Freud too often for anyone's good, especially his own. Occasionally and unknowingly she tore the hell out of their most tender areas.

On the flip side you had Ruth doing charcoals of A.G. on the field, or on the wrestling mat. She was so introverted she rarely met your eye, usually regarding her feet without a sound, so that after only a few minutes you found that you couldn't force a word in edgewise between the crashing cymbals of her silence. She'd repressed her memories of what had happened back in the caves, but he saw hints of her childhood power still. Talking to Ruth could make you feel like you were swallowing glass.

Jello Joe had this annoying habit of never taking anything seriously, laid back and so relaxed all the time it actually got on your nerves. And Jazz just couldn't help but be discovered with his Fruit of the Looms around his ankles, like some insane creature in heat that couldn't control himself no matter where he might be, and Bobbi May or some other cute chick clutching at him and laughing at his frenetic humor.

A.G. would read to Ruth more often than join in on the games, sitting on a picnic blanket and occasionally flicking spells across the grass that would either let you spot Spanish doubloons that vanished in the dirt or tadpoles that slipped out of your nostrils—it all depended on his mood and need for mischief.

Jelly Jane ate bushels of raw onions, and thought it was sexy for her not to wear a bra. Matthew knew it was more of an act than anything, her insecurities forcing her further and further into her own self-effacement.

The other kids never came back.

Among her other wonts, Jelly Jane also tried to jump Matthew's bones every chance she got. Jazz once wildly tossed a Frisbee so far out of range that Matthew had to scamper through the woods in order to chase it down. Two hundred and eighty pounds of Jelly Jane followed and leaped onto his back, her knees digging against his ribs, holding him facedown in the dirt while her hands reached around trying to untie his sweatpants. "Screw me," she snarled into his ear. "Now, damn you, do it now."

It was all another way for her to hate herself. He never found a way to let her down easy when she got like that, and he sometimes wondered if the book dealer had handed over the love potion made from Matthew's three pubic hairs to Jelly Jane, binding them like that together forever. She cornered him in the halls of school, got him in a headlock, and threatened to wring him into a piece of modern art—lots of laughter and smile, just a game, but an ugly one. The rest of the football team would laugh themselves into tears when they saw how easily Jelly Jane could beat him up—but none of them ever tried to help him. No, they knew she'd walk over them just as simply. Unlike Jello Joe, who took everything so casually, his sister was so pent-up you could see it even when she wasn't on the attack. Even with the weight problem she remained extremely attractive, with luring eyes and an enticing grin, but for all her beauty and Bosco Bob's wealth she was probably the unhappiest person Matthew had ever known, besides his father and himself.

The last time he and Helen had made love it was in the park, near the sandbox. Gus pawed at the ground there now, his tail brushing back and forth against the wooden corner of the box. Matthew tried not to think about how much she must hate him, even in their connected dreams, the silver chord of her spirit coupled to him by the nightmares of what their love had become.

He recalled everything of that last time, and could find no room left inside his head to keep it all stored away, like one of his plays spilling into the open: how Helen laced her fingers with his and gestured for him to grab her breasts, up and down strokes the way she liked it, tracing her large aureole slowly. His palms were almost painfully electric against her smoothness. She dug her nails in, shoving the heels of her hands against the sides of his face, angling his chin up and forcing him to stare directly into her soulful, understanding eyes. She knew nothing of him. Her slick hair swung down on him like a slicing pendulum slipping across his flesh, keeping to the beat of her bucking, fronds from the brush raining down.

He eased her legs farther apart, and she gasped getting to her knees. Helen shifted onto her side, arms draped over his neck, tugging him closer, always closer, and closer still, moaning in his ear and nibbling on the veins that bulged down his forearms. She bit his cheek and said viciously, "Love me," as if there were any chance he didn't, as if he wasn't. She laughed at the look on his face. "Love me. I love you." He kissed her, raw and thirsty, as though their first kiss had followed them through all their passion and needs. His bad ankle, as it sometimes did, throbbed dully with his pulse, with the three-quarter time of Helen's groaning, her furious breaths. She tried to touch the scar on his chest, but he gripped her hands and held them to her own breasts where she tugged at her nipples. The blue of the Krunch sign blazed even more brightly in her turquoise eyes. She grinned her askew grin, and it hurt him to see her as beautiful as this.

Afterward, he was startled awake by the moon. When he got home his father was lying on the porch soused out of his head, each hand twisted around a bottle of whiskey. As if the man couldn't get deranged enough as quickly as he wanted, already more doomed than Matthew's mother had been. Matthew helped his father to the bathroom and watched Dad kneel at another of the gods to vomit painfully. The man gurgled like an infant and Matthew carried him to his room, undressed him and put him to bed, waiting until Dad's shallow, erratic breathing became regular.

It was almost a blessing to know that his father had folded under the same kind of horror. Matthew tore hell out of his father's study until he found his mother's birth certificate and Social Security card cleverly hidden in his yellowing eighth-grade report card envelope. He left with a flashlight and a shovel, to visit her grave for the first time that night, and talk aloud to her about everything that had happened in the seven years since he'd last seen her.

He returned home to find his father hanging, the empty envelope on the floor.

He'd acquired the second mark of the Goat that night, knowing, even then, how stupid it was to run to his dead father as the man twisted in the air, and pull the power from inside himself as if by instinct, wanting to bring Dad back but hating him too much to resurrect him properly. He'd failed, of course, and lost another part of his soul for it.

Tears wouldn't come, they wouldn't ever come. There are minutes.

The night of his father's funeral, he left town without a word to anyone.

The park emptied by the time the sun fully set. Slivers of swift clouds tinged with silver streamed in from the north, threatening rain. The neighborhood grew frigid. Salamanders crawled into the black lake. A half moon hung low in the sky, and the lanterns were just bright enough that their pale illuminations lit the paths. Thin trails of smoke rose at the other end of the park, where his house burned. No one would even notice.

Matthew watched the shadow of Panecraft, his father's other son, rising up against the skyline, inadequate coils of barbed wire twining atop the high fences. It waited for him, and A.G. laughed, or wept, or did nothing, within. Gus looked up. The ocean was out of earshot, but it could be heard anyway, pounding as it had pounded against the walls of the catacombs.

His chest had completely healed. He touched the rise of the third scar through his shirt. Gus trotted to the bench, prancing and jittering excitedly—if he'd had a mouth he might have wanted to play a game of catch or chase a stick. Matthew stood and said, "C'mon, gorgeous." It was time to borrow a suit and go to Bosco Bob's party, and discover what lay in wait for him and the rest of those he loved. "Let's get the hell out of here."

They walked along the lake path, heading for the shortcut that would bring them out on the Avenue near the Krunch. Barking happily, Gusto bounded ahead past the children's water fountain, leaping over a boy's forgotten toy truck, racing and returning to prod the toy with his nose, shoving it across the grass. Matthew didn't know why Gus followed him, or what it meant when attempting to decipher these incidents. The dog, too, had been tied to him.

Gus pushed the truck into the brush until Matthew couldn't see him.

The night deepened.

It was already quiet enough to make him think he was in Potter's Field, above, or below, the earth.

He spun to his left, understanding that perhaps it might have been foolish to stay out in the open until the sun went down. He lifted his collar against the crisp air and called, "Gus, come here. Let's go, boy, come on."

An obscure shade moved against the bushes.

The asylum, focus of so much of his family's pain, pulled at his heartstrings with an almost palpable cruel joy.

In the woods Gusto growled low and mean and dangerous, a troubling and peculiar sound coming from him, made worse by the pervasive silence.

Something walked within the thickets.

His father's furious voice filled out the rest of the utter stillness—his mother's mirror a torch against his body.

Gus yelped twice and dashed out of the brush, limping with twigs and brambles hooked in his fur. Cowering, the dog dragged himself to Matthew, whining and peeing. The clouds closed over the half moon like shutters snapping shut.

This is not good, Matthew thought, raising his hands to rapidly scrawl messages in the wind, his fists burning as black fire rose. He listened to Gus howling madly as the bushes parted in the darkness and branches snapped, then realized at the last second that he'd been faked out again and stood facing the wrong way in the night. He turned a second too slowly and caught a face full of venom.

He cried out and stumbled backward, repeating the ballet of agony he'd performed in his bedroom, knowing the steps so well. Choking and sputtering, he dropped to his knees and clawed at his eyes, fighting not to scream and slinging hexes blindly in every direction. He got to his feet and fell over the cobblestone curb and tumbled into the grass. He felt the sagging weight of Gusto crawling beside him. Shrill wind rushed through the park, keening along with the dog's frenzied snarls.

Burning, greasy slime dripped down his face. The smell of decomposing meat and rotting fruit drove him to the ground, where he rubbed his sleeves against his nose, trying desperately to clear his nostrils. The poison bit in and held. Matthew wiped his palms over his cheeks, calling up spells and magiks of defense, yanking at the toxin. Revolting, bitter sweetness scoured his tongue and slipped down his throat as if alive. He reeled, thrashing, knowing this attack came from a human agent, not a djinn or ghost. His stomach lurched and he vomited, clearing an airway at last. Finally he was able to clean enough of the ooze off to breathe again.

Strands of moonlight unraveled, but not enough for him to get his bearings. He dove to his right and saw nothing. His misfired hexes hadn't come close, only scorched the earth and some dying bushes. Whoever had thrown the venom was long gone through the brush. Gus lay a dozen feet away whimpering, licking at his hind leg, black fur making the dog nearly invisible now in the dark.

The stench.

It clung like a living entity, rancid and rippling over every exposed pore. Smoke rose from his clothes. Fumes wafted about him, disorienting him even more. He retched and choked on the overwhelming stink, suddenly recalling passages from arcane tomes, where the pages had been written on dried stomachs, and to learn the lessons you had to taste the book.

Fog slowly drifted by his knees.

"Oh God," he whispered.

An elemental ritual, this curse. He couldn't distinguish between the herbs but knew what they were, remembering the proportions and exact ingredients. They'd called the brew by many names, but the most foolish remained the most accurate. Étienne Dupruis, the the seventeenth-century vineyard owner who'd slaughtered children and let their flesh fertilize his grapes, called it Lucifer's Perfume. He'd bottled and sold it until the local monks drowned him in his own wine vats. So ridiculous a name for an evocation as deadly as this.

Matthew ripped his shirt and jacket off, mopped his face, and flung the clothes from him. He heard his mother's mirror break. Some cryptic passage came to mind, so many rules that had to be followed without flaw; someone had a great deal of patience for this, and the most trivial mistake brought death to the conductor of the ceremony. The formula called for the invokers to slit their own wrists in the promise that their hatred would heal the wounds.

The runes and symbols of the magic circles had to be precisely spelled out in blood and oils. Strength of will and need for wish fulfillment could be nothing short of an all-consuming obsession. He understood the fortitude it took, the strength, and weakness, of character; prayers took hours of total concentration to complete.

And then came the petition to a higher order of daemon to perform certain tasks. Infernal hierarchies had been called upon. *Jesus, somebody sure doesn't like me.* He wondered if A.G. had taught Ruth, if she'd remembered everything from that day in the cave after all, and faked her own death. Could A.G. be in on it with her? All of this, just to bring him back home? He could see them roasting in their rage.

This specific evocation proved difficult, because the ritual had to be acted upon in person, without substitute or minion. The goal had to be stated aloud in the summoning, the conjured controlled through force of desire, venom thrown by the invoker's own hand.

Gus cantered toward him. Matthew tried to get the rest of the ooze off, pulling sticky chunks of it out of his hair.

Gusto sneezed.

There was a quiet laugh, and something lit a match.

Even his scars told him to flee, the Goat at odds with this new turn. The clatter of rampaging thoughts built to a crescendo. He held his breath, trying hard not to shiver in the cold wind, not to think, not to live, to be dead now even as his insane mother's singing tickled his hackles and resounded clearly in his ears as if she were standing behind him. The clouds filtered the milky light of the moon through a haze of October atmosphere—poetic, delicate, dreamlike, and hellbound.

By the flare of the match light Matthew saw their eyeless faces.

He didn't recognize them from any of the illustrations in the grimoires, but he didn't expect to—daemons rarely held to a specific shape for any length of time, their hideous narcissism pressing them further into new domains of vanity.

Even so, he understood the reason for the stench and so knew who they must be. *Adiel* and *Mauels* were the names men had once called them, two beasts from different hierarchies of the aethyrs, strangely working as master and pet, devouring prey together. Lovers, in a fashion, perhaps.

Transcribed tales told of their fondness for mental anguish above the physical, and yet, no matter what form they took, they couldn't alter those badges of their own damnation, if devils could be damned. These two were always blind, tracking victims by sorcery and the sweet, putrefying flesh scent of the venomous perfume.

And the human agent would be watching from a distance, scrying in some polished surface.

"I know your names," Matthew said, still coughing. "You'd do best to return to the aethyers now. Despite this poison, we've no quarrel."

This time Mauels had come like a freakish blend of toad and wolf . . . a contorted miniature mutant being composed of reptile and mammal, hairless and hunched, scraping at the earth, salivating and licking a serpent's forked tongue over sharp, broken teeth unevenly spaced in a mouth larger than any should be. No snout, though, no nose at all, really—merely two thick slashes of quivering wet nostrils trailing up the length of its entire face, from upper lip to the top of its forehead. The creature seemed to be grinning, if a visage like that could be amused in any mortal fashion. Its needle-thin claws clicked together. Matthew clenched his fists as his power wafted and glowed.

Adiel, the master, stood as a man, yet too different to be a man. Thinner and longer, stretched and skeletal, yet somehow the same as a man—tall and well-dressed in a cloak, wearing a top hat—*Good Christ, you've got to be kidding me*—and holding a doctor's black bag. The flame of the match reflected in the mirrored sunglasses perched on an impossibly long and thin nose that bulged and gnarled from cheek to cheek, lenses bending inward much too far because there were no eyes concealed behind them. The daemon now played a game of despair. The match it held burned out.

They starved. They were always starving and

would never be satisfied with his body or his pain, no matter how much suffering they inflicted. They stepped from the brush where the moonlight refused to fall. Matthew's pulse throbbed brutally like a knife repeatedly plunged into his neck. Patterns of flying white sparks traced symbols and sigils playing about his hands. His fear grew trenchant but remained oddly displaced, sinking deeper within, until it felt farther away than the other terrors.

There were faces yet to be seen, in the shadows of the asylum, in the caves, at the party tonight, waiting to swallow his soul personally. Hard contours of his body grew more rigid and defined as he tensed, the spells working in him now as he called forward his knowledge, preparing for battle in the park he considered a part of his own being . . . less than a mile from the stronghold of his past. The light swimming from his fists shone down on Gusto's shaggy bulk.

"Adiel and Mauels," he said, enunciating clearly. There was capability in the names, and in knowing them, he already garnered some strength.

Sparks spit over the short distance still separating them, where Mauels' jaws snapped at the flashes, its teeth clashing together with a demented hissing.

Adiel lit another match, looking so much like Jack the Ripper. "Everyone knows our names," it clucked softly. "That holds no sway over us." Its voice was like the sound of shredding vestments, harsh and unholy, almost more symbol than resonance. "Our evident attributes lend us a bit more credence and notoriety than most, though Asmodeus still runs about seducing nuns. Appellations mean nothing at this hour of your undoing, in this coven of ills. We quarrel with all."

"Who is your conjurer?"

The Ripper bowed politely, the game so obvious and yet so obscure. "Pardon. Privileged information."

"Have you been called to the village of Summerfell before?" Matthew asked. "To kill the children?"

"You will not believe me, but the answer is no. We have not."

"I believe you."

"More the fool, you, Galen, but you have my honest appreciation." Adiel tipped its hat. Mauels hopped and curtsied.

"Are you always such a gentleman?" To open conversation was to gain a greater perspective on character, on consequence.

"For the moment," the Ripper said. "But please have no delusions that my courteous manner is an authentic representation of my nature. Or that my curiosity and interest in you as a child mage will stop either of us from vivisecting you when the time comes. We will most assuredly enjoy your screams throughout the ages you'll be with us. And beyond."

"No," Matthew said. "I won't."

"You are already counted among the doomed, though you know not."

"I know it, but you're not my doom. Why the matches?"

Adiel opened the doctor's bag and began to search through it. "Inquisitive, eh? As all witches are, else why be a witch? In order to learn so much about the divine and grotesque as you do. I tire of questions." Of course, Matthew realized, but the Ripper would answer, else why be a daemon? Adiel crushed the match to his nose. "I enjoy the aroma of sulfur."

"Me too, actually."

Just enough moonlight for him to get a glimpse of Panecraft in the background.

Adiel extracted a scalpel. "Now, you will come here, won't you?"

With a snarling laugh, the human-size toad sprang at Matthew's chest.

Matthew brought both fists together in one swift motion that left streaks of liquid white fire spewed across Mauels' chin. Still, he wasn't quick enough to keep the sharp points of its jagged teeth from tearing into the meat of his left arm. He shouted, blood squirting against his naked chest, the scars opening to slurp.

Though Matthew hadn't hurt the beast, Mauels, like so many of them, refused to ac-

Tom Piccirilli

knowledge resistance, and so sat stunned, un-
believing, shaking itself as its tongue slithered
toward him, coiling around his wrist and lap-
ping at his streaming blood. The Ripper ran
across the field coming for him, its cape swirling about in the wind like unfolding wings.

Giggling now, its more genuine nature revealed, Adiel lunged. The blade glinted in the
arcane light as the daemon raised its scalpel
and brought it arching toward Matthew's ster-
num.

He sucked breath and urgently contorted
aside, the slicing blade missing his flesh by a
millimeter. The rage came on in one consuming
burst, and Matthew smiled. Mauels looked baf-
fled, cocking its head, the tongue hanging
limply. Matthew spun, grabbed the Ripper by
the shoulder, and slipped it over his thigh, the
strength of his body feeling so new and yet altogether familiar as he hurled the daemon into
its pet.

"You've forgotten a mage has pride, too," he
said.

Adiel fell in the dirt with a snarl. "In damnation one can afford all things proud. It makes
you all the more meaningless."

Gusto sat up and began to bay. He leaped forward, growling and biting into Mauels' throat
as the beast prepared to rake at Matthew with
its claws. Gus held on as Mauels heaved and

lifted the fat dog in the air, trying to rattle him loose.

Leaves whipped at them all, the field ferocious with winds that rose into a tempest. The Ripper stood in an instant, the lenses of its sunglasses full of spiderweb cracks, the empty paleness of ashen puttylike skin showing through. Its nose beat like a heart, twining and ballooning over its drawn face as Adiel joyously sniffed Matthew out.

No more manners. Shrieking, the fiend came at Matthew again, the scalpel aimed at his eyes. Matthew laughed insanely, and managed to parry the blade with his good hand. He didn't know what was happening, except that it felt good to laugh, even while terrified. Flames of mystic configurations shot over Adiel and raced along its body like a cocoon of electricity, its cloak flapping up wildly, the Ripper's elongated arms reaching out to crush Matthew's groin.

Matthew kicked at the scalpel and missed, shocked that he'd been smiling a moment before, twirled and let another of Adiel's stabbing strokes pass him, then twisted and brought his elbow down hard in the middle of the daemon's back. Something broke inside it. Physical contact, perhaps that was the reason for Matthew's mania—it had been so long since he'd lashed out at the Goat and its minions. The Ripper snickered.

Can't go toe to toe, they're simply toying with me.

Gusto's valiant efforts ended as Mauels viciously flung the dog against a tree. Gus squealed in agony and toppled with a sickening noise in the weeds. Matthew forced himself to concentrate, honing his fury, yes, like this, welcoming it as he must.

"Bring him to me, my friend," Adiel said. "My choice of bodies was again poor."

Matthew ran into the thickets.

Shoving past branches, he vaulted bushes in the dark, heading toward his house, trying to reach the lake again. Getting rid of the stench might confuse them long enough to escape— their time here was limited, the spell would lose its potency as he fought them. Matthew also fought his other foe. The human enemy watched but would feel his obsessed will constantly hammered upon.

"Can you see this, bastard?" he whispered while he ran. "Can you hear me now? You should have done it yourself. This isn't over, not a chance, not like this."

He pushed himself, thorns gashing his arms and cheeks as the daemons pursued him. His sense of self had been mislaid, and now it rushed to meet him again—thinking of Debbi and last night's dreams, Helen still hungering for him, crying after all this time, and hearing their crazy laughter behind, and his own inside.

He could almost believe that he ran from his mother, or was hurrying toward her, her songs were still so sharp in his thoughts.

He broke from the woods near the lake.

And just as he came to the clearing he and Gusto had walked across, the toad tackled him from behind.

Mauels straddled his back, lashing out at him again and again, tearing and pounding at his kidneys. Spells of defense ignited across its nails, barely protecting him. Matthew choked on dirt, heaved, and tried to throw the slimy fucker off, but it held on, cackling while its claws drew long bloody gouges. He grabbed tufts of grass trying to get a handhold and find enough leverage to flip the beast from him. His hands splayed and he couldn't get a grip on anything, as the Ripper came on.

His fingers touched something wet and soft, and he knew what he had to do.

He shrugged with all his strength, cursing, the words a fusion of systems and beliefs. Mauels laughed, rocking up over Matthew's head like a cowboy trying not to be bucked, about to bring its needlelike nails down into his eyes. They always took the eyes.

As the creature dug into his waist with its hindquarters, Matthew flexed his shoulders enough to keep the daemon off balance just one second more.

Then, without quite believing that this is

what would save him, he rolled and scooped up a double handful of Gusto's shit. He shook his head, reached up, and shoved his fists into Mauels' quivering wet nose.

The beast shuddered, convulsed, and fell backward screeching. Its hypersensitive nostrils, opening up into its brain, spilled a river of black ooze that coursed down its maw.

"Just like Mom's apple pie, eh, shithead?"

Matthew stood and took a running step up onto the back of the bench and dove through the air, coming down cutting into the freezing lake in a graceless arcing headlong plunge. Underwater he swam as fast as he could, rubbed at the perfume until most of the dried putrid grime dissipated and floated past.

He recited prayers, guarding him, warding the powers of the infernal, knowing he had not come this far to die so close to the ashes of his home. He was already numb, and growing more numb as he swam.

When he came up, Adiel squatted tending Mauels at the shore. "You can't win, Galen. If I'm unable to torment you now then I'll simply kill you and await our meeting in Hell, where you'll spend many cycles in my care. The blade is only a prop, as it always was, even in that slum Whitechapel. This shell is costume, you know that, and it is of no consequence."

Whoever had brought them here was surely weakening by now, so tied to him and unable to let go even now, since his death would mean release.

The daemon peeled its human mask and wormed into the lake.

It came after him, driving through the water, a turmoil of waves erupting around a giant buzzing, thrashing figure; this other form of Adiel's was built to ravage, though Matthew couldn't make out its hidden shape inside the whitecap foam and sediment it stirred. The hexes filled him. Spindly ropes and curving limbs chopped through reeds and mire and anything else they touched. The Ripper searched him out as Matthew floated, too cold and trembling in the water, *Jesus, not like this, not yet*, holding on because his enemy couldn't control the spell much longer. Adiel swallowed the water, following his trail easily. He'd been wrong to try this, *I'm so goddamn stupid*, it was on a perfect collision course. Another failure added to the heap of the night. There was no way for him to get away fast enough, nowhere left for him to escape.

Matthew hesitated for a half second before he made a decision, another wrong decision, regretting it and hating himself for it, yet knowing, of course, that it was his only chance, even as it was the worst thing to do. Watching the daemon hunting in this wet grave of the dark, he let out a grunt of resolve. He shut his eyes and raised his hands, kicking to stay afloat, calling up the power that was his and the Goat's, focusing on the pressure pounding in that space behind his soul, as he recited the words and launched these hexes, his fists incendiary, cursing the world and groaning. The blast of heat reached out for him in the same instant the Ripper's lashing limbs struck him across the temple, its jaws spread apart and flashing alien fangs to bite him into a thousand pieces. Matthew opened his eyes and looked into another pit, screaming for all the murdered, screeching for his God.

The lake exploded.

Chapter Seventeen

"Go over it again, Henry," Hodges said.

Charters glanced at the collage of snipped photographs, sat back in his chair, and wondered if his second wife, Melissa, would have eventually divorced him if only she'd lived long enough to grow tired of him. He sometimes believed that she, of all of them, was the one who would have stayed, making her death that much more ironic. Somehow, though, he thought, yes, even she would have learned to hate him.

"Henry?" the sheriff repeated.

"There's nothing more to go over." Charters took the ice pack off his swollen jaw. "After Roger and I left the boy's room we came here to my office. I wanted to speak with him at length over what he'd experienced, but after I shut the door he apologized and coldcocked me."

"Wakowski slugged you?" Russell Stockton asked, leaning back against the desk. "Guy like that has to think he has a reason. He apologized first and then actually slugged you?" Russell sort of grinned, as though it would be funny to walk up to somebody, say you were sorry, then land one on the button.

"How perceptive of you, Deputy." Charters tossed the ice pack across the room, feeling where his dentures had come loose, the few remaining teeth in his mouth having shifted now thanks to Wakowski's fist. "What was your first clue? This bruise or the fact that I've repeated myself a half dozen times now?" There was still blood seeping from his gums, and he took a breath, held it, knowing how much Melissa despised when he'd lost his temper, and let it out slowly. "I'm sorry."

Russell nodded. "There's a mass of nerves there that will lay you out if the punch is thrown just right, and the guy doesn't even have to be strong. It's happened to me, hurts like a bitch."

"That's just it, your question isn't as superfluous as I took it for, Russell. Wakowski didn't actually punch me. His fingers pressed into the spot, almost gently, and he merely poked me. Makes me feel goddamn ridiculous as well as ineffectual." He sighed. His teeth hurt like hell. "Forget it. Are you protecting the boy?"

Hodges said, "I have one of my men over there now."

"I don't think Roger would harm Richie, quite the opposite actually. It appeared as if he was guarding the child. Something horrible spooked him, but even if I'm wrong your deputies won't be able to stop him."

"Okay, he poked you in the face, but get over the Superman crap. Listen, Henry, I know this guy was a Marine, but please, don't tell me my goddamn job."

"Nor you mine. We've got to move Richie Hastings to a safer place."

"We're in a damn asylum for the criminally insane already, what's going to be safer?" Hodges looked out the window and saw the beginning smears of rain pelting against the glass. He turned and regarded Charters, glancing back and forth between the doctor and those photos he was so interested in. Hodges waited a moment longer, considering the camera's point of view, and said, "Wakowski isn't here, so to take the kid out would only increase the risk of putting him in danger. O'Malley will do his duty and shoot the fucker if he comes back." He shifted his gun belt, wondering, *Jesus, where did this stomach of mine come from?* "I'm going to tell you something, Doctor, and that's only because I need for you to know it. You won't tell a soul. No one. Are we clear on this point?"

Charters kept a steady gaze. He knew Hodges

was a man beyond either subtlety or exaggeration. "Yes."

"We found one of the missing girls this afternoon. Joanne Sadler. She was mutilated, and only been dead a few hours when we discovered the corpse. Which means that the psycho we've already got locked in your tower has a partner . . ."

"Or is innocent."

". . . and that partner might still have the other kids alive. And now on the very day we find the girl, that nut's best friend, Matthew Galen, shows up after having been gone five years, and your chief of security cracks his pot. You don't have to be a cop for half your life to be a bit suspicious of that. And we all know that Galen doesn't come from a family with the most stable background, don't we?"

Charters's eyes narrowed.

The sheriff continued. "I won't accept your professional opinion on whether you think he's involved, because I know you and he go a long way back, and far as I'm concerned, anybody who spends much time in this place is crazy anyway. Don't bother hawking him to me. Galen's a suspect, and I fouled up and blew my stack and now may have lost him. When I get him back, though, I'll keep him under wraps. I'll also tell you that I don't think this hospital of yours is worth the sweat off a flea's balls."

"How poetic."

"Shut the fuck up, I think you shrinks screw up more people than you could ever possibly help, and that you let too many of the wrong ones back on the street again."

"I believe a good number of people agree with you."

"And now this thing with Wakowski might, or might not, have something else to do with it, and the whole mess is giving me the runs. If he's involved with A.G. it would explain a lot." Hodges sneered, at Charters or perhaps everyone. "Maybe he was trying to kill Richie because the kid could identify him somehow, but then why not just do it? And why go to the trouble of pretending to be caught in a flashback, unless he wanted to get off on an insanity plea, get the jury to wring their hands for the vet? What's the point? From every angle I've looked at it, this thing falls apart."

Insanity in individuals is something rare—but in groups, parties, nations, and epochs it is the rule, Nietzsche had said. Charters wished he could remember more. "I'll give it to you as clinically as possible, whether you want to hear it or not, but I believe Roger isn't involved in any of this."

"Now who's cracked?"

"He's got problems, but whatever they are, he understands them and is fighting them in his own manner. He remains a soldier, and has survived by living and adapting to the insanity of war. I believe you can understand that."

"Not quite," Hodges said.

"I also think he would agree with you on the value of formal psychiatry, but whatever Wakoski is, he is not a sociopath in the clinical sense, despite what he may have done in war. I also don't accept that A.G. is your kidnapper or killer, and since he doesn't say a word or respond in any way to treatment, there's no way for me to reach him. He is where he belongs, but I think he's innocent of the crimes you've charged him with. You're looking for someone other than these two men."

"Jesus Christ, is that a lot of horseshit. A guy sitting with a skeleton, doing God knows what to a kid, something so awful the boy's flipped his wig too, but we're not looking for him, huh?" Hodges swallowed the bitter taste in his mouth, knowing from experience that there were two things you could do when you couldn't do anything. You either flowed with this tide instead of allowing it to drown you, as he'd done on the search-and-destroy missions he and Karragan had been party to, or you simply went without answers. "I want to talk to A.G. He's got answers, and I want them, and he's going to give them to me tonight. Now."

Melissa's left eye peeked out from beneath her sailor's cap, regarding Charters, reminding him of just how firm a hold this place had on him, even then. "No, he's my patient. I can't allow that. You have no authority here, Sheriff."

"Shove your moral dilemmas, Henry. Are you really that naïve?" The sheriff walked over, sat on the desk, and pressed a finger to Charters's chest, wondering if he could poke him hard enough to knock him out too. He whispered though he didn't want to, couldn't seem to find enough humanity to put into it, and coming out with a snarl. "If he doesn't tell me what I need to know, I am going to put a bullet in the back of his head."

Russell stiffened. "Umm—"

"Shut up, Russell." Hodges kept poking Charters, shoving harder and harder, understanding that it was causing pain, with another nice mass of ganglia near the clavicle. But the doctor took it like a man with hardly a grunt, you had to give him that. "And you will swear in a court of law that it was justified, Henry, or I promise that I will shoot you as well." He turned and eyed Russell closely, wondering about him. "Hey, you got a problem with anything I just said?"

Russell thought about it, about how you couldn't really run fast enough or far enough, not to Canada or anywhere else, and so sometimes just had to make a stand on your own. "No, I just wanted to say it was about fuckin' time, Sheriff."

* * *

As the three of them walked silently together through the garbage-strewn tunnels connecting the buildings, Henry Charters looked out at the rain and thought of things he hadn't thought about for a long time. Details, denials, repressions that even a psychiatrist could fool himself into not noticing, but only for so long.

It had been years.

The harder he tried not to recall Mattie Galen's mother, the more fleshed she became in his memories, the smooth, pale, graceful arch of her chin now so firm in his mind that he could feel his palms tingle: her intoxicating white smile, that laugh, her ebony hair that flowed so thickly, and all the other qualities that would not fade from his mind. He chewed the inside of his cheek until more blood ran against his teeth.

The worst part of all was that, though she'd been dead these many years, she still wouldn't vanish from his most urgent fantasies; the vividness of them could be hideously tactile. He remained as jealous of Galen now as ever—realizing he fought a ghost for the love of a ghost. There had been times when Charters had been invited to their home only to find himself so anxiety-stricken and incensed at watching the two of them together that he couldn't bear the sight of their loveplay any longer. Spilling his drink, knocking plates to the floor and reveling in the sound of breaking dishes, apologizing as he was forced to make pitiful excuses and scurrying off like the mighty mouse. His jealousy drove him home, where he'd stop Sophie or Melissa or Maureen from doing whatever they were doing, grabbing them from behind wherever they were, to start making love to them wildly right there. Heat devoid of real poetry, angst, and humor. Merely a sad mockery of himself screwing his wives while envisioning himself with a different woman, so lovely, even now bending to clean up the broken glass.

They walked out of the last corridor and came to the elevator of Tower C. He pushed the button for fourteen, the ride up too slow, and Charters felt anxiety beating away inside of him, looking for a place to be freed. Once he'd been more comfortable here in the asylum than in his own home, knowing his wife was not the woman he wished her to be.

Now he couldn't help but feel as if he were about to witness yet another portion of his life, and this town, coming to an ugly end, first ruined and then destroyed for incomprehensible reasons. Hodges stood beside him like an escort to an execution, and Russell moved with the wary alertness of an animal. The video cameras captured them for something more than posterity's sake. He tried to soothe his stomach by rubbing on it gently the way Melissa used to, or Maureen, or his teenage wife Sophie stroking him and kissing his navel. He thought he might vomit.

When the elevator doors opened at last, Charters flashed his ID badge at the security desk. Despite his warning glances, the men went through their usual formalities to an extent. Hodges and Stockton were known, of course, and wouldn't hand over their guns or turn out their pockets or be frisked. Breaking procedure like this could get you killed no matter who you were. Charters could see a small yet very real danger in his men's eyes, as if they thought the police now invaded a sanctum that ran outside their influence. One of the violent offenders could make a move, grab a gun, kill everybody all in the name of Hodges's pretension. "Leave your guns here."

"Fuck you," the sheriff said. "You really want to get into this, Henry?"

Why bother? It served no purpose, so far down this path already. "No."

The three of them proceeded down the hall and came to the secondary gates, where Wakowski had been posted five nights a week since A.G.'s arrival. *Perhaps evil and insanity can be contracted through osmosis*, he thought, *absorbed through the flesh by being in close proximity to madness*. It wasn't a new idea. He wouldn't deny his own questions any longer: *Why did she go mad? Why had he allowed her*

*into this filthy purgatory? Why couldn't I save
her? Why didn't she love me?*

The locks opened for them, noise of the gates
scraping across the floor loud enough to crack
the walls. Charters had one of the orderlies
open the door to A.G.'s cell.

"Here," the doctor said tersely, voice hoarse
as if from all the shouting he did in his head.
"You son of a bitch."

"You're coming with us, Henry," Hodges replied.

They entered.

A.G. was gone.

"What in the hell!"

Eugene Carmichael rushed out of the
kitchen, looking ready to grab his shotgun from
the closet, consternation marring his cherubic
face. If that damn Jello Joe was back bothering
his daughter again, he'd point the dubious par-
ticulars of that out to him, for sure.

He found himself gagging, taking a whiff of
something long rotten and thinking that the
freezer in the basement must've broken. "Good
Lord, what . . . ?" Checking the door to the cellar, he saw that the latch hadn't been tampered
with, nobody'd gone down there.

Carmichael turned and jumped as something
brushed his leg. He backed against the kitchen
doorjamb and Gusto limped by more asthmatic
than usual, wheezing horribly, brushing past

apparently unaware that Carmichael stood there beside him. Gus slowly gazed up without interest, and Eugene moaned, stooped, and took the dog's head in his hands, unsure of what to do. "Boy . . . ?" he whispered.

The blood all over.

Gus was covered in mud and blood, and seemed to have been in a fight with a pack of dogs. It had happened a couple of times before, but never like this. A terrible slash parted the hair down the length of his flank, still dripping fluid, and the pouring rain hadn't allowed a scab to form. Some kind of black sludge dribbled from the dog's chin, striking the wooden floor with increasingly loud *pip pip pip*s. Thorns and brambles spiked his fur, and wounds of all sizes covered his rotund body. Eugene looked at the basement latch again, the smell so bad. His arms were covered with gooseflesh. "Gus, oh, oh my pal . . ." His voice shook. "You're gonna be just fine, boy, just fine. Here, let me . . ." He didn't know what he was supposed to do.

Thunder rocked the verandah, and Gus peered behind himself. Farther back in the hall Eugene saw another figure in the dark. The light switch was over there, and he couldn't reach it to see who the guy was first. He gritted his teeth and moved forward quickly but cautiously, coming closer and lifting the heavy statue of *The Kiss* from the table, hoping he didn't have to splatter anyone's brain with it. He thought that it might be Jodi, his baby girl lying there. My God, *my God*, why are you doing all of this to me now?

Matthew rose and stumbled into the foyer, and with a muted groan fell against the wall, knocking *La Pietà* off the table. Carmichael stared at the broken pieces of the statuette on the floor until Matthew's knees buckled and the boy joined them there. He splayed into a pink puddle of water and Carmichael hurried to help him, muttering frantically, "My God, what's happened to you? Here, here, hold on, I'm right here." Where was Jodi? *Jesus*.

Rain lashed the screen door and kicked it back open just as Matthew managed to get to his feet. He reached out with a bleeding hand and threw an arm over Carmichael's shoulder, the stench so incredible that the old man backed up a step, then another.

"It's all right," Matthew said.

"All right? That's what you say, that you're all right, bleeding like that?"

"I'll be fine, Eugene."

Poison still clung to his shredded, burned clothes, as he watched Carmichael drop the other statuette, it too crashing and bursting into fragments.

"Sure, sure, you'll be fine, son, I know you will." Carmichael looked around searching for help. "The one time I need them two goddamn no-talkin' chess-playin' antisocial immigrants and neither one of 'em is in sight!"

"It's all right," Matthew repeated.

"Ain't you hearin' what I'm sayin' to you, son? What was it that happened? I gotta get ya to a doctor."

Waving him off, Matthew stood on his own and moved to the staircase. "I got mugged."

Eugene Carmichael looked at Gusto as the dog crawled over to his mat by the kitchen door and lay with a whine and a huff of air. "Jesus God! And the sons a bitches mugged my dog, too? Ain't there any shame left in this world? Did you see who done it?"

"No. Couple or three wild kids, I think. Came up behind me. Couldn't see anything in the rain, in the night. Gus helped me out."

"It's 'cause of that damn Bosco Bob's party, I bet! This whole town goes shitstorm crazy when that rich man decides to throw a shindig. He's a regular goddamn Caligula, if anyone's got mind enough left to ask me. And you should still go to the hospital. And the police."

"Nothing to report."

"Well, you don't worry about that. Hodges will probably already have them kids in custody anyways, if they're out there harmin' decent folk. I'm gonna go find out if I can get some damn lazy doctor to get over here and come see you, son. Your head's lookin' a little dented, if you don't mind my saying so."

"I'm okay, just a little shaken up," Matthew said.

"Well, then, what the hell is that stink, you cross tracks with a skunk? What'd them rotten kids do to my dog?"

They got to Matthew's room and he pulled away from Carmichael, his ribs protesting when he bent to open the satchel, grabbing other clothes, the chills chopping at him deeply. His frozen arms were still blue. "Gusto's beat up, but he'll be all right. You should get him to a vet." *Go, anywhere, leave me.*

"Anything I can do for you, though? A drink maybe? A shot of whiskey or two? Got the good stuff under the sink. Some of Emma's liniment? She's got all kinds of that grease around the house, and it won't make you smell too much worse."

"No, thank you, I just need a shower."

"Yeah, well, I ain't arguing on that." Carmichael grimaced and stood back, his concern apparent but with little reaction, the man just staring and not moving, until finally he let his hands drop to his sides. "I sure don't like the look of that cut on Gusto's back, either. I'll be getting him to the vet, then, he's gonna be needin' stitches. Of course, that's only supposing that the doctor hasn't gone off to the party by now. Mebbe I just better go into Gallows, at least there people are still in their right heads."

"Yes."

"I'll be back soon. You remember to take it easy on yourself. It ain't in my nature to mother, but I wish you'd let me do something for you. But if not, all right, then. Jodi'll be back any minute, I suspect. Okay?"

"Thank you," Matthew said, able to grin for an instant.

"All right, then, but I got some Man-O'-War cologne on my dresser that you're more than welcome to use."

Matthew shut the door and began pulling off his tattered clothes, blisters on his chest flattening and draining, healing now, even as he watched. His kidneys were bruised badly, back covered with scratches, welts, and bites. He quaked, a rush of nausea and dizziness dropping him forward over the bed. He snaked out of his pants and underwear. The cold sweats came and his bad ankle beat like castanets. After a moment the vertigo passed and he brushed his wet hair out of his eyes, got up, and made his way to the window, knowing that he was just being corralled. He deserved what he got, so stupid, but at least so human.

A few overlooked dead luna moths lay crushed in his tracks. His reversal charm should have vanished these as well, but he'd been missing the finer details. Lightning blazed from ground to sky in the distance, impossibly igniting in the cold night. He drew back the curtains and watched Carmichael lead Disgusto into the passenger seat of his car and back out of the driveway. Gus looked up at the window and wagged his tail once. Matthew couldn't help himself and actually waved as Carmichael sped off toward Gallows.

The dog had saved his life.

Outside this window, the trellis had pickets along the edge, and Matthew gathered his clothes and hung these rags from the points. Tired and weak, he still focused himself enough to speak the Enochian spells: Images of the Seraphim flooded his mind, Debbi moving behind him but just out of peripheral vision, making him turn to look, to turn and look again. His tongue twisted to fit the melody of the language of angels, in and out of time with his pulse. He placed the hand that Mauels had bitten through on top of the cursed clothing. Words worked against the buffeting wind. Soon flames licked at the lifeless brown vines and his clothes were on fire, burning perfectly until there was nothing but cinders left to blow in the strange storm.

Something would happen soon—maybe A.G. knew what, but he wasn't telling. This reaping of the whirlwind.

Naked, he moved down the hallway to the bathroom and checked himself in the mirror, assessing damage. The fourth scarred point of the inverted pentagram—the Goat's other ear—had already scabbed over. Flecks of dried blood flaked off the burns. He touched the scores of

259

bruises and gashes on his face, neck, and torso. He was lucky that he hadn't drowned when the backlash slammed him down to the bottom of the lake. In two days, the gray gray streaks in his hair had grown into rivers twining through his curls. He snatched a towel off the shower rod and stepped into the tub, his knees cracking. He scrawled the seal of Solomon in the soap scum on the tiles.

Aiming the shower nozzle to spray into his face, he turned on the water. Steam started rising, but it still didn't seem to be hot enough for him. There was a chunk of malformed soap already in the dish, and he briskly lathered up, over and over again, letting the scalding water flush away the daemonic perfume and lake sediment, his blood so thick swirling in the drain. Vapor floated into his face like the ghosts of friends and family.

He dropped the soap.

"No," he whispered. "Oh no."

He bent and retrieved it, looking deeper into the yellow wax of the soap, peering closer as if words might be written in it. He shut off the water, hearing the souls now whispering across time, so distantly he almost thought he imagined them.

Almost.

"You maniacs!" he shouted.

He flung the soap from him, disgusted, but after what had transpired tonight, he realized it

didn't matter much anymore. Soon he'd simply
be one of them, another of the desecrated dead.

He got out of the shower and dressed.

Ready to party.

A sound, or the lost ripple of a sound, drew him
to the dimly lit den. The silence of the empty
boardinghouse made the groaning and rumble
of the invading storm all the more desultory
and definite.

A.G.? he asked, but felt no return psychic reverb, none of the crossing of life force he could
note. He stepped farther into the room, glancing to the left and right while leaves blasted up
against the windows. He went to the table, at
last realizing that the chess set wasn't composed of normal Civil War pieces, as he'd orig-
inally thought.

There was much to be said about bones.

Matthew knew them well: how they looked
up close, straight from the earth, old and broken, treated and polished like ivory, used according to ritual, as locks and keys. He knew
skin. He knew human fat.

Chess pieces of the body and spirit, taken
from corpses. He understood that immediately
as he touched them, the soldiers stern and vicious and callous, young, belligerent and posed
to strike. Some of them grinning and handsome, but all of them cruel; the victims' agony
engraved into every crevice of their starving,

hollow faces, wearing nothing but rags and agony; each body poised in some ultimate torture, shrinking from boots and bayonets.

The years it must have taken.

The hatred honed to perfection, perhaps as fine as Matthew's own, perhaps far better—this rage needed to keep the dead past alive long enough to faultlessly remember each face of never-ending torment and ceaseless, sadistic pleasure. It could happen like this, the bones on the table, the human fat in the shower.

The front door opened and Kessner and Hoffman trudged through the foyer. One of them was crying.

Kessner entered, coughing hard into his fist, and proceeded to hang his overcoat on the rack in the corner. He spotted Matthew, nodding slowly and walking over to his seat: the Jew's side. "So, you have noticed."

Each movement of his fragile body appeared as if it might be his last. "That is a start." He picked a pawn off the board and turned it in his fingers, carefully, as though the bones were his own. "This is me," he said. "I am only fourteen." He replaced the piece and took another, one that might have been the Queen. "This is my mother. Her name was Tzipora. It was her grandmother's name. It is also the name of Elie Wiesel's younger sister, who did not survive the camps except in the dedication to his fine book *Night*. You know Wiesel?"

Matthew nodded.

"I am glad that there is at least one such book dedicated to my mother's name. It is befitting, I like to think." Kessner leaned forward and chose a Nazi pawn from the front line. "This is the soldier who killed her. He was little older than me, this boy of seventeen, straight from the Hitler Youth. He lived most of his young life in the city of Munich, the birthplace of Herr Himmler." He held the two pieces together, the woman lying on the ground, arm raised to avert a blow, frightened eyes pleading while the soldier kicked out, his foot coming down on her throat at the precise angle. Placed together, the bones were each consummated. "This other boy . . . his name is Hoffman."

"God." Matthew nodded again, having no idea what else to do, the extent of evil so concrete in the town, in their lives, this room, that its influence was staggering. So much power in those shards of splintered bodies. His own flesh was now covered with the flesh of others.

Kessner replaced the chess pieces and said, "I no longer believe in God, which is not such a bad thing, despite the fact that my forefathers were all rabbis. I go to temple, but that is out of respect for my parents, and because I worship the past. It lends my existence a little more credence, and puts fate a bit more firmly into my own two hands." He gestured to the doorway, and beyond to the living room, where the weeping persisted, though now lower. "We have just returned from temple, he and I, and now he goes and sits in front of the television and is forced to watch the rallies where the gay men and women hold their lovers without shame. He watches the homeless, who are something like the gypsies, shouting obscenities at their own president of the United States, decrying your very own government officials. These freedoms."

Kessner laughed under his breath, and there really was humor in it. "He sees the Berlin Wall come down and sobs all night long. He was not a soldier who whined that he only followed orders. He believed. He truly believed." Kessner smiled and ran a palm over the board, tapping at the black and white squares as though listening to the blackshirts marching in step. "Oh, he wants to kill me, this is true, but he does not dare. For he, too, worships only his memories, of which I am now the greatest part. This is his torment, to see how badly his precious Thousand-Year Reich has failed him and the Fatherland. I can think of no better vengeance."

The scars on Matthew's chest twitched, speaking, having tasted the murdered again, and wanting more, so much more.

"Yes, your skin sparkles," Kessner said. "He still has many bars of soap. He bathes with them on occasion, washing his sins with all of the families. I see no reason to stop him. I enjoy the idea that the dead are here with me, forever upon him as much as on myself."

Kessner brushed his shaggy beard down, and said, "She's in the basement, you know."

"Who?"

He waved Matthew on. "There. Go. See for yourself. It is not my place to bring sadness to another innocent old man's dream."

Matthew left, with the Goat rippling beneath his sweater. In the living room, Hoffman sat on the couch, sobbing, watching the news, his mouth moving but no sound emerging.

"Come!" Kessner shouted from the den. "Come! Kill my mother again tonight."

Hoffman shut off the TV and went.

Matthew unlatched and opened the basement door, feeling for the light switch but not finding it. He descended the rest of the stairs in the dark, and at the bottom, reached up to pull the chain he hoped would be there. It was. The single lightbulb glowed effusively through the unfinished basement. Boxes, cabinets, toolboxes, and other assorted junk of decades piled high all around.

He listened to the hum and drew closer.

He opened the meat freezer and stared into the face of Emma Carmichael's corpse.

At least she was smiling.

Chapter Eighteen

Debbi laughed and flashed her braces, stuck her tongue out, threw her hands out, and *poo-poo*ed him again in her mother's fashion. "Smile!" she ordered, fist held to his chin. "Don't be so grim and creepy all the time, this is an adventure! Like you've got something much better to do? Today's the day we've been waiting for!"

No, it wasn't, he hadn't been waiting for it at all, but trying to dissuade her from this—he'd been reading, he'd already learned so much. She didn't care about anything he said and just laughed. Debbi whirled around, like the way his mother danced with his father. "In a couple of hours we're going to be stumbling on pirate treasure, listen to me, I'm telling you." She told him, she was always telling him. "It's down there in the ground. Pearls and diamond tiaras. Jewels and silver chalices." No, witches abhorred silver. "Rubies, emeralds, gold doubloons and jade stolen from Chinese emperors. Anything you can name, everything you could ever want!"

He wanted her to forget about it.

Her eyes grew moon-wide and bright with anticipation. She bopped him gently on the jaw, bent and grasped the metal handle on the floor of the lighthouse, exerting herself until the blue veins stood out on her skinny forearms. "And even if there's not we've still got nothing better going on in this dumpy town." She grunted and heaved at the antiquary trapdoor cut out in the slates, but couldn't budge it alone. Nobody could move it all the way, all the way open *into there*, wherever it led to, because of the locks and wards upon it. He could sense that now, and worse, whatever was in *there* could sense him.

She scowled at the rest of them and smooshed her smile into a frown. A.G. and Ruth bent to grab the handle with her, the three of them pulling but still not getting anywhere. Even if they opened it they wouldn't be going anywhere except down the stone stairs.

Only he could slip through the wards. The counterspell wasn't difficult, but not especially easy either. She said, "Well, are you going to help us or just stand there?"

Tom Piccirilli

He didn't know what to do. He stood by them, so curious to see if he could open the door *all the way*, his breathing becoming ragged now in the heat, so close to Debbi. She smoothed the backs of her knuckles over his cheek the way his mother used to do, and a sob welled in his chest but thankfully didn't come out.

Debbi said, "Come on, help us out with all them muscles."

He bent and strained at the handle, the words reciting themselves in his head, sweat breaking on his top lip, and he knew in his heart that they were going to *open* this, and whispered so low under his tongue that she asked, "What did you say?" The rusted hinges finally squealed like an animal, rolled back, and the door flapped open.

"It wasn't that tough the last time," she said, puzzled, and Ruth added, "This is stupid."

A.G. moved closer to him and got him into a headlock. "Yeah, well, that's because Mr. Muscles here has been spending all his time in the library and bookshops for you, Deb. He's pale and weak."

"No, he's beautiful," Debbi said.

His face burned.

The flowing of the craft came so easily, as if he had been made for it.

Sunlight filtering in through the rotted planks covering the windows seemed absurdly distant. The highlighted dust looked like falling snow. Waves boomed on the beach and seagulls continued to *cawwww* nearby, but he still felt as if the lighthouse itself stood much farther from the ocean than it should. He pushed A.G. away, wishing he could explain it to them, wanting to warn them but too excited that he was pleasing her and had the ability within him, happy to perform anything she bid.

"Holy digs," Ruth said, looking through the trapdoor and seeing the first few stone steps. The stairs receded into the darkness below, and she bent and wiggled her fingers at it, as though testing the waters. "Freaky. How'd you ever find out about this, Deb?"

Debbi oohed and aahed in some exaggerated Alice in Wonderland astonishment. "I found it the only way you can find rabbit holes like this," she said. "Pure luck. Those chains fastening the front door are so salt-eaten they've broken through, or maybe older kids cut a few links, I'm not sure. See, the door still looks chained shut, but it's not locked. Anyway, I was hunting around the Point looking for seashells for Mr. Smiley here a few weeks back, and I just, y'know, stumbled into here. The trapdoor just looks like a storage basement." Others had spent time here, beer bottles and condom wrappers scattered about the room. "But you'll see that there are cracks in the rock down there, and the caves open up beyond it. It's great! So now here we are. Soon to be millionaires."

Ruth whirled. "You sneak! You mean you've

known about this for weeks and you only told us about it last night?"

"Yeah, well . . ." Debbi looked sidelong at him. "He wanted to do some research. Kid spontaneity. There's some marks on the walls he got really interested in. Anything to keep his nose in the books."

"Do you really think there's treasure down there, like all the gossip says?"

A.G. softly hip-checked Ruth, knocking her off balance. "Oh, please, don't be ridiculous. Like if there was, they wouldn't have discovered it by now?"

"There could be. They still find treasure, they haven't found it all."

"There could be sea turtles the size of Buicks resting down there, too." A.G. turned to him. "What do you think? What's it for, that room? Fallout shelter maybe, at one time?"

Ruth said, "Escape route for the Underground Railroad? I bet that's what it is. This is old. Cool."

"Yeah," A.G. said, smirking. "But the Underground Railroad didn't actually go underground, Ruth."

"Choo-choo." She giggled. "Yes, it did, in some places."

Debbi took his hand and interlaced fingers. He hoped he could siphon some of her excitement into himself, but none of it wore off. He shook his head and stared into her smile. And that, for the moment, satisfied him, despite the fact that he knew there was more to come, so much of the unknown here besides all his love for her. Still, he wished he didn't care about all this—this game of hers, this adventure that the others didn't know was already too real, as she *poo-poo*ed him every time he tried to speak seriously, as A.G. got him into a headlock whenever he mentioned anything about the darkness. He was nearly certain they concealed something from him as much as from themselves.

The trapdoor had been camouflaged beneath a number of slates that covered the outer edges of the lighthouse's base. It was shabby in design, almost as if put down as an afterthought, in order to make the interior more attractive, or to provoke another arcane pattern. The slabs had split, shards scattered.

"What cracked the tiles?" A.G. asked, taking a flashlight from his backpack at the edge of the room and shining it down the stairwell. The light barely pierced the gloom. "I was afraid of that. This cheap thing isn't nearly strong enough. Somebody go out to my bike and get my father's lantern. I forgot to bring it in with me. That sucker can light up Etcher's Point."

Ruth checked over A.G.'s left shoulder and Debbi stared from his right. The three of them peered into the blackness, only the barest hint of the scrawlings, signs, and badges seen as the beam from the flashlight panned this way and that.

He went to retrieve A.G.'s father's lantern, shoving hard against the front door, the ineffective chains rattling but not holding the door shut. He realized in a brilliantly rational moment, too crystalline for truth perhaps, that he was free. He had made it out, and he could leave. Staring out at the surf, a strange and solemn thought pervaded: *I want to go home*. It confused him now, whether he should run, until he wondered just what home he wanted to go back to, and where it could be found. He hurried across the sand and swung A.G.'s handlebars around the other way so he could unload the lantern, then returned. He stood a moment in the shade of the catwalks above, knowing he was going to go back in, for her, of course, but more than just her, he wanted to go all the way in for himself.

He handed A.G. the lantern. Ruth grabbed A.G.'s hand and angled the flashlight, and now the lantern beam, too, against the walls of the stairway.

"What are all these marks?" she asked.

"Is that the writing you were telling us about? The runes? What'd you call them, sigils?"

Ruth kneeled on the tile, reached out, and touched the nearest sign. "Cool, funky digs, what language is it in? What's it say? Can you read it?"

"Who cares?" Debbi said. "Come on, this is boring! Let's go and get on with it." She flipped on her own flashlight. "The worst thing that happens is there's an earthquake and we all get sucked into a river of molten lava."

"Well . . ." Ruth said. "That won't hurt much."

Glancing back, A.G. said, "We set?"

"If you are," Ruth answered, "but wait a sec, I didn't bring anything. Give me your flashlight." With considerable effort, she finally managed to shove the switch up. "Okay, I'm ready, Griddly."

Holding the lantern before him like a lance, A.G. descended first. Ruth held on to the back loop of his belt and followed, the powerful shaft of lantern light playing wildly across the pictures carved into the rock, flashlight beams weaving like lost souls gliding. Debbi went next, virtually skipping into the darkness, *tra la la la* as she wound down the stairway. He followed her, reaching forward and clasping a hand around her wrist, because he'd turned the keys in all of these locks, and would learn the meaning and price of this particular brand of madness. He counted on it.

"Don't be such a baby," she chastised him, but tightly held on to his hand.

Their feet dragged against the rock, Ruth's sandals making an awful racket. Debbi shivered with jubilant energy. She was always so damn bored. He'd tried several times to explain what the runes meant, and she'd called him grisly and creepy, still searching for her father out at sea. Is that what she hoped to find here in the cave, some remainder of him?

Crrrt, Ruth's sandals went against the stone as they descended. *Crtt crtt*, her footsteps fell.

"You were right about one thing, Ruth," A.G. said. "No way is this a fallout shelter."

"How many times have you guys been down here?" Ruth asked.

No one else had been down here the way they were now.

Debbi played her fingers up and down his wrist as the sweat of their palms began to loosen their grip on each other. "I've been down twice, but only to the bottom of the steps. It's more fun to explore the caves now, with all of you."

"Yay, fun." A.G. couldn't help keep the reality of awe from his mocking voice. "Yay, if we meet any subterranean troll people down here do you think they'll worship us like gods because of our advanced scientific knowledge?"

"Caves?" Ruth said. "I guess I wasn't really listening when you said that before. That's impossible, we're at the beach, there can't be any natural caves here. Whoever heard of such a thing? Maybe just an alcove." Now at least Ruth picked up on it, as he muttered more spells under his breath, so low yet still so powerful, feeling the arcana that thrived here almost reaching out.

"There can be a cave, can't there?" Debbi said. "What are you talking about? Where do you think the pirates hide all their treasure on them desert islands?"

A.G. stopped short. "Be careful you don't trip. That's the final step, and the last four or five are smaller than the rest and all jammed together. God, we're down far. This is kind of freaky. I counted one hundred eleven."

"Me, too," Debbi said. "Last time."

"That's what?" Ruth asked. "Something like eighty feet maybe?" She reached and took a handful of Debbi's hair, pulled it gently, and flipped it back, her hair always everywhere, merging with the darkness. "I can't believe you came down here alone. Why, Deb?"

"Why not?"

"That's a reason?"

"Sure, it's the best one."

A.G. turned the lantern to his face and the glow lit him in eerie penumbra, none of them realizing the extent of these shadows. "Stay together, everyone, this was very stupid of us. There's no way we can explore, we'd be lost in a second." His voice snapped around them all, echoing. "Jeez, this is much bigger than I thought. Nobody ever mentioned anything like this." The powerful beam of light arched and faded into the depths without showing anything more.

"It looks kind of different," Debbi said. "Why's it so dark? It wasn't this dark before, not really. You could see the cracks in the walls, but that's it."

"This isn't a cave. Listen to how far those echoes go. It's a cavern. There might even be catacombs."

"Oooooh," Debbi went.

"Ruth, keep holding on to my belt."

Ruth nodded resolutely. "I ain't letting go."

A.G. looked at him, reached back, and said, "You were reading that book on numbers the other day, I remember. Called *Numerology*, right? One eleven. Do you think there's a significance to that?"

"What's that rumbling sound?" Rush asked.

Debbi said, "Lava?" She burst out laughing, the sweet and high tittering warbling into the distance and whipping back at them from every angle.

A.G. drew his hand along the rock, finally starting to feel what had to be felt, his other senses opening. It was clear, just look around. He understood, to some extent, what they were entering. "That's spooky. I think it's the ocean beating against the walls."

"It's so loud, like giant lungs."

"It's Goliath," Debbi said. "That little wimp David didn't do the job after all."

"The waves."

"Shine the floor," Ruth said.

A.G. did.

"Look at that," Debbi whispered. "Hey, now we're getting somewhere."

From between the scattered ugly drawings and odd designs on the floor rose stalagmites of all sizes, some cylindrical and others sharply tipped like icicles extending upward. It was unnatural here, like this, like his father killing his mother. A mindless merging of earth and perverse artistry.

Ruth gasped.

Debbi said, "We'll come back with more lanterns, and miner's caps, and sacks for the loot. Rope lines so we don't get lost, and we'll chalk our path across the floor."

A.G. shook his head and carefully swept the area around him with the light. "Miner's caps, huh? Somebody's already marked up the floor. But why? What does it mean?" A.G. turned to him now, expecting an answer, but seemed undisturbed when he didn't get one. Water dripped nearby. "Hold hands and form a single line. Spread out as far as you can without losing the stairs. Watch out for these rocks." When they were as far into the cave as they could go without losing contact with the stairway, A.G. illuminated the path they'd chosen.

And they saw it.

There. Only a dozen feet away. Untouched for

so many years because no one else had been able to unlock the labyrinth.

The four of them stared at the altar.

Ruth shivered. "Is that a painting of a goat on the floor?"

It was Baphomet, looking alive, its blind malfeasance now turning an eye toward them. *Oh God*. His grip tightened on Debbi's hand, and he tugged her. He may have even tugged her forward.

"We'd better get out of here," A.G. told them, beginning to back up.

"I'm with you," Ruth said. "I want out. Look at that sicko thing. It's got a dick."

Yes, look at it, that's what they'd come here for, to find what had been forgotten, searching for Debbi's dad, looking for his own father here too, and all the other answers. He heard a sound to his left.

Something shoved him forward, or he tripped, and his heel lost contact with the bottom stair. He entered the darkness, and, however briefly, welcomed the invitation. He tried to keep his balance and grabbed on to Debbi, but again it felt like he was pushed.

"Hey," Debbi said as her hand was torn from his. "What the hell are you—?"

Chapter Nineteen

Now it had come to this, and Charters found it more pleasant than he'd ever imagined.

Rather than becoming either manic or depressed—which he had a penchant for—he remained at rest. Intense cold helped to contain and calm his thoughts as he sat huddled and shivering on the frozen ground, hands thrust deep into his pockets as the wind rose furiously and the rain thrashed.

Sitting Indian-style in the mire and weeds of her grave made Charters feel like a teenager again; it was the sort of jejune romantic gesture that a sensitive seventeen-year-old boy would feel compelled to make in order to seal a pact with love. He only felt sorry that it had taken him so very long to understand how out of touch with this life he had become, to realize that the hold she had on him even now, after all these years, was not something to be ashamed of feeling. Frigid air made crying difficult; the rims of his nostrils felt sliced by razors. Sentimentality used emotional crowbars to pry up every buried and half-covered passion.

And yet perhaps this too was exaggeration, but the moment called for it. He reached into the mud, hoping to come to terms with such aggrandizement. *Go on, what the hell do you have to lose? Live a little. Wax poetic.* This was a perfect time for such youthful hyperbole and melodrama, in the shadow of his life. Especially when you considered that he was now making the supreme overstatement.

He hoped someone else would fully consider this to be his reasoning; Richard Karragan, the M. E., was the one friend who might. It truly was like being thirty years younger again, when his desire grew to be more than he could control, but still he managed to handle it well, he thought. Feeling so wonderfully alive.

The irony, of course, was quite apparent at the moment. Mud ran down the banks of the hills and flowed into an eddy at the base of the woods below. Rain drove past his hat and into the collar of his coat, like the tongues of his wives.

After they'd found A.G.'s cell empty there had been a long and jarring beat in the air. A rupturing of the minute as several events came together for a precise fit in Charters's mind. He instantly and quite placidly accepted truths previously unacceptable, and felt damn good in doing so. Like finally facing the bully who'd chased you around the school yard for years.

Charters simply turned to get his first unclouded look at what he'd been running from.

Hodges, though, stuck to the facts and his hatred, checking videotapes and ranting the way you'd come to expect from the bitter sheriff, borderline himself and a hairs breadth from a complete nervous crackup. Hodges slapped his gun belt a lot, and Charters was afraid there would be a shoot-out between the police and the thin-lipped hospital guards. How the sheriff hated A.G., the fury just another element thrown into this case, everyone's anger, spite, and frustration playing meaningful parts. Charters had been surprised that he hadn't been arrested. Sheriff Hodges hissed savagely, suggesting that the doctor had let him go.

But Charters hadn't let A.G. go free any more than he'd allowed himself to be released from the asylum.

The tape revealed nothing; another glitch, and this time Charters grinned, understanding, in a fashion, what was at work here. Nothing except wafting fog figures and static-filled smoke that sent shudders through him, because there were faces to be made out in the picture, if you searched for them. Charters ran and checked Richie Hastings's room to find the boy awake and alert, and telling the nurses he was hungry for something called a Garbage Deluxe Krunchburger. To see the boy animated and stable proved to be at least as amazing as having watched the once amicable A.G. so silent and deranged in his own way.

Charters was glad that, in the end, A.G. had let the kid go.

Lightning creased the sky. Charters sneezed and shook, rain beginning to annoy him. His backside slid a bit in the mud of her grave, his fingers clawing into the dirt. He could remember how good it once felt to be this close to her years before, regardless of their surroundings, regardless of reason, loyalty, ethics, honor, or essential sanity. In the rouge light of those early mornings he would dismiss the nurses and watch her in her cell, dancing with invisible angels, mashing her kisses against the soft walls until he broke into sobs. Her passions remained unhindered by the straitjacket—arms twisted about her shoulders, head thrown back in some unfulfilled, unfathomable howl—and still, with his chest racked with the weeping, he could feel only love and total resignation to that love. He smashed things in her name, running through the streets before dawn and throwing rocks through his neighbors' bay windows. Christ, how he'd often cursed every aspect of this existence, from his grandfather to God, and back again, to himself and his wives and pets and patients.

He'd handed her the poison in a teacup, china he'd stolen from her husband. There was poetry in that, he believed.

She took it daintily, and when she'd finished drinking he thought—he hoped, *oh holy God in Your Heaven*, he had to have faith—that she'd mouthed, *Thank you*. He prayed for this to be true above all other truths, but perhaps it was actually only another part of his warped and lonely, hollow fantasies.

"I love you," he'd whispered as she fell back into his arms. She gagged and coughed, but there didn't seem to be much pain. She reached and touched his face with the backs of her fingernails, before she closed her eyes and the sweetness of her breath blew one last time into his face, and she died for him, for him, only for him, at last. He repeated it now to her gravestone. "I love you." More words unbridled themselves, but he didn't want to taste them, because now came a gush of honesty that he wanted to hold away—everything couldn't come up. Let it be over before then, please.

But he didn't stop, his voice sounding so unlike himself he almost imagined he, this man in the mud, was not Henry Charters. "You understand now, don't you? I had to do it, darling. I loved you too much to see you rot in this hell."

Yes, that was good, he could survive intact with that, his soul remaining at large, as long as he shut up now. He saw so much inside his mind, and couldn't stop himself. "I had to do it. *He might have cured you.*"

The disease.

The disease is love.

Dr. Henry Charters, former husband and one-time best friend, traitor, hypocrite, adulterer, and director of this madhouse, laughed briefly and sighed, placed the shotgun under his wet chin as the wind stole his hat, and blew the top of his head all over Potter's Field.

Chapter Twenty

Jazz spritzed his ex-wife Bobbi May with a seltzer bottle, and she yelled, "Asshole!"

To say that everyone who was anyone showed up at Bosco Bob's parties wouldn't be fair to the nobodies. Considering the narrow strata of hierarchies, it proved to be virtually everybody. Everyone was there whether they were someone or not, no one or not.

How could you miss out on Big Bosco Bob's parties? You couldn't. How could you not feel inclined to go? Everybody he knew crammed into the mansion, so that the place now writhed like the town itself, thrumming with the same life and heat, and the underpinnings of every secret of Summerfell. This was a tradition, he invited and they went, what did anyone else have better to do on a Saturday night?

Bobbi May kept at it. "Jasper, you jerk! What is wrong with you?" He grinned and held the bottle up as if to nail her again. He was just daring her to give him any more backtalk. Her boyfriend had graduated from high school the year before, a kid who now worked in the gas station and spent his free time in tattoo parlors having all the Merrie Melody characters squeezed into his flesh. Bobbi May had some shit scrawled around her wrist, something on her shoulder now too, it appeared, but Jazz didn't get a close enough look. When she didn't move fast enough he blasted her again until she ran away, pulling the kid with her, who looked warped on downers, probably Bobbi May's Valium, and was easily led off.

Jazz grabbed an hors d'oeuvre off the tray of a passing steward, thinking, *Poor serf*, took a bite out of the smeared cracker, gagged on the slimy, lubricious taste of it, and started to chuckle. He'd seen this scene once in a flick, and it hit him funny. He looked around to see if there was a dog around that might take it off his hands. No such luck, so he hid the rest of the cracker in a napkin, crumpled it into a tight ball, and made a terrific hook shot back onto the butler's tray as the servant bowed and spun from couple to couple.

Jazz slurped down his fourth scotch and soda, glanced across the dance floor, and saw that Mr. Spinelli was doing the Jitterbug with Florence Needlebaum, of all people; she had to be eighty years old and was dancing Spinelli's ass into the ground. "Go, Flo!" he shouted. Spinelli undid his tie and unbuttoned his suit jacket, made eye contact with Jazz, and signaled him over. Oh no, hell no, forget that. Jazz lifted his seltzer bottle in a toast and turned, stalked past an enormous table covered with a magnificent layout of fruits and melting ice swans, and went to look for his friends.

His neighbors crushed against him as he made his way through the halls; it became weird, seeing them like this, people appearing to lose distinction as they wandered toward him en masse. Maybe the scotch was catching up to him a little. Some of the faces he knew but couldn't quite recognize at the moment. Bemused and cocky, Frank Farlessi and his wife stepped in through the portico, and he saw they could look like any normal loving couple when they got out of the bedlam of the Krunch. It could happen. They strutted by without bothering to even look at him, though her hand sort of dragged by Jazz's groin.

Jazz sighed, turned down another corridor, and thought he saw the gleam of Helen Bretnor's auburn hair in the crowd, going by him at high speed.

Mattie had never come by for the suit he'd wanted, and Jazz wondered if that meant Mattie didn't intend to show, that he couldn't handle facing Helen again after stiffing her, along with the rest of them, five years before.

"Hey, Helen! Hey!"

He shouted her name again and made a move after her, but before he could take a full three steps he ran straight into Gigantor Davidson's granite elbow. Jazz bounced into a breakfront and listened to all that highly expensive and easily shattered crystal clattering inside, thinking he'd wind up as Bosco Bob's personal chauffeur for a year if anything broke.

All six feet nine of Gig looked down at him in slow motion.

Jeez, everybody had the good stuff, it was clear that the giant stood stoned, drunk, maybe just stupid, or any combination thereof. It was like watching a coked-up *Tyrannosaurus rex*. *Mama*. Gigantor took a deep breath, wiped his mouth on his sleeve, and said, "Sawweee, Jazzpeerr." Every syllable dragged out beyond its normal length. Gig dropped his head back, opened his cavernous mouth, and continued to simultaneously pour two half-filled bottles of Jack Daniel's down his throat. A circle of his buddies clapped and hooted, urging him on. There were possibly three working brain cells left in that cranium.

Jazz bolted.

Helen had shifted into the throng, nowhere to be seen. A rush of something black passed in front of Jazz's face, and he snatched another hors d'oeuvre from the same serf; this time he managed to finish the cracker, getting into the rich but slimy taste of it. *It's not too tough being wealthy*. He opened a door at random and poked his head into a linen closet the size of his apartment, but with more shelf space. Flustered, he walked to a set of stairs right out of *Gone with the Wind* and made it to a different floor, a different wing. *Space Quadrant 34E secure, Captain. All prepared for colonization*. Christ, this place wanted to swallow you whole, you could feel it.

Kathy Marinello's new hairdo made him stop short and do a double take, especially since it beat her into the hall by a good foot and a half. Corkscrew curls and dreadlocks and all kinds of dynamic waves and loops and ribbons snaked out from atop her head. He went, "Whoa, hey there now, this I might like . . ." She too was drunk, what else could you expect, and kept walking into the furniture, but didn't spill a drop from either of the glasses of champagne she held. She smiled hideously, and Jazz trembled.

She giggled, hippity-hopped over to him, and cooed, "Hello, lover," and started to say something else, maybe about that night when the Domino's delivery guy found them in his truck, but she got her heel caught on the carpet and nearly fell. He reached out to steady her, but she took it as a come-on and tried to kiss him as she sprawled against his chest. He wound up with champagne fizzing all over the front of his two-hundred-dollar blazer. He groaned and spritzed her big hair, and she screamed.

Direction grew meaningless in Bosco Bob's mansion. You could walk for hours up and down these corridors and chandelier-lit stairways without ever getting to where you wanted to go—at least such was true in his case. Maybe Jello Joe and Jelly Jane knew the ins and outs, maybe they probably didn't know them all. Although he'd made love to Jane several times in her bedroom, he had no idea how to get there from here. She'd sworn she had only one private bedroom, but he was pretty sure that someone this rich wouldn't settle for that. What was the point? You're going to have fifty rooms and only put your Barbie dolls in one? There still wasn't enough space to fit all the clothes and shoes she owned.

Jelly Jane would prove difficult to miss amid this bog of milling bodies, but so far he hadn't caught a glimpse of her, Joe, or their father. Big Bosco Bob was probably over there telling bad jokes and playing the piano, wherever the piano happened to be today. Jazz was in the ninety-nine to one hundred percent range of certainty that Jello Joe was at the moment making up with his girlfriend Jodi Carmichael in his bed on the fourth floor somewhere, the east wing—

or the third floor, east wing? West wing? *This is still North America, no?*

"Where am I?" he yelled, getting dizzy, and for the first time not liking how it felt.

"Here!" someone hidden in the masses answered. A few others laughed.

"No shit, I think I knew that! Where's here!"

"Here is here and nowhere else!"

"Fuck you!" Jazz shouted.

He cut down another corridor and thought he recognized some of the paintings on the walls. Was he anywhere near Jello Joe's room? Maybe. It didn't matter, he couldn't disturb them anyway, it might imperil his record. So where was Jane? This became frustrating now, and the anxiety grew as the crowd pressed in on him even more. He yanked a couple of drinks off a passing pushcart, his hand forcing past all the other hands, Jesus, like there were wads of money falling off the thing.

It struck down on him like a mallet. He felt a sudden and urgent need to find a friend, one of the gang, all of them, in fact—he could feel the storm outside working its way in. It was important that they talk about . . . hell, what did they have to talk about? Well, everything, about how far the whole gang had drifted, and what that might mean, and where was Ruth. He needed them more now than ever before, and found no shame in the fact—damn, was he alone in that, too?

"I'm not that drunk," he said. "I'm not." *I shouldn't be babbling*. Only they would be able to talk him through it, whatever it was. When was the last time any of them had really been here face-to-face, with meaning? He couldn't remember, and hoped that it had happened at least once, at some point, and that he wasn't just imagining it all.

"Jello Joe!" he shouted. "Joey!" Others picked up on it, repeating his cry. "Jello Joe! Joey!" And farther on, like a wave at a baseball game going around the circuit, up to the cheap seats. "JelloJelloJellloooo!" Jazz sat in a chair cradling the seltzer, ran a hand over his face, and tried to shake away some of this goofy fugue.

When he looked up again Sheriff Hodges and Russell Stockton were standing in front of him totally drenched, their faces tight with fury and resentment.

"Oh damn," Jazz said. "Are you going to beat me up?"

The sheriff stared down at him, and it was all there written into the corrugation of his face: weary, crimson-eyed, and indignant. Enough to make Jazz perk up even more in his seat, like a school kid being called on to solve nasty algebraic equations. Hodges *always* had a mad-on, it was part of the fucker's charm, but tonight there was something different. A feral quality, definitive, and now *devoid* in the man.

Somebody shouted, "Happy New Year!" A

party favor flew by, and a cork from a champagne bottle shot into the wall. *No*, Jazz thought, his stare locked with the sheriff's. *No way, you bastard, you are not going to force me to think about her. I am not going to ever talk or dream or think about what I saw this afternoon hanging from the station ceiling, thank you very much. Not now, not ever again. Hey, hey, you got a question? Go ask Mattie.*

For all the mental bravado, his willpower couldn't constrain the flow of images now, so young and pretty and cut up like that with her organs piled beneath her. Somebody really had a ball doing that.

Corded muscles of Hodges's neck threatened to burst. "Metzner."

Jazz stood quickly and bowed. "I live only to serve."

"Where?" Hodges asked. He rubbed the tips of his fingers together like Doc Holliday warming up at the OK Corral.

"Where?" Jazz repeated. "Where what?"

"Where are they?" the sheriff said.

"Who they?"

"Them."

"Them who?"

Hodges grabbed him by the lapels and lifted him up onto his tippy-toes. Stunned, Jazz couldn't quite believe the amount of strength the man had, holding him like he weighed nothing.

"You know who!" Bloodshot glare burned up close, his wrinkled nose snarling and canines prepared to rip, ready to kill, lips skinned back. Jazz reacted the only way he knew how.

He spritzed the growling sheriff dead in the face with the seltzer.

Roaring, Hodges whirled like an enraged beast, as if he'd had acid thrown in his eyes. Russell just stood there completely dumb-founded for a second, scowling, now sneering, shaking his head, and his hand reaching for his cuffs.

Jazz fled down the corridor with the seltzer bottle held high before him like the winning football. He didn't have any idea just which "they" Hodges might have been referring to, and, *Heavens to Betsy*, he didn't ever want to know. There were too many theys and you-know-whos to worry about. How gauche for a cop to be so vague. He had to find his friends. *I'm dead I'm dead*.

They chased after him, the sheriff howling now and people laughing. The scene had to be pretty funny from the outside, but from here, from in here, Jazz knew the danger. He still re-membered enough football plays to let him weave through the crowd. Notes from a piano fluttered off in a direction he couldn't get a bead on. "Bosco Bob! Help!" There were no returning shouts of "I'll save you" from any cavalry, and Jazz just knew he was going to wind up in a road gang chained between guys named Bubba and Maurice.

Russell yelled, "Stop!" Women screamed now, amid the giggles. Jazz scooted down another flight of stairs and then up another, sprinting crazily. He tried doorknobs, but the rooms were locked. *Argh! They're getting laid, and I'm going to be sent to the Okeefenokee.* The crowd thinned down here, and he wasn't sure if that was good or not. The more blockers the better. *What did I do? I'm going to jail for the rest of my life, and all because that son of a bitch wanted me to think about that girl hanging like that . . .*

"No," he said. "Not now. Not ever."

"Huh?" some girl asked.

"Shh, baby, it's a dragnet. Say, you're kind of cute."

He ran down another hall and was about to clamber out a window, but at the last second something caught his attention and made him twirl and rush into an open room that seemed nebulously familiar. He shut the door behind him and leaned against it trying to barricade it with his own body. In the darkness he took in quick, short breaths, just waiting for the sheriff to shoot through the lock, come in, and shove a gun into Jazz's eye for no reason. Sweat dripped down his back, soaking his shirt and pooling beneath his ponytail. He reached into his jacket for a cigarette, only to remember he'd smoked the last one; immediately the craving intensified. *The things they'll do to me in jail*, he thought. *I'll have to give up my scrawny ass just to get a smoke.*

Turning, Jazz saw something out of the corner of his eye flicker by him in the dim reflection of the moonlit mirror. The wind pounded against the window, chopping at the latch, and it appeared that the trellis had yanked loose from the side of the house, or that somebody climbed it at this very second. There was a slight tickle in his throat.

The latch didn't give, but it certainly seemed to want to, as rain hammered the glass, panes quaking in their frames. He coughed into his fist but couldn't clear his throat.

"Hey," he said, and yet . . . no, wait, no, he hadn't said that at all.

He fell back a half-step and faced the door, felt the light switch pressing against the side of his face. It seemed easier to hit it with his nose. A lamp went on across the room.

The seltzer bottle dropped from his fist and rolled away. He wondered how he'd protect himself now.

He was still hunched over and staring at the wall. Fatigue swamped him. He grew too tired to move and couldn't help but think that if he passed out now, the scotch so good in his head, the sheriff really would kill him.

Gravity pulled. Heat filled his chest as though

he'd just had another couple of shots, and he couldn't figure out why it should be. He wanted a cigarette desperately.

The back of his neck itched. He couldn't keep himself from spitting now, his mouth flooding, as if watering from the thought of the cigarette, the scotch, the seltzer, whatever. Disgusting, he knew, but he had no choice. He hacked against the wall, and something dark ran.

Blood?

That couldn't be right. After a dazed moment he managed to drop his chin an inch to his chest and saw the blood gushing out onto the floor. *Holy God, hey hey, holy God, my throat's been cut, and I don't even feel it.*

Footsteps moved behind him in this moment of realization, but he was unable to turn his head, thinking that it would fall off. Delicately balanced, he stood with his brow resting on the wall in front of him, legs bent just so, useless arms dangling at his sides. He listened to the smooth *slup slup slup* of his life leaking away from him, painting the wall red.

In another three or four seconds he dropped over.

On his back now, Jazz stared at the ceiling, too weak to be frightened and almost thankful that the end hadn't come from cancer, the way it did for most of his family. A hand and a blade moved into his line of sight. So there it was, the weapon of choice. *No wonder it doesn't hurt, that damn thing is honed fine.*

This is just something else for me not to think about.

But he really couldn't help himself when he saw who it was that had murdered him.

Chapter Twenty-one

Lines crossing, spheres converging.

Music rolled from the vestibule. Every window blazed with light, drunken shadows, candelabra, and slow dancers touching. Maniacal laughter merged with guffaws and fluttery giggles. Laughter and songs dripped into the storm, out past the floods of moonlight spreading over the washed-out gardens. Trees at the north ridge of the estate recoiled in the wind, leaves rushing across the great lawns as if filled with purpose. Statues of water nymphs remained poised and aware in the night, rain running from their mouths.

You there?

A presence drawn back and stopped in

muddy tracks. A wary hesitation, stoic and suspicious delay.

More silent than silence, there were words without voice. *Yes*, Matthew said. *I'm taking the shortcut through Patterford's backyard.*

Coming to the party? Hell is already here. He seemed oddly jubilant, now that the endgame had finally started. *You can feel it.*

I'll be there in fifteen minutes. Wait for me. Don't go inside on your own. And tell me more about Richie Hastings.

Vibes rang through the cochlea of the inner ear, a mental sigh, stifled chagrin, or an exhalation of remorse. *I had no choice, the kid came onto the porch to collect for the goddamn gazette while I was using the bones to lock the caves up for good, and the Goat played into the irony, a paperboy meeting the paperboy, coming to collect. Get it? Some fun. Find the humor in it? Nothing to do, I had to connect the kid to me.*

You could have let him go afterward.

I wasn't sure of that. I'm not as adept as you, Mattie.

And you let them put you in Panecraft?

What difference did it make? Where else was I going to go? There's nowhere to hide, you know that better than anyone, damn you.

I do. But you should have told me what you were doing.

No, I don't trust you anymore. You're going to miss all the fun.

A shudder passed through him. *What can you see?*

I'm in the grove freezing my ass off. Big Bosco Bob playing the piano, a lot of people having a good time. There are so many of them, Jesus God, the whole town's been lured here. Jazz's father the hippity-hop king is going loopy on the piazza. I can feel the charge of evil.

Running through the rain in the shadows, swinging through the yards again. *Crappy wooden fence gave out under me. Gotta take a rest, can't catch my breath.*

You're out of shape. I can hear the scars. You've got four of them now.

Branches overhead scraped together like the swords of children playing King Arthur. *Who's the enemy, A.G., do you know?*

Biting the tongue, a break in the speech rhythms, the circles all jerking sideways now in so much feedback. *In this town, who can tell? Don't you think I've been trying to figure it out since you left? Ever since Ruth disappeared I've been waiting to get my hands around someone's throat, and I'll do it. We can't tell what's going on with them, to them, behind their doors, and behind their eyes. Do you have an idea how many of them have already been hexed? How many would be dead or insane already if not for me? For years I thought it had stopped, but you knew better, and that's why you ran, bastard. The Goat simply became more subtle.*

Keep your eyes open.
Shut up and hurry.

Matthew hurled pieces of the broken fence out of his way and kept going, running through the yards, repeating the actions of his childhood. He felt even more tense and ill than earlier, knowing the homes were empty, all the madness centered in one spot. He heard a chain clinking to his left and turned toward the sound; a Doberman's wet moonlit eyes warned him of its attack an instant before it came charging out of the doghouse, barking ferociously and galloping across the few feet of swampy grass between them. The Doberman lunged for his face, jaws snapping shut next to his ear. He barely completed a scrambling dive over some bushes before the dog's chain reached its full length and yanked the animal backward with a strangled yelp. Matthew's fists burned with arcana, glowing blackly in the night.

Garbage cans rattled and screeching cats leaped for gutters. Matthew came out at the mouth of an alley and ran up toward Bosco Bob's vast property, rubbing his shins and squinting in the downpour. He could hear the ocean. Broken tree limbs and dead leaves clogged the sewer grates and the whole road was flooded, surging waters rising over the curbs and enveloping the sidewalks. Spray blasted into his face and he could imagine himself at the seashore again, in the sand with Debbi, and in the middle of winter cuddling with Helen in his sleeping bag, defending his aspirations. *Who are the mad? Who's been murdered?* Driftwood floated by with rats clinging to it.

He wasn't certain he could trust A.G. anymore, either, especially with Ruth still missing. Possibly, she kept in hiding, perhaps her memories had returned and she knew what lay at the heart of their world. There was also the chance that she was the agent of the Goat, this enemy he'd been searching for—but in his heart he knew she was dead. Ruth already seemed dead to him, not enough of her left. She couldn't contribute any real performance in the final act of this play, nothing other than what she'd helped set free in the beginning, and what her blood would establish now. Had A.G. loved Ruth in that same curbing way Matthew had loved Helen? Matthew had still been able to walk away from his love. What had A.G. been able to do?

There was knowledge that could not be attained unless it met you part of the way; pain had come between them, and passion, and a great deal of hatred in the learning of these lessons. There was no telling just what games A.G. himself might be playing, whether he would run now that Matthew had returned to take up the mantle and bring it back where it belonged. What tricks and traps had he already set to snare, what tempest of revenge was he rightfully harboring?

But it had felt so good to talk with him again.

Floodwaters churned past Matthew, yanking at his legs, swirling and pulling him farther down the road. He splashed across the street, not feeling the cold anymore or noticing the chafing from his wet clothing.

Stone lions snarled and raised their paws to the sky. The walls and spear rails of the gates to Bosco Bob's estate stretched out before him.

Festivities.

The evil emanated, but not from merely the mansion anymore. Matthew wheeled as the hedges at the ends of the gate hung in the wind and battered his shoulders. He couldn't quite peg it, this electrical feeling of his enemy crawling on his flesh, through his head, inside his history and soul, making every inch of him sting.

A web of malignancy blanketed the area, now rising from the soil itself, as it always meant to do. It extended through the air, under his feet, wrapping him in a cocoon of the runecraft. He knew the bloated sac of disease in Panecraft, from the caves, was more free than before, coming for him now. Alone with him. *It's inside me*.

Chanting his personal catechisms, he bowed his head in the storm, beneath the weight of guilt and horror, clasping his hands tighter as they flamed within the darkness, his power great and his own rage even greater. He visualized his chest free of these burns, his conscience clear, his mother and father alive and happy again in the days they danced beneath the mistletoe. His fantasies flared.

He honed his illusions to sharpness . . . what it would be like to be a normal man, to have Helen in his arms, to have Debbi in his arms, to have anyone besides the Goat in his arms. A slithering of mutant chemicals in his brain. Desiring these dreams more than he desired his life.

There would be a choice to be made eventually, between these truths. He willed his thoughts to life until his gums began to bleed from the gritting of his teeth, lifelines of his palms writhing now upon his hands, changing . . . fingernails cut new paths and the blood could force a different course of events . . . crying though he didn't know it out in the rain, so focused now upon this fusion of past and present, lie and fact, that he could feel his consciousness shift along with this existence, if only he cared enough.

Enochian prayers gushed from him like his love and blood, invoking the Seraphim and begging, commanding, that his call be heeded, and finding a resistance even in himself. For an instant he was a different man who had never given up his life to his love, to this beast that lurked beside his love. And at the apex of his willpower and needs, his wants and hopes, his life and death, he threw a binding hex around himself in an attempt to confine the black sorcery and bottle the whirlwind harvest corrupting the town. Sparks skittered up and down the railings, arching and popping into the trees. Flames swirled against the pouring rain. The wrought-iron spears became red-hot, then white-hot, sizzling, steaming, and melting.

"I am Matthew Galen!" he screamed.

His words echoed, and thunder growled along with him.

Everything knew his name now, and in the name was torment and mastery. He pressed his hand against the gate and felt no pain. Sheet and ball lightning spun and waxed in front of him, welcoming him here as burning branches fell into the floodwaters.

Shielding his eyes, Matthew looked at the grove in the distance where A.G. had said he was waiting. There was nothing to see. He could barely make out the entrance to that circle of pine, the place where Bosco Bob had built a barbecue pit and cooked hot dogs and hamburgers every Fourth of July, Jelly Jane chasing Matthew into the woods. *Can't see you.*

Beneath the canopy trees. Can't see you either, where is all the energy coming from? You aren't insane enough to invoke the Seraphim?

It didn't work. The angels won't come.

No, that's what I meant, you can't be crazy

enough to think they would help you. They enjoy atrocities. They know your name now.

It doesn't matter. I need to speak to Helen and make sure she's safe. I'm going through the portico, you enter from the vestibule. Let's finish this, one way or the other.

It's going to be the other.

A psychic nod of assurance.

One more thing, Mattie. Distraction, another beat, and the stillness under the whistles and keening of the living wind. Now a different pressure throbbing in the cortex, jammed and heavy with mental reverb of long-controlled viciousness ungluing, even the psychic voice flat with self-righteous contempt. *Why?* Shivering in the cold, disconcerted face scrunched and his forehead furrow. *Why did you leave us?*

Fire consumed by the tempest, explosions of thunder stepping behind him like the feet of Christ. Insanity stroked his flesh, nuzzling and promising the love he had never found anywhere else.

Because I didn't want to end up like my mother.

Chapter Twenty-two

Diamond necklaces and glass beads glittered, faces and facets reflecting in his drenched hair. Matthew entered the crowd, this throng his only home now, more at home than ever before. The horde swallowed him, and didn't spit him back out despite his long absence. It laughed and drank and flirted and danced, visages familiar, most of them smiling, or eating or kissing. Fingers pointed, a few mouths lolled and gaped in surprise, one was vomiting into a garbage can in the corner. Some legs ran up to him, followed by dry-lipped smooches and innocuous questions. He offered no response.

Jello Joe pounced, his face red with the flush of recent sex. "Mattie!"

Heat and claustrophobia intensified, spells

weaving among them now from different stations. Matthew grabbed the arm Joe threw around him and stopped himself a moment before he broke it, realizing this was his friend— whatever might be at work upon Joey, this was his friend. They all were. His neighbors pressed closer.

"Sweet Jesus Christ, Mattie…you…you…!" Joe sputtered, dropped his stein of beer, and hugged him with such passion that Matthew couldn't fight the nausea that rose up his throat. One terrible sudden racking heave worked through him but came out sounding like a hiccup. "Son of a bitch! I don't know if I should bust your chops or kiss you!"

Jodi Carmichael's elfin features moved out from behind Jello Joe, and she said, "Give him another hug. You can always punch him out later."

Consenting with a smile, Jello Joe said, "Right you are, baby," and hugged Matthew again, then held him out at arm's length and planted a kiss on Matthew's forehead. Joe made a face, as if tasting the poisons in Galen's skin. "Un-fucking-believable, look at all these gray curls, what the hell has New York been doing to you? Being on Broadway is taking its toll, huh? C'mere, come over here and let me get you a drink. Hey, you need towel? You're dripping. Over there, get a towel. Talk to me, buddy, we've got a lot to catch up on. I want to know, Mattie, I want to know it all."

Matthew said, "Joe, have you seen Helen?"

Jello Joe waved a hand in the air. "She's here someplace, you've got to know that, everybody is here somewhere tonight. I think I saw her over by my dad a while back. Go on, get, it's okay if you've got to find her first, it's gonna be a long great night, it already is. I need to talk to you, though."

Jodi came over and kissed Matthew's cheek, her empathy endearing and powerful; she was special in ways he could put no name to, and he hoped they'd both survive the night. "Don't mind his antics, Matthew, he makes a good play at sounding sober, but believe me, he's sloshed out of his gourd, and he doesn't want you to leave either. He's been talking about you today, telling me about all the high school mischief the two of you used to get into. And how you wound up breaking your ankle on his head during your big ninety-nine-yard run. You were out of the house so fast this morning, I didn't even get a chance to say hello and make you feel welcomed back home."

"Thank you, I appreciate it," Matthew said, understanding that this too was truth. He trembled with anticipation as the maleficia glided over him like a dead snake skin returned to sheathe the snake.

There was the loud sound of popping, laugh-

ter, and applause when the cork from a bottle
of champagne ricocheted off the snout of a
roasted pig laid out on the banquet table. Other
corks rolled on the floor, kicked by dancers.

Your mother is dead, he could tell her, *and
your father sits with her, too frightened to let her
leave him.* "Sorry I can't talk more now, Jodi,
but I have to find Helen." He backtracked a few
steps and made to leave.

Jello Joe stooped in disbelief. "You don't want
talk to me?"

"It's not that, Joey, I just have to get to her—"

"I know what you have to do." Joe hung his
head, cheeks flushed with more than sex now,
the anger rising. "Run. Whether ninety-nine
yards or a thousand miles. Jesus, you never
stop, do you? Not even after all this time?" He
shifted his weight as though he was going to
throw a punch, deck Matthew, get the evening
really rolling, offended and furious. "Go on,
you. Keep on running. Shit. I was hoping we
could . . . that it might be like it was in the old
days. Even if only a little bit." The old days.
They'd passed by only a few years before. Impossible, so many lifetimes had passed. "My
fault."

"It's not like that, Joey, really, listen to me."
No, it wasn't, and there was no way to explain
what had truly transpired; how these friends
could possibly still save him, even while he continued to hurt and betray them.

Tom Piccirilli

"Some buddy! Running off for five years, Mattie, five fuckin' years, without a single postcard, you rotten son of a bitch, not one phone call! Nada. Why'd I think it might be different, now that you were back? Didn't the rest of us mean anything to you? Did you only come back to visit that psycho in the nuthouse?"

Jodi tried quieting him, saying, "Joey, shhh . . . shhh . . . it's the beer talking." She looked at Matthew with eyes filled with condolence.

"And now her, of course her," Joe ranted, "of course you've got to see your Helen now, after you trampled on her. It's called abandonment, what you did. She isn't going to forgive you, bastard, not like I was going to. And you proved me wrong."

Scratches of lightning brightened the room, engraving the black night sky. Afterimages cavorted. The crowd lurched away from the windows, sighing, cooing, like a one-celled creature slithering from an electrical prod.

Matthew had that double-edged sense again, as if he stood in two places at once, lived dual lives that had simply converged into nightmare, but might be pulled apart again into redemption. Those twin feelings, as experienced on his mother's grave, and when seeing A.G. and Charters and Jazz and the old house: half shame, half gratification.

Jodi stared down in embarrassment as Joe continued his tirade. Matthew's stomach plummeted when he saw the depth of these harbored feelings. Jello Joe began to weep. He said, "Joey, listen to me . . ."

"Get the hell out of here."

He shoved Matthew aside. Yanking Jodi's arm roughly, with a sobbed growl escaping him, Jello Joe pulled away. He stomped off, dragging her behind him, pressing rudely through a gaggle of elderly women swapping tales of angelic grandchildren, knowing nothing.

Shadows fell as walls grew bright, panes of glass glistening with rain and illumination. Matthew couldn't follow, but the urge was still there, like the tide of the washed-out streets tugging at him again. Freakish, high-pitched cackling made him turn and glared at Mrs. Farlessi, waving a chicken wing above her head, lying back and giggling in the arms of a man wearing thick glasses.

Witch work abounded, though none of the high holy days here except Samhain, All Hallows' Eve, came so close that it tempted and flirted like a brazen lover wanting your love and lust.

He scanned neighbors, trying to spot his enemy, knowing his foe's gaze was upon him in the mass, wondering what the next move would be. Blank eyes stared at him from every angle. This had become a cancer ward, and none of them were aware. Fever in him ran higher until he thought another spell had been cast, his skin still burning in that strange way, the Goat mouth chittering on his chest, babbling and ranting. He snatched a beer from the bar and drank it down without a breath, and chugged a second one, as well. What may have been swans hours ago had melted into grotesque hunch-backed iceworks of ghouls in which he saw scenes of depravity and torch-fire persecution of witches. Sweat rolled off his chin, and he wiped his sleeve against his eyes.

He realized how similar the mansion was to the asylum.

The migraine had grown much worse, voices of hell thickening in tone and timbre, sounding too much like his own thoughts. He walked out of the dining room, shrugging off old acquain-tances heaping praise and pecking at him like worm-starved ravens. He wandered into a corridor, feeling foolish and defenseless, mur-muring charms like lullabies, wards that meant nothing now but helped him feel calmer. *Cut me up all you want, I'm still going to stop you.* This peevish, glancing-over-the-shoulder crap got him nowhere. Too many people were dis-tracting him from what he had to do; they were a means to an end, all of them. Summerfell it-self had simply become a consequence of a war being waged forever.

Matthew tried to find an empty room where he might be able to meditate and track the vir-ulence. His scrying mirror had been shattered, but the shards still held enough power for him to glimpse unfolding events. The doors he tried were locked.

Jelly Jane's room was on the next floor, he remembered from back when she'd had a penchant for pink: pillows, curtains, teddy bears, china dolls, expensive fresh pink roses stuffed in crystal vases every day.

Crisp chords from the grand piano floated beside him like a living presence. Down the long corridor from her bedroom was Jello Joe's room, and the stairway to his left would take him out to other quarters, down to the garages and winding even farther to the wine cellars. He wondered where Helen, Jazz, and Jane were, and hoped the spells he cast would keep them safe here, as the beast coveted their town.

You in the ballroom? he asked, and after a lengthy pause called again, *Are you here?* No response from A.G. The headache interfered, and he couldn't be sure if he was in union anymore, or how far his voice might be heard, or even whom he was calling anymore. Did it even matter? A.G. might or might not be on the level, he couldn't tell anymore, and not having faith wasn't the worst of these sins on his hands now. *It ends tonight*. He took the cramped flight of stairs off to the cool majesty of the wine cellars. Maybe this would be it.

Slowly, one stair at a time, his descent fell into perfect alignment with some other descending. Vertigo and fearsome déjà vu sliced him into still more separate sections, one here and one somewhere else, some*when* else, some-*one* else. Collisions of past and present sent him reeling, so that he had to lean against the hand-rail for support, his mother so clearly in his mind that he could not free his vision from her. She walked at his side, so real he felt her breath. His footsteps sounded louder against the walls of his mind than the walls of this cellar. Debbi, too, with his father, wafted in and out of view. Only the dead would walk with him now.

There are minutes when you are out of contact with the rest of your world's movements.

His mother and father, the lighthouse, Pane-craft, this cancer spreading through the centuries but waiting to be unleashed by him, now come collecting.

In the air and . . . under his feet.

"The catacombs," he whispered, looking at the floor, with all the slain in the cellar with him now. "My God, how far do they go?"

And his head splintered with memories, the Goat's mouth hissing its unhuman knowledge, teaching him about the inferno.

At the bottom he swung, looked back up the stairwell, and saw Helen staring down at him.

Her turquoise eyes didn't share the weak humor of her thin smile. She flipped an auburn curl off her forehead and his entrails bucked: On another woman a move like that would have seemed an obvious sensual gambit for power, but he recalled how her bangs made her eyebrows itch. It had the same effect on him, a little thing like that making him sweat so much.

There was nothing obvious about Helen, despite his being so familiar with her. Years had refined and cultivated her teenage cuteness into beauty. She took a step down to him, her mouth moving silently as she struggled with what the first words would be.

A sort of erotic groan escaped her, and he took a deep breath. She looked at him to speak first, but must have realized from his awestruck face that he wouldn't be able to say or do anything again unless she helped him along.

"I saw you," she said. "People have been talking, and I wasn't sure if I should believe them, or whether it was true you were back. Bobbi May had me cornered in the dining room, telling me what a horror Jazz was, and then I watched you cross the room and slam a couple of beers back. You really needed that drink, didn't you? I followed you here."

She came down the stairs as slowly as he had.

"I needed to talk to you, Mattie, I . . ."

He saw the other man he dreamed he might be, taking her now with a sigh and a laugh, always laughing that one, to sweep her into his arms and cuddle her now as she stroked his cheek, and he swept her hair off her eyebrows. She might urge him to make love to her against the stone wall, lunging forward to mash her lips to his, stifling all complaints, promises, and pleas, though this other man with the other life would have nothing to complain, promise, or plead for.

She would giggle madly and he would laugh against her throat and bury his face in her breasts, and the wild passion would pluck their heartstrings to an even more wild tune. Her voice would not fade out with the other Matthew Galen, as it did now with him, bottom lip trembling until whatever stoic mask she wore crumbled in the cold reality of his presence.

With her eyes set that way she moaned once, from deep in her chest, and tears ran down her face. She kept her arms folded over her breasts to hold in the grief and anger, acting so much like she did in the shared nightmare where she cried in the snow before the whirling pages of the book of his life and death.

He couldn't take it anymore, and whispered, "Come here." She turned and turned again, as if to go back up, then wheeled and flew down the stairs.

He opened his arms to hold her to him, a sob breaking in his chest. "Helen . . ."

She kept coming at him until she was too close, drawing back but not fast enough as she hauled off and punched him in the face.

Then she viciously backhanded him.

She wound up her arm, hand hard as stone, and brought her fist to his chin again, then backhanded him once more until he took her wrists.

"Why?" she cried, breaking loose and clenching handfuls of his sweater. Red-faced, he held her as she furiously pounded her fists against his chest, sobbing as he stared off behind her.

Jesus, he'd gone so far into the fantasy it shocked him to rewind back into his own body, and know that none of that other man had ever been real. She cursed him until the fury seemed to burn out, and she weakened enough to slink forward into his arms.

He could do it now, live out part of the lie if he was a great enough failure, and he was. They might all die, but he had to press his mouth over hers and hold her as their tongues met and they had this moment. Their bodies swayed in the damp air, rocking back and forth as their passion resurrected itself from the dead past. Her thighs ground against his. He tasted her sanity, sweet and delicious. He pulled her backward, his fingers scrawling curing charges and sheltering stamps of the *agnus dei* upon her forehead.

They broke and gasped, both whispering. She still hated him and always would, and he murmured against her cheek and begged forgiveness in a child's voice he hadn't heard in decades. She said, "Your hair, it's so gray . . ."

"I love you," he told her.

From above came to the scream.

Screeches so full of blood lust, desperation, and despair that he didn't understand how a human throat could have held them. Startled, Helen moved closer as the shrieking continued, seething and agonized, echoing from far off, and now followed by other screams. She pulled from him.

The rest of the pieces of evil dropped into place.

With an almost sympathetic grimace he knew who it was who hated him enough to give the Goat more than its due.

"What the hell is that?" she asked, clutching his arm, realizing it had something to do with him, of course.

"Let's go."

"But what's happening? This is because of you, isn't it? Who is that?"

"I love you, Helen. Despite all that's happened, you have to believe that. I love you and always have."

She gave a sigh of exasperation. Words were easy, but real, and he knew she believed him. In one regard, that was all that mattered, and part of the battle had already been won. He felt the silver chord of her soul tighten further to him. *Thank God*.

She ran with him up the stairs. As they emerged into the banquet hall they witnessed their neighbors bursting open like the poked bellies of dead animals.

Hidden infection of insanity leaked out and seeped to the surface, gangrenous, leprous.

They performed the waltz as some of them yelled, chortled, and bubbled with glee, others eating food until awareness grew from within as much as without; arms and legs thrashed on their own accord as though tiny creatures hung inside muscle and ligament, testing each tissue. Severed souls, as other personalities stepped forward to claim what they'd been waiting for. All the Hydes emerged, smiles widening even greater than that of Mauels, all the infection rising like cream floating to the top. He'd seen them dance like this his entire life, in the halls of Panecraft. His mother had heard the music, and taught him the song.

Dementia remained the same here as it was behind the rows of cube windows, not so different from the rest of the turnings of the world, just kicked up a couple of notches. He understood why: The tunnels below the lighthouse extended farther than he'd thought possible, the catacombs trailing under the entire town, dozens of miles' worth of twisting, diseased veins spreading the arcane cancer from house to house like paperboys delivering the news. They'd had to stew in their own mad juices for more than a decade, unaware of any change, all of them too bent already to notice the difference. He recalled Cherry Laudley's baby, and the matronly voice on the other end of Judy Ann Culthbert's telephone, the look in the fish-boy Elemi's gruesome gaze.

"What's happening?" Helen moaned, trying to find her friends in these unrecognizable faces as they let loose with greater laugher and more shouting. "What's going on? What are they doing?"

"At last," he said. His redemption was at hand.

They drooled and babbled like infants, squealing and biting their own wrists, muscles locked like those of epileptics caught in seizure, but laughing too, having so much fun. They fell to the floors groping one another, some dropping to make a careful and precise kind of love, others masturbating and bleeding. They'd be going for the knives and forks next.

Not everyone, though: Some still hadn't been overtaken by the Goat, even after all these years. Thank God, he and A.G had actually managed to do some good, countering the hexes. Pregnant pauses bore the damned. It took only a minute.

Mr. Spinetti threw up when he saw Mrs. Needlebaum using a pair of cleavers to hack off her own drooping, wrinkled breasts. Helen gagged and wheeled, but Matthew yanked her close. Gigantor Davidson guffawed on the floor, his pants around his ankles—all of this so infantile when you thought about it, the devil took great pride in the adolescent and inane— fumbling at the empty spot of his crotch while the mewling Mrs. Farlessi snugly fit his castrated penis into her own ample cleavage.

Helen screamed, and he held her wrist tighter as she tried to make for the door, dry heaving in his arms. He wouldn't let her hand go the way he'd lost his grip on Debbi. Outside the tempest roared, sheet lightning slamming down like a guillotine time and again, shearing the grove.

"You think you know how to hate," Matthew whispered to the human agent who listened from afar. "Maybe, but not nearly as much as I do."

There were more ugly scenes, but he didn't linger on them: white, headless dervishes like nerve stems wrapped about his ankles, daemonic familiars that wagged their tongues at him, some form of hybrid djinn grown here in Summerfell instead of in the infernal hierarchies where they belonged. He blew them off with hexes flaming in his fists, hoisting guttural names and words of power. Helen jerked away, and he had to grab her by the hair to keep her from flailing into a murdered man. Buzzing green flies stuck to the contours of Frank Farlessi's face, eating his nose and lips off while he happily hummed the Our Father.

And it would get worse if he didn't move fast.

More symbolism had been made into truth, the same lack of subtlety turning lethal: Robbie

Landon had a three-pound leech draped around his neck—no, not around, but issuing from him like his bottled anguish—driven to hack Terry Mareco's head off with a butcher knife. Matthew caught Robbie's arm and brought his knee up into the guy's nose, even while his spells discharged across the room. He stuck his fingers down into the leech's back and watched it blacken and curl. Terry picked up the knife, gushing blood, and slashed at Matthew until he was forced to pop her shoulder out of the socket.

More entities from the other side emerged into the mansion, appearing like smears of blood across the living: Giles Corey, the only real witch of Salem, his body crushed by the rocks placed upon him by the judges, now holding fist-size stones and hobbling forward to smash in skulls; Father Urbain Grandier and Jeanne des Anges straying in together, his skin still bubbling from the flames of his enemies, clenching the rope about her neck and twining it tighter, tugging the Mother Superior behind him as she dropped to her knees and crawled behind him throughout their mutual, eternal damnation. She clambered to the table, filled her hands with ice water from the melted swans, and poured it over his charred face. Both of them turned their gazes upon the rest of the screaming room, their sorrowful smiles working into smirks, then leers, realizing that now they could share their vicious devotion with others. They stretched the rope out between them and began strangling women.

"No," Matthew said, reaching for the noose.

Emma Carmichael turned to face him, ice riming her wrinkles, opaque eyes as ugly as Joanne Sadler's as she approached from across the room, limping slowly but then faster, showing her teeth as her mouth widened, a clawlike finger outstretched to point and accuse him, coming for Matthew, who had found her body and shut the freezer door again.

And the maniac, Beast 666, Aleister Crowley, looking like he did more at the end than the beginning, in a stupor and swaggering drunkenly, naked with an erection. He scrambled atop Kathy Marinello, ripping out handfuls of her hair as he tore her panties away and guided himself into her. Matthew growled and kicked Crowley in the chin, relishing the contact between the soon-to-be-dead and the dead. He rushed forward and grabbed Crowley by the throat with one hand, clenching the back of the dead bald head with the other. He wondered if the Beast 666 was actually the reincarnate Eliphas Levy, if this foolish caricature before him was somehow truly the father of Baphomet. Someone in hell had carved swastikas into the jelly of his eyeballs, and ichor streamed from the ghost's face and ran onto Matthew's fists.

With a roar he flung Crowley aside.

Bosco Bob's piano playing continued, pounding out a sick and deranged song that everyone by now knew by heart.

"Stay close!" he ordered Helen.

She paled, her chest heaving in the throes of hyperventilation—all of this occurring in a few minutes, only seconds after seeing him again. She tried to run again, and he yanked her to his side again, hoping she wouldn't pass out. "What are you doing, Mattie?" she shouted. "Christ, your hands are on fire!"

Hysteria wasn't so much a mindless orgy as it was a well-performed melody, orchestrated by the conductor of daemons. Jeanne des Agnes tightened her own noose. Ballet became liquid, coordinated and exact, movements beautiful in their own revolting fashion.

"Don't move from my side. It'll be all right, I won't let anything happen to you, Helen."

"Oh God," Helen said. "Why did you come back to do this?"

He tugged her down the hall, muttering counterspells and defending her from whoever wandered into his path, whatever attacked. On the floor, in front of the fireplace, Jello Joe struggled with one of the Friedman twins, while her sister struck at him with one of his football trophies.

"Joey!"

The sister turned, hissed, and raised the trophy over her head to kill.

Matthew dodged and held the girl off, as she cocked her head and grinned in ecstasy. A scorpion with a lascivious smile crept from the trophy and stung his hand . . . twice, three times . . . until he could hear its mind plainly in his blood. The *Baal-birth*, it called itself, infecting him. It giggled and uttered, *You're mine, Mage*, before he could crush it in his burning fist. The third stab had left the stinger embedded between his thumb and index finger, and from that source he found the daemon's circle, a lower-caste beast without much real power.

Jello Joe kicked the feet out from under the Friedman twin he still wrestled and sucker-punched her as she sat up. She twisted once more and continued to club at him, but he caught most of the blows on his arms.

Helen said, "You," and struck the girl on the shoulder. When the Friedman girl spun, Helen drove a fist into her stomach, brought the butt of her palm up under her nose, and dropped her.

Dazed, Jello Joe looked at Helen. "Rape defense course," she said, wiping tears from the corners of her eyes.

"I'll bet," Jello Joe said. "Thanks."

Matthew wondered how insane Joey might be, and as the awful infirmity hit he managed to inscribe a partial sigil in front of his friend. Pain flowed up his arm.

"What in the deepshit is happening, Mattie?"

Helen said, "Can't you tell us?"

A stab of agony hit his belly. Doubled over and gripping his stomach, Matthew fought off the shock of Baal-birth's stings. The scars vividly described all of Helen's sexual encounters in his wake, all the men who'd loved her. His skin grew ashen, turning splotchy for a moment, as he dropped to his knees. His bones creaked as he collapsed, elbows and knees thick with arthritis, his body so slow he already felt like a corpse, as Joe and Helen stooped beside him.

He wouldn't speak the name of God; Baal-birth could hurt him but not damn him, and the Goat would rest with nothing but completion. Carefully, even as his jaw went numb, Matthew pronounced the nineteen keys of Enochian magik—speeding his pulse and driving the stinger up out of his hand with a loud splash. He rolled onto his back, and Helen took his head in her lap and tried to lift him by the shoulders.

"I'll be okay," he said.

Jello Joe punted more of the filament, nerve-stem djinn hybrids into the fireplace, where they burned. Real djinn had been created in fire before the creation of Adam; his foe had been experimental and brilliant but hadn't proved infallible. Matthew gasped for air, his breathing returning to normal and blotches fading.

He stood, and Helen fell against him, and they both nearly went over. "We've got to get out of here," she said. "It's awful outside, but we can make it, I think. They're out on the lawns, the storm is right above us, but come on, we can make it."

"No," he said, "not yet."

"What's happening outside?" Joe asked. "Where's Jodi? And my sister, and my dad? Where's Jazz?"

"I haven't seen any of them," Helen said.

"Hallucinogens," Jello Joe said, in shock. "We've all gone fuckin' nuts, no other way to think through this, nothing else it can be. I've got to find them. Go get some help!"

Before Matthew could stop him Joe ran off, hurling bodies out of his way.

"We've got to leave!" Helen shouted.

"It's even more dangerous outside, Helen."

"It can't be!"

Matthew dragged her up the stairway, tossing hexes when he had to, wondering where A.G was and whether another disaster loomed ahead. Blood spattered the walls, never dripping naturally, but forming phrases from the *Goetica* and the black grimoires, painting faces from Hell. Someone had nailed Winnie Sackett to the banister by her lower lip. Frank Farlessi, without much of a face, was too busy humping her to care about the ravens tearing at the side of his head, eating at the maggots. Winnie thrashed, eyes wide with terror, mumbling and pleading with Farlessi right up to the moment that he orgasmed, already brain-dead, wrenching her hips in some expired ecstasy as he fell backward, a happy vegetable. Her lip stretched until snapping, leaving her with only the grinning lower half of a skeleton's shrieking smile. She crumpled to the carpet semiconscious. The scene grew worse yet even more ridiculous, as disgusting as it was horribly misplaced here at the end of their battle, the Goat without enough respect for him to even keep it at some level of esteem. A decapitated head with a large section of clavicle still affixed bounced down the steps and landed in the crook of Farlessi's arm.

Helen puked over the banister. When she'd finished she wiped her mouth and said, "That was Paul. Boswell. My next-door neighbor."

"I know."

"Why is this happening? *What did you do?*"

"I'm sorry, Helen." He couldn't keep the whine out of his voice.

"You're sorry, is that what you said, you son of a bitch? You're what!"

Because of me, he thought, *because of my hate and love*.

"What are you looking for, Mattie?" she asked. "How are we going to get out of here alive?" She sobbed faintly, stern, more composed now, everything having already become second nature for her, as it did for him back then when he'd begun on this path. "Your hands."

And he saw it.

There.

At the end of the hall.

The room as he remembered.

He tugged her to him and tried the doorknob. It was unlocked and turned too easily in his hand. He gritted his teeth as all the stenches of lust and betrayal drifted so strongly from inside. "In here," he said.

He opened the door.

To see Jelly Jane on the bed.

"Well, well," she told him, stretched in a nice pose. "About time you got here. I've been waiting a long time for you, Mattie."

She'd lost all the weight, every bit of fat, and you could see what it had cost her, and that she didn't care.

Now reclining against the same pink pillows he remembered, laying herself out before him like a porno movie starlet ready for bad behavior at the urging of her director. Dressed in tight black leather and crimson lipstick, she was radiant in a way he could have acknowledged but never fully believed. Depression must have driven her to this, but hadn't drained the life from her—instead, she'd been vitalized, given new hope. This would be her gift. How long ago had she lost the weight, when did she follow his left-hand path into the bookshops of Gallows and the dustiest shelves of the library? *Six months ago*, he thought, *right after she killed*

Ruth and started to feel her way back toward Matthew.

On her night table were the *Divine Pymander*, *The Hermetica*, and the *Emerald Tablet*, books that had become a part of him, and now Janey as well. Their sweat, stink, and souls had been absorbed into the passages. She had drawn him from the pages.

At her feet, Jazz lay dead on the floor with his throat cut, a lurid smile sealed to his face.

"No," Matthew whimpered, "no, not you, Jazz."

Helen said, "Jesus, oh Jesus, isn't it going to end?"

Jelly Jane licked the tip of her pinkie and moistened her lips with it.

She said, "So?"

And that truly was the question.

So now what? Where do we progress from here, as his foe rested before him, so steeped in hatred and unrequited love that he could still see the gross pain heaving in her heart. His every movement had been caught under her watchful eye, since they were teenagers and he'd shoved her into the buffalo wing dip. She'd become a part of him, he'd been so blind not to see it, how he'd shackled her and dragged her into the black evil of his life.

"Janey." This luscious creature, this poor girl. She was quite possibly stronger than he. Perhaps the lessons had gone by more quickly with the Goat's help, with its promises and prices, and payments demanded. "You killed Jasper for this?" he asked, but couldn't be sure if she heard. She purred on the bed, a kind of chuckling, maybe. She'd learned, and in learning she'd discovered that sometimes life tasted better with bloodletting.

He almost apologized. He almost begged for forgiveness, as he wanted to beg them all. But Jazz on the floor, even with the grin, forbid that.

In the catacombs, the Goat trudged beneath them all.

Singing its enticing songs, waiting for someone else who'd heard the call to come and make friends. Jelly Jane had listened and met true love at last, for the Goat was nothing if not loving in its corruption and depravity. She'd most likely killed Ruth after forcing her to tell about what had happened in the caves when Debbi disappeared, plucking the memories from her mind, digging them out with a witch's blade. She's prayed to the Goat and offered up the sacrifices of the missing kids, of course, a nice setup, here in a mansion where you could hide yourself away and no one would even come looking, much less find you, in its recesses. She'd kept them alive for how long here? . . . Weeks, months . . . drawing the circles in their fluids and experimenting with different prayers, and ways to feed flesh to daemons. . . .

Jello Joe and Jodi ran into the room, both of

them bruised, Jodi near collapse. "Sis," Joey said, "thank God you're all right, I thought you might be . . . I . . ." He let the sentence trail when he saw Jazz's body. "Oh shit, no, Jasper . . ."

Licking her lips now, as obvious in her intent as the devil, Jane got off the bed and smoothly stepped over Jazz—how long she must've dreamed of this moment, this final unveiling of strength and purpose—pulled back the drapes of the window, and stared out at the thrashing, hideous night.

Matthew moved, threw a shoulder into what had once been a flabby stomach. It didn't work; she didn't back up an inch. Jelly Jane tossed him backward with a tremendous spell, and pulled the *athame*, the witch's blade that she'd used to cut Jazz's throat, from the back of her skirt.

Jello Joe cried out, "Stop!" and dove onto Matthew's back, and then the others were screaming more, the hallway filling with whoever had survived, drifting into the doorway. Helen pulled at Joe, and Jodi yanked at Helen, the four of them fighting like this for all the same, but wrong, reasons.

Matthew heard the spells in Jane's voice, but she didn't seem to be saying anything as he pulled her to him and—knowing it was the right thing, the only thing, here among all his own sins—wrapped her in his arms and kissed her with all the tenderness he felt for the fat Jelly Jane, his friend, but had never been able to express, having driven her to this. She whined then, but not nearly as loud as his father's weeping in his mind, as he shrugged Joey off his back and took the *athame* from her strong, slender hand. She kissed him again, as he wept for the girl he'd destroyed, the knife ready to plunge into her heart if that's what he had to do.

"Jane, oh God, where's the Goat? Tell me. Answer me. *Where is my mother?*"

Chapter Twenty-three

Debbi had tripped, or been pushed, into the darkness, away from him. He heard her breath knocked from her as she hit the ground, an audible *whuff* as she hit the dirt.

"Hey, Deb, come on, knock it off," A.G. yelled, swinging the lantern in her direction, the beam slashing into the miasma of black flowing through the cave.

She was coughing.

Spitting, and trying to say his name. "Mah . . . ? . . . mah . . . ?"

When the light finally struck her it ignited the red spittle strings hanging off her chin. All around them, on the ground, her blood began filling the marble canals chiseled into the cave floor, the Goat's face painted over the carved pentagram.

Ruth shrieked.

Debbi weakly touched his ankle, and he flinched from her hand, too stunned to do anything else. Her crimson mouth dribbled, the stalagmite lifting the back of her dress like a tent, but it hadn't torn through yet. She blinked and tried to speak, tears rolling down her cheeks, in agony. "Maa . . . ath . . . ewww . . . ?"

The altar began to glow.

A.G. and Ruth both screamed for more than their lives, running down the tunnels lost without any sense of direction, now heading the wrong way, searching for the stone stairway that led back up into the lighthouse, where he had brought them.

Debbi clung to the cuff of his pants, stroking his ankle with feeble back-and-forth motions, eyes pleading with him to help her, his love, to do something, but he could only watch the syrupy blood dripping off her braces and trickling from her nose outside the tracks. No time for it to well or pool beneath her as her fluid was siphoned into the trenches, flowing down the rock.

Her tented dress ripped apart and she groaned as her body roughly slipped another inch down the sharp stalagmite, ripping open the rest of her stomach. The pretty dress tore in half and he saw the rock gouging her body, viscera sticking to the tip of the point. Her finger-nails caught in his sneaker laces.

The catacombs echoed with the cries of A.G and Ruth, footsteps stumbling for the stairs. An insane animal laughter rose from the edges of the altar.

He clamped his teeth together in case it was coming from him. It wasn't. And it was. He felt a certain recognition ringing within him, a re-turning to place, a comfortable familiarity in the moment. The altar brightened. Debbi kept her eyes on his, pinning him to the pentagram he stood over, his feet on either side of the stone channel running with her blood. They were both in the center of the Goat's face, her red liquid streaming in little rivers along the outline of the five-pointed star. The Goat grinned at him, and it was a smile he knew.

When at last her hand fell away from his foot and the wet red lines met, Debbi was dead.

(Debbi was dead.)

But her eyes pursued him still.

A blast of force, a whirlwind of pain, mad-ness, and malevolent joy reached from the altar and broadsided his soul, slamming him back-ward in a wash of malignant energy, where he struck the wall and crumpled facedown in her gore. The rumbling of the ocean beat into his ears. His shirt burned, on fire, and his chest siz-zled.

He listened to the laughter.

Through his slit eyes he watched a blurry white motion coming closer to him and easing down to his side.

Something bent and kissed his face.

He opened his eyes and saw his dead mother's deformed and decomposing body recede into shadow.

Through his tears he understood the meaning of evil, the love that it makes its own.

But he soon forgot.

Chapter Twenty-four

His senses slipped.

Like a black box closing, everything folded from him except Jane's face, the lovely tanned skin, those tempting, thirsty lips. No sounds for an instant.

Her eyes rolled back into her head, and he looked and saw that his hand had found her throat and he was throttling her, though she smiled. Her witching reached out for him like a spouse returning. They were two of a kind amid a town that couldn't contain all that they were. With a jarring sensation Matthew realized that Jane was now the only woman who could ever understand what he truly was, the extent of knowledge in his possession. She knew what fueled him, and they were inextricably bound.

He drew away jerkily, releasing his grip on her throat. Without malice, her erotic eyes acknowledged and pinned him. Sexed, his hands moved on their own, traveling gently down her neck to where he laid his palms over her large, firm breasts and squeezed as she sighed in his grip. She writhed beneath him and shoved herself out forward to meet his touch, whipping her black tresses over his skin.

Heat that had remained bottled inside her escaped and licked against him. Matthew felt the tightly muscled belly and smiled as Janey raised her chin up to longingly kiss him, and he lowered himself to meet her lips. It took only a moment. *My God, she's got me in her power, and I know and love it. She's so much like me, all devotion and scorn.* Perfect, more perfect than any woman he'd ever seen, and she wanted him. She was so incredibly enticing. And then, through these crazy thoughts, he saw how easily she was *bending* him. Matthew grappled and threw his arm across his eyes, thrusting from her, as she reached for his crotch again.

"You know I'm the only one who can give you what you need," she said.

"It doesn't matter." The smell of Jazz's blood made him gag. He leaned over and grabbed Jane by the throat again, and raised the crusty blade to her carotid. "She's in the basement, isn't she? Show me how to get there."

The others in the room, like those in the hallway, now snapped to attention, and Jello Joe dove onto his back trying to get him into a headlock. Matthew shrugged him off and threw him against the headboard. "Enough, Joey."

Matthew knew there wasn't enough time for any vengeance of this kind. Both of them shaking, he and Jane sneered at each other, aware of what ran beneath their skin, in back of their eyes. She pouted and blew him a kiss. If he lived through the night perhaps he would return and kill her, perhaps make his love to her the right way this time. But for now he needed to get into the basement, find the Goat, and stop the paincraft before it grew too late to save anyone still left.

On the floor, aroused and gasping, Jane laughed grimly and said, "I'll punish you, Helen." The words came out as an afterthought, shocking Matthew that Janey hadn't killed Helen instead of Ruth, torturing his love in lieu of himself.

Joe dropped to his knees beside his sister, eyes glazing with astonishment. "Janey . . . ? What in the hell are you doing? What's this all about? Has everybody gone insane?"

Helen flung Jodi Carmichael aside, this fight over with, though they were all still holding on. She ran to Jazz's body and held her hand over her mouth as she tried to do something, looking here and there, and knowing it was all too late. She stared at Matthew. "You were kissing her?"

"No," he said. "This has all been a lie, this entire night." He shot Joe a glance that left his friend openmouthed, Jello Joe putting his arms around his sister while Jodi sank to the floor and wept beside him. "Lock the door behind us, Joey," Matthew said. "You hear me? Keep the door shut. It's all going to come together now, it'll be all right in the morning." Joe nodded absently.

Matthew drew Jane's *athame* across his thumb, his blood welling against the edge of the blade. He leaned over her and let the binding spells come to him now, as his knowledge of her increased, his blood seeking out her name in the knife. "Your name is mine now, and I bind you with it. You're going to go to sleep now, Janey."

"You're a vain bastard, Galen." She wriggled, excited, still so hot. "You don't have the strength tonight, Mattie. Come back to bed."

"The Goat's played you for a fool, too, Jane. You're not in control either." He drove the heel of his palm against her jaw and felt teeth break. Joe cried out but didn't move, just kept cradling her. She moaned once, her body contorting for another moment before she passed out, straining against the leather.

Jodi crawled, crying hysterically, and Joe

hugged her with one arm, holding Jane in the other, keeping their faces turned from the blood.

"I should kill you, Mattie," Jello Joe said. "Whatever's happening, I know it's because of you."

"Remember that I love you, Joey," Matthew said. He held his hand to Helen, thinking she would not approach him, that if she understood anything it would be that she should stay away from him. But reluctantly, languorously, swaying as if slow dancing now, she moved to him, took his hand, and led him out of the room. The neighbors, hollow-eyed and so pale that some of them might be dead, let them into the hall.

"What were you saying about your mother?" Helen asked, no more whimpering, already accustomed. "You know what this is. Tell me. About your hands, about all of . . . this." She gestured to those torturing themselves in the other rooms. Jazz's father, the hippity-hop king, hippitied on top of Mr. Dobson's corpse, unaware that his dead son lay only feet from him, unaware that the man he danced on was still laughing, but without a soul, all of them nothing more than the pulp of men.

"It's an infection. One that's been in remission for years but started growing again, and only I can stop it."

"That scorpion talked, the cats, and . . . what,

nerve gas, something your father did in the asylum?"

A good guess, maybe she would go for it for now. "Yes. A strain of virus."

"What are we going to do?"

"We've got to get back down to the cellar."

"Why?"

"The disease is centered under the house at the moment."

"How? In canisters?"

"Yes," Matthew answered.

He heard a gunshot as they cut through the hallways, watching the rest of the crowd still playing out this sabbat, wild in the moonlight and lightning flashes, the doors open so that the rain and storm was let in to thrash against their skin, Lucifer here among them.

She tugged his hand and he felt his wards snap, one by one, as their sweaty hands made it tougher to hold on to her. He lost his grip and she whispered, "Glorious." Helen tried to scramble away and join in with the hysteria, eyes glazed, the wanton smile affixed. He wasted what power he had left in order to reattach the protection spell. She collapsed in his arms at the top of the wine cellar's stairs, and he bit his tongue in frustration.

His name sought him out.

"Galen" came from behind him, hushed and guttural, seeking an end.

Sheriff Hodges stood in the doorway heaving

for breath, battered and bleeding with a silver knife handle protruding from his upper thigh. His face was so ferociously contorted that he didn't even look like a middle-aged man anymore. He became a wood carving that had had too much splintered from it. "This is your fault, Galen, I know." His revolver smoked, and at his feet lay the naked, quivering body of the half-faced Winnie Sacket, her lipless mouth gnawing on his boot.

Without moving his gaze from Matthew, Hodges kicked Winnie away and took two limping steps forward.

He grasped the handle and tugged the knife out of his leg with one steady, gruesome pull. There was no more room for pain in his snarl. "Your fault," the sheriff repeated, as right as he'd ever been about anything in his entire life. "I know it." He pointed the gun at Matthew's head, but it was apparent that Hodges would rather skewer him with the knife. Silver, the witch's bane. Hodges grinned.

With one swift, precisely executed movement, Roger Wakowski appeared from someplace he hadn't been an instant before and broke the sheriff's elbow. Hodges went down on his bad leg and, still gripping the silver handle, thrust the knife out in front of him, slashing at Wakowski's abdomen. Wakowski dodged and brought his fist down on the sheriff's shoulder and, loudly and neatly, broke that, too. Hodges floundered for a moment and dropped onto his belly beside Winnie, still conscious, his lips puckered against the agony, licking the floor.

Wakowski looked past Matthew, staring down into the cellar. "It's down there, isn't it?"

"Yes, right now," Matthew said. "Did you feel it at the hospital?"

"I did."

Wakowski didn't even care, Matthew could see that in his eyes; more accurately, he cared as much about this as anything else, with no real questions, curiosity, or fear. There was also no remorse for anything he'd done or seen done tonight. The fever couldn't break him because he'd lived through it before, adapted as he had to, and would live through it again. "You're lucky," Matthew told him.

"No," Wakowski said, even his voice cut from stone. "But I'm alive, and I still will be even after this is over."

"I'm not so sure about me."

"Go on. I can't help you with whatever's down there. Give me your girl. I'll keep her safe and try to save as many of them as I can. Do what you have to do."

Matthew placed Helen in Wakowski's arms as she slept. He kissed her brow, and Wakowski nestled her and tenderly carried her off, without worry, into the maelstrom.

Matthew's scars told him to *come home, come home, come home*.

He would do what he had to do.

*   *   *

Hodges had screamed it at him back in the abandoned train station. *You're going into the ground!* Another prophecy fulfilled. Matthew rushed to the cellar and tossed hexes against each of the four walls, his will as much a part of the arcana as his past, as his memories. The north wall burst apart in a cloud of brittle brick and dust, to reveal the mouth of a tunnel leading into the rest of the caves and catacombs.

"Mother!"

Of course he knew the Goat.

This counterpart risen from whatever circle of Hell it had come from was not his mother, but the Goat had raised him into this life as surely as any parent. His mom was more of a beautiful myth than a woman who had changed his diapers and danced with his father. The crackling sheen of fiery sigils wafted from his hands and lit these tunnels. He called out for her again.

The Goat's mouth whispered to him, marks of the Beast chattering and pulsing in his own flesh.

Matthew ran through the catacombs, following the directions that the scars gave him. He passed by the area he thought should be directly under the grove; stopping and looking above, he saw rivulets of rainwater sluicing down from a muddy hole at the top of the cave wall.

He kept running, feeling lighter as he came

closer to his assertions and his acceptance.

Soon the walls vibrated with the thrashing of the ocean, as he stumbled, gasping. Sweat stung his eyes, but he put the miles behind him. He turned through the catacombs the way his scars told him to go.

Leading him back to where it all began.

He needed to see Debbi again so much. Though A.G. had taken her bones in an effort to relock the Beast in the earth, her soul would still be there where her gore had set the evil free.

Soon he came to the altar, these same carved tracks ready to be filled with more blood.

His hands lit the cavern so much more than A.G.'s lantern had done those years before.

He saw.

His mother.

Sitting on the altar before him, within the magik circles of the painted Baphomet. The dress she'd been buried in had been nothing but a rag to begin with, and had become even more tattered after all this time. Matthew was stunned to see that the Goat had bothered to keep it on.

The face he'd loved was long gone, shredded worse than the dress, more mutilated than the first time he'd seen her in the cave, leaning over him to peck his cheek. Only a skull with scraps of dried flesh stuck to it, a parody of her beauty, cheekbones without much by way of cheeks. Some scraggly clumps of her hair remained attached in uglý weavings, cut to prepare knotted cords in order to perform greater rituals of maleficia. He couldn't tell if she had eyes, but a piercing stare emptied out from the depths of her head. Her mouth was black and grisly.

The rock on the ground where Debbi had died remained an icon to torment and betrayal.

A.G. had never made it inside to Bosco Bob's party.

She cradled him in her arms. A.G. slumped, covered with dirt and blood from where he'd fought her as she'd sucked him down through the muddy hole in the grove. He lay across her lap like some godforsaken version of *La Pietà*, Mother Mary cradling the dead body of Christ.

"There's no need to kill him," Matthew said. "I'm here now, Mother."

She dumped A.G. off her lap, and he struck the cave floor with a thud.

Matthew pointed, and she did her best to smile animatedly, so alive, and even lovely, in its own way. Her mouth didn't work so well anymore. "You're the same as anyone else," Matthew said. "You got greedy. The more you had the more you wanted, isn't that the way of it? Just another simple human trait."

The Goat nodded happily. His scars chanted, *yes yes yes*.

"My mother and father weren't good enough for you. Debbi wasn't enough. The bits and pieces you nibbled from town only whetted your hunger for more. Janey and those kids couldn't satisfy you, no, you had to have everybody, and failing that, you still want more."

Her eyeless glare glistened.

"She was special, my mother. Even down here in this darkness you felt her above, like a love that could threaten your possessions. Maybe whatever it was that made her so special is what woke you from your stupor."

Yes, yes, yes.

"You started to feed on her, little by little, saturating her with your cancer. Killing wasn't good enough, you even had to take her body from the nameless grave. The humiliation made you stronger, but believe me, it didn't hurt her. This doesn't hurt my mother."

Skin like parchment fell from its face.

"My father knew it in his fashion, knew that my mother walked, that the insanity you plagued her with wasn't a natural one, or else he would have cured her. Debbi's blood made you stronger, too."

Now, the ultimate truth. Could he face it?

Within him, this tumor of reality, shifting as he dug for it, not wanting it to be real. He could fantasize forever, live out a dozen more false lives if need be, or come back to where his love resided, surrounded by seashells on the beach.

"I pushed her for you."

The echoes of the ocean rumbled through the cavern like laughter.

"That night when I found my father drunk, I discovered my mother's grave and went to it, dug it up with my own hands to see if I was right, if what I remembered was true—that you'd taken her, too." He glanced down at his palms, covered with the black flame of hexes.

"You waited for me to return, shaping events to bring me home again, and when the last point of the inverted pentagram is filled, my soul will seep out and you'll take over this witch's shell, and be a thousand times more powerful on earth."

The body of his mother held its hands out to him, clacking its teeth together.

Matthew approached the altar, and his mother opened her arms to embrace him. He bent from her and grabbed A.G.'s wrists, dragging him from the circle. "Wake up," he said. "C'mon, man, you've got to get the hell out of here." The Goat talked to him through his chest. "Shut up! Let him go, it doesn't matter now, nothing matters now that we're back together again."

Yes yes yes.

A.G.'s eyes fluttered open and focused.

"You've got to get out of here now," Matthew said. His scars made kissing noises, loving A.G. nearly as much as they did him.

· A.G. swallowed and said, "You're coming with me."

"Later."

"No." He wavered and held on to Matthew. He wiped mud off his face, cleared his mouth. "I know that tone of your voice. You never made it out of here with me the first time. You're going to give the Beast what it wants?"

I've been dead all these years anyway, ever since that first blast of arcana threw me back against the cave wall. The stone is cracked, I couldn't have lived through that, every bone would have been broken. It's the cancer inside, that's what's been keeping me alive.

"We can beat it," A.G. said.

Yes, I can, I can destroy the Goat, but only if you leave me alone with my mother.

"No."

A.G. began to weep now, all of these missed emotions welling at such a wrong time and place, but also the only time it's ever completely mattered. *I love you, man. Tell Helen how much I—*

"I know. I will."

They hugged each other, and A.G. spun and spat at the Goat, then turned and ran up the stone stairs that had brought them down to this level in the first place, going back up into the lighthouse, the only survivor.

Matthew took off his sweater. "Let's get this over with."

His mother reached out and tapped the un-scarred portion of his chest.

The fifth point.

A triangle.

Three lines to fill out the pentagram.

She drew her shard of a fingernail through his flesh, as he groaned beneath her touch again, stealing the fever and fatigue from him now, the juice that he'd been living on. She carved in the second line, and his blood pumped from the wounds congealing and drying into powder.

The last stroke proved the easiest, his skin as thin as communion wafer by then. When the Goat finished this new baptism his mother's body pitched forward onto him, released at last.

"Rest," he told her.

He stared at the stalagmite and whispered God's name.

Matthew positioned himself as best he could. He felt the hot wind brush against him just before the final segment of his soul was ripped from him, and he was thrown back up against the cave wall the same as before.

As his consciousness heaved, he felt himself splitting again, becoming, at long last, the other Matthew Galen, on the beach with Debbi and staring at the lighthouse, as he took her hand and led him from that place and said, "Come on, Deb, let's go swim," and she assented with a grin.

He was alive.

* * *

The deafening sound of stone cracking, these moments sometimes planned, sometimes not, but he had hoped.

The Goat stood inside its son's body.

The inverted pentagram flamed on its chest, blue and red fire swimming in skin.

Its eyes had turned crimson, and it smiled, waving blazing configurations of doom before its face now, rearing back and howling laughter that was a second reborn but screamed the agony of millennia.

"I . . ." the Goat said.

The cave wall cracked open where Matthew's body had struck it twice in the course of his life and death, and a billion gallons of ocean roared in.

The tremendous waves lifted the Goat up, and for all it had sown, it hadn't reaped enough understanding to know that it stood where Matthew had trapped it, directly in front of the stalagmite that had murdered his love.

The surging curl of the first massive swell swung Matthew Galen's body down with immense power, plunging it onto the point of the rock where he'd killed Debbi, tearing away the lungs and scarred chest before the Beast that was only itself could complete its first selfish breath.

Chapter Twenty-five

The end came mercifully quick.

Nearly everyone who lived through the night stayed in town despite the horror. Wakowski had done an impressive job of saving these people. Out of almost a thousand neighbors, more than six hundred lived through Bosco Bob's party as the paincraft came to a close in the tempest. Maimed and blind and shattered and alone, they still managed to live.

Roger had personally broken forty-three jaws, yanked a bucketful of nails from seventeen of the crucified, placed tourniquets on the amputated, cauterized slit arteries. Of the six hundred less than a third were immediately placed in Panecraft. Dr. Patterford was promoted to the status of head director of the mental facility, but soon after was replaced by Doctor Moser when Patterford barricaded himself in the girls' lavatory of the Gallows elementary school, holding a shotgun and three children hostage, and it took three hours for the SWAT team to shoot him in the head.

Anyone who hadn't attended the party realized their good fortune and decided not to push their luck. They moved, all of them, even if only to the next county. Bosco Bob's mansion took no worse a beating than did Bosco Bob, who had played piano throughout the night while the town died around him and the sea ran under him. He had only nicks and bruises, but all of his fingers were broken from playing so long and so hard. He would never play again.

The next-to-worst part of it all—so it seemed to him—was that he was a good man who would never understand how these atrocities had decided to use him as benefactor; the seventeen private detectives he hired to discover the reason returned without answers.

The worst part was that his daughter had disappeared.

One detective had phoned to say he was close to Jane and would call back later with more information.

He'd been found with his kidneys compacted into his nostrils, no other part of him touched.

Neither Joe nor Jodi Carmichael could think about the events of the party much, even when they were married and moved to Hawaii, without nightmare or delirium of fevers, never tormented—they were a happy couple, proving the resilience of well-placed ardor.

On the beach at night, after the storm, Helen and A.G. and Wakowski stood on the shore and watched the lighthouse being swallowed by the ocean as the cliffs rumbled all night long and crashed into the waves. Like the Leaning Tower of Pisa it tilted only slightly at first, then gradually more and more and the ocean rushed through the tunnels under Summerfell. Before dawn the catwalks had fallen, and a little after sunrise the entire structure crumbled. A.G. threw stones into the water. Helen sat in the sand, crying, watching the seagulls. Wakowski sat beside her, holding a bullet in his left hand, a periwinkle in his right.

After a few minutes he threw them both high in the air. A seagull dipped, searching for food, and dove. It caught something in its beak. Wakowski wasn't sure if it had been the bullet or the shell. He didn't care enough to let it bother him.

Helen and A.G. often came back in the following months after Summerfell was a ghost town populated by ghosts. They sometimes drove through the mostly deserted streets and regarded the empty houses and those where no one entered the light anymore. The asylum didn't fold—it did more than continue, it thrived.

They would sit in Potter's Field and stare at the rows of cube windows, wondering which of their friends were where, what the sheriff might be thinking about in his cell. Helen would take off her jacket and ball it up into a pillow behind her head, or else lie against A.G., both of them on a nameless grave, watching the windows.

Wherever Mr. Carmichael had moved to it was still close by, and on warmer days Disgusto would be there waiting for them when they arrived. The three of them would lie beside each other, ears to the ground, listening to the ocean roiling in the catacombs, the last vestiges of Summerfell.

As Helen fell asleep in his arms, the back of her neck would begin to quiver, as though silvery hands caressed her. She dreamed of Matthew.

So did Panecraft.

DOUGLAS

HALLOWEEN
THE

MAN

CLEGG

The New England coastal town of Stonehaven has a history of nightmares—and dark secrets. When Stony Crawford becomes a pawn in a game of horror and darkness, he finds that he alone holds the key to the mystery of Stonehaven, and to the power of the unspeakable creature trapped within a summer mansion.

HORROR THAT WILL HAVE YOU CHILLED TO THE BONE!

Rough Beast by Gary Goshgarian. A genocidal experiment conducted by the government goes horribly wrong, with tragic and terrifying results for the Hazzard family. Every day, their son gradually becomes more of a feral, uncontrollable, and very dangerous...thing. The government is determined to do whatever is necessary to eliminate the evidence of their dark secret and protect the town...but it is already too late. The beast is loose!

__4152-9 $4.99 US/$5.99 CAN

The Neighborhood by S.K. Epperson. Abra Ahrens's neighborhood looks like quintessential smalltown America. But it doesn't take her long to notice that beneath the Norman Rockwell exterior a hideous darkness is festering. Someone in town is decidedly *un*friendly, but she couldn't know how grotesque it really is. And the more she finds out, the more she wants to hide her welcome mat.

__4109-X $4.99 US/$5.99 CAN

BLACK RIVER FALLS
ED GORMAN

"Gorman's writing is strong, fast and sleek as a
bullet. He's one of the best."
—Dean Koontz

Who would want to kill a beautiful young woman like
Alison...and why? But whatever happens, nineteen-year-old
Ben Tyler swears that he will protect her. It hasn't been easy
for Ben—the boy the other kids always picked on. But then
Ben finds Alison and at last things are going his way...Until
one day he learns a secret so ugly that his entire life is
changed forever. A secret that threatens to destroy everyone
he loves. A secret as dark and dangerous as the tumbling
waters of Black River Falls.

"Gorman has a way of getting into his characters and
they have a way of getting into you."
—Robert Block, author of *Psycho*

——4265-7 $4.99 US/$5.99 CAN

Cold Blue Midnight

Ed Gorman

In Indiana the condemned die at midnight—killers like Peter Tapley, a twisted man who lives in his mother's shadow and takes his hatred out on trusting young women. Six years after Tapley's execution, his ex-wife Jill is trying to live down his crimes. But somewhere in the chilly nights someone won't let her forget. Someone who still blames her for her husband's hideous deeds. Someone who plans to make her pay . . . in blood.

___4417-X $4.99 US/$5.99 CAN

Elizabeth Massie
Sineater

According to legend, the sineater is a dark and mysterious figure of the night, condemned to live alone in the woods, who devours food from the chests of the dead to absorb their sins into his own soul. To look upon the face of the sineater is to see the face of all the evil he has eaten. But in a small Virginia town, the order is broken. With the violated taboo comes a rash of horrifying events. But does the evil emanate from the sineater...or from an even darker force?

___4407-2 $5.99 US/$6.99 CAN

DRAWN TO THE GRAVE
MARY ANN MITCHELL

"A tight, taut dark fantasy with surprising plot twists and a lot of spooky atmosphere."
—Ed Gorman

Beverly thinks that she has found something special with Carl, until she realizes that he has stolen from her. But he doesn't just steal her money and her property—he steals her very life. Suddenly she is helpless and alone, able only to watch in growing despair as her flesh begins to decay and each day transforms her more and more into a corpse—a corpse without the release of death.

But Beverly is not truly alone, for Carl is always nearby, watching her and waiting. He knows that soon he will need another unknowing victim, another beautiful woman he can seduce...and destroy. And when lovely young Megan walks into his web, he knows he has found his next lover. For what can possibly go wrong with his plan, a plan he has practiced to perfection so many times before?

___4290-8 $4.99 US/$5.99 CAN

Dorchester Publishing Co., Inc.
P.O. Box 6640
Wayne, PA 19087-8640

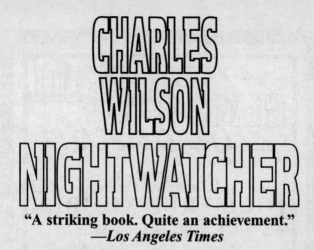

CHARLES WILSON
NIGHTWATCHER

"A striking book. Quite an achievement."
—Los Angeles Times

The staff of the state hospital for the criminally insane in Davis County, Mississippi, has seen a lot in their time—but nothing like the savage killing of Judith Salter, one of their nurses. And with three escaped inmates on the loose, there is no telling which of them is the butcher—or who the next victim will be. Even worse, as the danger and terror grow apace, the only eyewitness to the nurse's death—a psychopathic mass murderer—begins to reveal a fearsome agenda of his own.

___4275-4 $4.99 US/$5.99 CAN

Dorchester Publishing Co., Inc.
P.O. Box 6640
Wayne, PA 19087-8640

Please add $1.75 for shipping and handling for the first book and $.50 for each book thereafter. NY, NYC, and PA residents, please add appropriate sales tax. No cash, stamps, or C.O.D.s. All orders shipped within 6 weeks via postal service book rate. Canadian orders require $2.00 extra postage and must be paid in U.S. dollars through a U.S. banking facility.

Name_____
Address_____   _____
City_____ State_____ Zip_____
I have enclosed $_____ in payment for the checked book(s).
Payment <u>must</u> accompany all orders. ❏ Please send a free catalog.